DIMITRY SALCHEV

JAMES DOBREV

The Cold Murder

A NOVEL

ISBN: 979-8-9865719-0-4 (Hardcover)
979-8-9865719-1-1 (Paperback)
979-8-9865719-2-8 (eBook)

Revised Edition

1

It was a bitterly cold Saturday night on the 20th of November, 2021, in Chicago. The temperature was below 0 Fahrenheit. One of those cold nights in Windy City where people avoid walking outside to prevent getting sick the next day. The streets were so frozen that it made the city look like a gigantic refrigerator with icicles hanging like Christmas tree decorations. Many of the roads were covered with slush, which had piled up from an unpleasant blizzard a few nights ago. Despite the bad weather, two men lingered in a car, parked at the corner of Halsted and Belmont. The two men in the car, which was a black Dodge Challenger model SRT8, were Rocco and Joe. Rocco was as big as a brick shit house, his body looked like the WWE star, Braun Strowman. Rocco was an Italian man, 6'7" tall with 255 pounds of muscle. He spent three to four hours a day lifting weights at his apartment. He was twenty five, but many people thought he was over thirty five. His eyes were blue, but when he got pissed off, his eyes turned black. Rocco had the power to smash the skull of a teenybopper. He had tried to become a professional bodybuilder and participated in a few bodybuilding contests. Besides lifting weights, Rocco loved guns. He visited shooting ranges twice a week and was better than a gunner in the US Special Forces. One day at the shooting range, Rocco bumped into a guy named Freddy Limo. Freddy offered Rocco a job doing '*things*' for a guy called Mr. D.

Joe Smith, a muscular, Irish-American cruiserweight street fighter, was in his early thirties. He had started training boxing when he was thirteen, and he had competed in twenty amateur fights. Joe won all of his fights with outstanding performance. As a ferocious and arrogant boxer, he had the natural flair for knocking people out cold. At the age of seventeen, he got into a fight with his coach, and they kicked him out of the boxing gym. Joe Smith was an aggressive brawler because he grew up as an orphan in a foster house somewhere around Logan Square. He never celebrated the holidays and Christmas was an ordinary day to him. One day, Freddy Limo saw how Joe beat up two bouncers in front of a strip club. Freddy was impressed by Joe's boxing skills and offered him a job working for Mr. D.

"Hey, Joe! How long you think we will have to stay here? I'm cold. Turn ON that frigging clunker," Rocco complained.

"I don't know, Rocco! Take a chill pill. Mr. D gave us an order to wait in the car with the engine off," Joe Smith exclaimed, getting a bit annoyed at hearing the same question for the third time already.

"Are you sure that is the right place?" Rocco questioned.

"Yeah, Mr. D said Jim's Liquors at the corner of Halsted and whatever the other…"

"Belmont!" Rocco cut him off.

"Yeah, Belmont!" Joe got pissed when someone interrupted him. Usually, he would jab those who dared to do so, but not Rocco. Joe liked Rocco. He secretly admired Rocco's ability to shoot with guns. Joe had heard some gossip about Rocco getting a job offer to work for the Secret Service, but Mr. D had said NO. When Mr. D said

NO, that was equivalent to a decision by God. Not many people could mess around with Mr. D, and Rocco and Joe knew that perfectly well.

"What are you doin' for Thanksgiving, Rocco?"

"I don't know, man. My girlfriend wants me to visit her parent's house in Minnesota. I guess I will eat turkey with my girlfriend, unless something else comes up at the last minute." Rocco was trying to answer despite the fact that he hated talking about the holidays. Rocco's mother had died from cancer when he was ten, and he had never met his biological father. That's why he disliked the holidays.

"You're saying, that you are gonna eat your girlfriend's turkey?" Joe asked, and Rocco gave him the look as he was saying, *"What the fuck are you talking about?"*

"Naw, I'm not gonna eat my girlfriend's turkey. What I said was that my girlfriend and I will eat turkey at her parent's house. I don't like eating the turkey of my chicks. Okay?"

"Okay, okay. So, how long you've been dating this chick?"

"Bro! What are these weird questions?" Rocco was getting frustrated which was the reason why Joe had teased him.

"Rocco, I'm breaking your balls. Stop crying! It was just a question. That's all," Joe murmured, regretting asking this meaningless question.

"Joe, I have to take a leak!" Rocco announced. It was dumb saying it, but he had to inform Joe because he wasn't supposed to leave the car. That was the order they had been given by Mr. D.

"What, right now? You went a half an hour ago!" Joe exclaimed, puzzled by Rocco's proclamation.

"Yeah, and I have to go again. What do you want me to do? I can't piss in my pants." Rocco said angrily.

"Okay, hurry up. Watch for the police and keep it low profile," Joe said quietly. He became agitated when Rocco acted oddly.

"Okay, Dad!" Rocco sounded irritated. He didn't comprehend why Joe was hectoring him like that and making it a big deal. The truth was that Rocco was scared of Joe. He tried to camouflage his fear by answering and pretending that he was mad. What Rocco didn't know was that Joe had already sensed his fear. When he used to box, Joe could sense the fear of his opponents, which gave him a green light to fight in a better way. Not only that, but Joe wanted to beat up his opponents even when they were lying on the canvas. One particular day, Joe was disqualified from a boxing tournament because he knocked out the referee. Everyone thought he did it on purpose, but it was an accident.

Walking on the sidewalk, Rocco was trying not to pay attention to the chicks who waved to say "Hi" to him. He waved back, but he didn't stop walking. Rocco wore a thousand dollar leather jacket. He looked like he was a member of a biker club, but that was how he dressed. A few minutes later, Rocco hopped back into the black Challenger. He was so big that when he sat on the seat, the whole vehicle jolted.

"I said hurry up! You can't goof around. We are working."

"Okay, Joe. There were too many people around me. I had to find a safe place to… you know."

"What, are you scared they might see your small pecker?" Joe laughed his ass off. Rocco didn't like Joe's snarky behavior and swung a punch. That was a bad idea because Joe blocked the punch and countered by throwing jab that stopped right in front of Rocco's face.

"You don't want to do it, Rocco! Stop acting like a high school senior, and let's focus. Okay?"

"Yeah, I hear ya," Rocco said with an emotionless face, indicating that he regretted doing something unwise like that.

"What time is it?" Joe asked.

"9:30 p.m.," Rocco said while looking at his cheap wrist watch.

"The store is closing soon!" Joe declared, trying to speak quietly. They both watched the door of the liquor store. Instantly, it became dead quiet in the black Challenger. It was so quiet that Rocco could hear the beat of his pounding heart. A few minutes later, two guys were leaving the liquor store, and Joe exclaimed, "That's him. Shoot the motherfucker!" A fuzzy sound of the window rolling down, and Rocco pulled out his 9 millimeter, and BAM-BAM-BAM! The two guys dropped on the ground at the door of the liquor store, and the sound of screeching tires rang out. The Challenger sped off as if it was already being chased by the police. Upon hearing the gunshots, terrified voices filled Halsted Street with screams. The scene looked like something out of a crime movie.

"WHAT HAPPENED? SOMEONE IS SHOOTING! CALL 911. OMG! STAY INSIDE." Voices were chanting from elsewhere and a shriek of a female voice blasted out loudly along the length of the street. A minute after the shooting an ambulance and a few police vehicles pulled onto Halsted. In ten minutes, the intersection of Belmont and Halsted was blocked by dozens of police patrols and a couple of EMTs.

***

Around twenty minutes after the shooting, the black Dodge Challenger parked in an industrial area on Elston Avenue. Joe and Rocco hastily hopped out of the vehicle. Joe popped the trunk, fumbled for a Milwaukee drill, and took off the vehicle's plates. While Joe was removing the plates, Rocco was dousing a can of gas over the entire vehicle.

"C'mon! Hurry up, Rocco! We only have a minute before the police will be here! Move your fat ass!" Joe was being bossy. He got nervous when work was behind schedule. In this business, people cannot afford to be slow. Otherwise, the cops would bust them down. If the police arrest them, that's it. They're out of the game. Even if they are lucky enough to get bailed out, their boss would kill them and make it look like it was a suicide.

A black Ford cargo van came over and parked on the street.

"Let's go, Joe!" a voice echoed from the black van.

"Rocco, you got a lighter?" Joe asked.

"I'm not sure!" Rocco answered, trying to find a lighter in his pockets.

"Here. I found one!" Rocco announced.

"Don't look at me, meathead! Fire up the vehicle," Joe gave the order. Rocco did as Joe said, and both threw the gloves that they had been using into the Challenger.

"Let's go!" the same voice rumbled from the cargo van. Rocco lit up the black Dodge and jumped into the cargo van. The Ford van sped off and was soon out of sight. In no time the Dodge Challenger exploded in flames.

"WHOOHOO!" Joe and Rocco were yelling from the cargo van. Ten minutes later, firefighters and the police circled the burning Dodge. The firefighters put the fire out, but it was too late. Any evidence had been burned up.

2

An unpleasant hangover awoke James Dobrev. His iPhone 12 displayed 10:05 a.m. *"What a nimrod! I shouldn't have been drinking that much last night!"* his inner voice proclaimed. A couple of minutes later, James snailed to his bathroom to do his morning routine. Dropping a number two, brushing his teeth, and then doing a quick wank. James lived in a townhouse located in Lincoln Park, which he had bought a year ago. Dobrev occupied the second floor in a two-bedroom condo. He spent around twenty grand, remodeling the entire condo and making it look sumptuous. The first floor was rented by a Mexican family who were quiet and always paid the rent on time. James liked that Mexican family, despite the fact that he didn't remember their names.

James was 6'1" tall, a thirty-two-year-old white man. His body wasn't ripped, although he sweated four times a week at a boxing gym called 'KO'. As a kid, James had fifteen amateur fights in the light- heavyweight division and made his pro debut in his early twenties, winning by unanimous decision. Actually, his debut happened to be the last fight in his career because he seriously injured his knee, which forced him to stop his career as a boxer. A year after he got injured, James wrote his first romance novel, which became a lucrative project for him. This stimulated his self-assurance, and he had worked harder to publish five more novels in the past ten years. People loved his books, but James didn't think of himself as a successful writer. In fact, he disliked calling himself a writer. He referred to himself as a man who wrote books. James had never been recognized as a writer. People could buy his books on Amazon, Barnes & Noble, and most bookstores in the US, but he wasn't well-known and had never given interviews or podcasts about his books.

It had been two hours since James roused, and he was still fighting against the unpleasant hangover. "*Gosh! Why did I drink that much last night? I can't remember what happened! I was talking with that girl, and then what? I must have passed out on the bar! Wait, what! What was the name of that pub? Ah yes, Pint! I think that's the name. Gosh, I have to talk with Charles.*" Those were the thoughts whirling in his exhausted mind. At noon, James started working on his novel called *The Cold Summer.* He was excited about this project but he had some issues developing his characters. James loved to write, he could type on his computer for 8 to 10 hours a day. Normally, he wrote until afternoon then his mind forced him to swig bourbon. At 3 in the afternoon, James got a phone call from his buddy Charles. "*Speaking of the Devil, and there he is!*" he thought.

"Hi, Charles"

"James! What's up, you frigging heavy wino? How you feeling?"

"I feel like a clunt baby," James replied apathetically.

"What do you mean a clunt baby?" Charles got confused.

"A clunt baby is a baby who gave his mother an orgasm when she gave birth to him." Hearing that, Charles laughed his ass off.

"You writers are weirdos," Charles declared.

"I heard the same thing about architects," James quipped.

"Stop pulling my leg. I'm a prosperous Chicago architect, and I've never heard anyone calling me a weirdo."

"It's never too late! Charles, what happened last night? I can't remember anything."

"Bro, as we were drinking at *Pint*, you started talking to that gorgeous chick. After she left, you were chugging shots until you passed out. I had to Uber you to your place. That's all."

"I'm sorry, Charles. Usually, I don't drink like that. You know that.

"Yeah. That's fine. See you at *Pint* at 10, right?" Charles asked.

"I'm only drinking water, though," James replied.

"Yeah! You said that last night. HA-HA-HA." They both laughed happily. A few minutes later, Charles and James ended their conversation. James had met Charles in a bar somewhere in Lincolnwood a year ago. Charles had gotten divorced after finding his wife cheating on him with an African-American pimp at his apartment in River North. Since then, Charles had been regularly hanging out with James.

The writer overlooked the recent chinwag with Charles and focused on his novel. A second before he started writing, he was disturbed by another phone call. This time, it was Michelle, his mother.

"Hello, mom!" James said lazily.

"James, dear. I'm just calling to remind you that you have to spend Thanksgiving with us in Schaumburg. We will be expecting you any time after 6:00 p.m. I will make your favorite salad. Listen, if you're going out tonight, you need to dress warmly. It will be very cold. As you know, the virus called Zener has killed millions of people across the world. The newscasters were talking about vaccinations that are available for anybody over the age of nineteen. Please, dear, get your vaccination as soon as possible. I'm worried about you. Okay! I have to go! Love ya, bye."

"Yeah, Mom!" James answered, even though he knew his mother had hung up the phone already. Michelle was a widow. She had been living with a tax attorney named Frank for the last fifteen years. James hated going to his mother's house because he detested Frank's peculiar demeanor. Michelle's boyfriend loved to talk about politics, and that was the subject that James purposely avoided. Ivan Dobrev, James's biological father, had emigrated from Bulgaria back in the 1970s. Ivan was an honored man and had been a prominent plumber in the Chicago area. One particular night, Ivan Dobrev went to celebrate a friend's birthday and never came back. The police found him shot to death in the parking lot of *Lakers* Casino. Investigators had never solved the mystery of Ivan's murder. Twenty years later, no one could tell why Ivan Dobrev had been killed. James bottled up the loss of his father and he never talked about him, but he wanted to write a biography of his old man.

At 8:00 p.m., James Dobrev stopped working on his novel. The lust for alcohol had been bothering him for a while, he decided to turn on the TV to refresh his mind. The gogglebox* was streaming the nightly news on NBC. The newsreaders were jabbering about the free vaccinations fighting against Zener. Moreover, they urged everyone above the age of nineteen to get vaccinated and yada-yada. This news additionally depressed Dobrev, and he turned off the TV. The Apple news on his iPhone displayed the same topics about people getting vaccinated. The commercials on YouTube and the radio were streaming the same subject. It seemed like the crushing blows about vaccinations were coming from every source that James used. He wasn't averse of getting vaccinated, but he felt forced by reporters and social media to do it. James felt that the world was pressing him to do something against his will. "*Okay! I need a break. I'll swing by Jim's liquor store to grab a bottle of Jameson,*" he contemplated. As

---

* British slang for televsision.

he walked through his apartment, the writer noticed that the ceiling lights in the kitchen were blinking. *"That's weird! I just changed those. I guess the light bulbs are defective."*

***

It was around 9 in the evening when James entered the store with a huge sign that read 'Jim's Liquor.'

"Hey, James! How you doing, buddy?" the man working behind the cash register greeted him.

"Hakim! I'm doing fine. How's your family?"

"They're fine, you know. The kids are growing up, and so are the bills," Hakim said, showing his thumbs up. The only reason why they knew each other was because James had been visiting the same store for many years. Hakim had been working in this store for over ten years. He was a man with very bushy hair, making him look like he was Tarzan's twin brother. Hakim had the dead serious face of a serial killer, and at the same time, he was generous and genteel.

Jim's Liquor was packed that night. Wherever James walked, he had to squeeze past at least one person because the store was crammed as if they were giving out free alcohol. James grabbed a bottle of Jameson and a pack of peanuts and paced to the cash register where Hakim was working extremely fast.

"Did you find everything you needed, James?" Hakim asked politely.

"Yeah, I got it! Considering the fact that I can't find a pair of socks at home." Hearing that, Hakim was laughing out loud. A man around his forties, with unkempt hair and tattered clothes that were too big for him, was waiting in line next to James. The man's body suggested that he wasn't eating regularly. That stranger looked like a homeless man, but he acted as if he was a tourist. *"This man is not from here! Maybe he has a gun. I better let him go ahead of me!"* James' inner voice cried out. The man had a sinister look, he tried to avoid eye contact as if he was regretting something he had done already. He bought a pack of American Spirit. After getting his change, the man sensed that James was surveying him and glanced back at him, as if he was saying, *"Please, don't look at me!"* The unknown man wasn't belligerent, his face was telling James that something ominous was about to happen. The writer opened the door and let the man go first. James and the stranger passed through the threshold as if they had known each other. In a split second, there were several gunshots. BAM-BAM-BAM. James and the unknown man collapsed on the floor as if they had slid on ice. The ruckus was raising panic on the street. Confused voices were chanting from everywhere.

"OMG. WHAT HAPPENED? THEY ARE SHOOTING! HIDE! HIDE. CALL 9-11," somebody bellowed. People were scared to death as the terror floated over the corner of Belmont and Halsted Street. Parents were covering the eyes of their kids. Everyone who witnessed the shooting was hiding and waiting for the cops.

"Ugh!" One of the victims screamed, lying on the ground covered in blood. He had burning pain in his arm and a heavy headache. The man was shouting some gibberish while holding the top of his arm. He got on his feet, but vertigo made him wobble as if Tyson Fury had walloped his ass. A few minutes later, sirens blared from the north side. Dozens of police vehicles and two ambulances occupied the perimeter. The picture in front of the liquor store became grotesque. Bystanders were horrified. Both victims were prudently placed on gurneys and immediately transported to the nearest hospital. The deputies evacuated the premises, some of them were controlling the traffic.

"You will be okay," one of the EMT providers assured one of the survivors during the ride to the hospital. The man who had been shot merely nodded. It took a few minutes before he closed his eyes as his low pulse pressure caused him to lose consciousness.

***

Chris Jackson was making hibiscus tea at his condo in Hyde Park. His place faced the south shore of Lake Michigan. Jackson lived on his own; he was an African-American man in his late thirties. He felt heartbroken from his recent failed relationship with his partner, Princeton. They had had many altercations about their future. Princeton took a job as a pianist at a church in Houston, Texas, but Jackson couldn't leave his job as a homicide detective working for the City of Chicago. Jackson had the insightful look and charismatic smile of an intelligent philosopher. He was 6'1" tall, with a tapered curly haircut. He loved to run and ride bicycles on trails next to Lakeshore Drive. He was a vegetarian and disliked eating food from animals killed by humans. It was around 9:30 p.m. when he sat down on his couch and put his hibiscus tea on the coffee table. He grabbed the remote and played Hamilton on his 65 inched TV. A few minutes later, his iPhone disturbed him. Jackson picked up the phone and said, "Harry, what's up?"

"There was a shooting at the corner of Belmont and Halsted," the man on the line said.

"I'll be right over," Jackson mumbled tersely and hurried through his condo to get dressed. He knew he would be working extra hours that night and stopped his favorite musical before it started. Fifteen minutes later, a red Camaro model 2020 ZL1 parked fifty feet from Jim's Liquor store. Jackson hopped from the sumptuous Camaro and scuttled to the crime scene where many people crowded the corner of Belmont and Halsted. News reporters were trying to get any information about the shooting and a local news chopper was hovering overhead.

"Harry!" Jackson yelled as he made his way to the crimes scene. Harry Burns was the lieutenant of the 19th police department in Lake View. He had an obese body that made him look like a big doughnut. He had a big mustache and bushy eyebrows, and his silvered crew cut glowed. Burns was a white man, pushing his sixties who grew up in Northbrook, Illinois. He had always wanted to be a police officer, just like his father. Harry had served in the Chicago police for thirty-five years, and he counted the days until his retirement. During his work, he had seen too much crap on the streets on the south side of Chicago. After that, he was transferred to the police department in Lake View and has been working there for about ten years. Burns hated when there was a homicide in his jurisdiction because he had to make sure that all the evidence had been collected. Moreover, he had to refuse any comments about the questions asked by reporters.

"Seems like we will work tonight!" Jackson greeted the chubby lieutenant.

"Hello, Jackson," Harry said, subdued.

"What happened?" Jackson asked while looking at the puddle of blood on the curbside of Halsted Street.

"Two guys have been shot. One is in the hospital, and the other is in the morgue. Witnesses saw a black Dodge Challenger speeding away right after the shooting. I'm pretty sure the people in that Dodge are the killers.

"Have you identified the weapon used" Jackson asked, he couldn't take his eyes off the crime scene.

"All the bullets were 9 millimeter," Harry reported.

"All 9 millimeter?" Jackson repeated as if he hadn't heard the response from the chubby lieutenant.

"Yeah. It doesn't make any sense to me, though. Usually, there are no shootings in this area," Harry attested.

"It's not about the area. It's about the people who were shot," Jackson proclaimed. Hearing those words, Harry's eyes widened.

"Excuse me, lieutenant," an African-American deputy interrupted the conversation between Jackson and Harry.

"Yeah," Burns said, his face was saying, *"What do you want?"*

"There is a burning car twenty minutes away from here! The dispatch said the car is Dodge Challenger," the deputy declared. Jackson and Harry exchanged puzzled glimpses. Then Jackson said, "After you!" Harry nodded and scuttled his doughnut body into his vehicle. Harry accelerated his police vehicle, flashing the lights and blaring the sirens. Behind him, Jackson was speeding his red Camaro. When Harry and Jackson arrived, a couple of fire trucks and police cruisers were encircling the burned Dodge Challenger. The fire in the Dodge had already been extinguished. Jackson hopped out of the red Camaro, his face grimacing as if someone had just done a circumcision on him. He wore a Gucci coat that cost over a thousand dollars, a Versace sweater and dark Diesel khakis. The price tag for his outfit was over $2000. Given the way he was dressed, Jackson wasn't expecting to walk around of a burned vehicle.

"What do you think?" Harry asked. It took a few seconds before Jackson answered.

"That's the work of professionals. It could take us a year before we find something crucial. Also, I'm sure that the killer had been using gloves. In other words…"

"Forget about it!" Harry finished Jackson's sentence.

"Exactly!" Jackson sighed and asked, "Has anyone found the plates?"

"No! They had been removed," a voice familiar to Jackson echoed from a couple of feet behind. He turned around to survey the man.

"Paul! What the heck are you doing here? I thought you went on vacation in Italy?" Jackson exclaimed, flashing his charismatic smile.

"Yeah, cripes. We decided to postpone the vacation because of Zener. I mean, my family and I have been vaccinated, but you never know," Paul Mancini asserted. He was an Italian man in his late thirties. Everyone called him Rocky because he looked like Silvester Stallone. Paul was 5'11", his body resembled an eggplant because he loved eating stuffed pizza and drinking Miller Lite while watching baseball. Paul and Jackson had graduated in the same year as homicide detectives at The Police Academy in Illinois University of Chicago. They had been working together on criminal cases for five years. Both knew each other very well. In fact, Jackson spent many holidays with Paul's family.

"What are your thoughts, Paul?" Harry asked, feeling alienated from the conversation that Paul and Jackson were having. Paul looked straight at Harry's pupils and declared.

"Cripes, I believe Jackson's analysis is correct. They covered their tracks well enough. We are not sure how many people were in the car. In my opinion, they were at least two, but I could be wrong. I think our next step is to trace the VIN number of the burned vehicle."

"But first, we have to check the body. Paul, are you coming?" Jackson asked.

"My Range Rover broke down! I had to Uber myself to come here."

"Jump in my ride! I'll be your Uber tonight!" Jackson quipped.

"Cripes! You won't charge me, right?" Paul asked playfully.

"Paul, you are a stingy dago! I don't want any money from ya, but you're buying me lunch tomorrow."

"Where, Carson Ribs?" Paul asked, his question came out as an offer.

"Carson Ribs is a good restaurant!" Jackson declared.

"Yes! They are Italian!" Paul announced, feeling proud of his wisecrack.

"I don't care what they are. You will cover the check plus the tip," Jackson uttered.

"Okay. Okay! Cripes, let's go. I need to be home by midnight." They hopped into the Camaro, and Jackson sped to the Morgue of Cook County. Jackson was a good man but a bad driver. He spent around $5000 annually in red light and speeding tickets. The way he drove was making Paul regret taking the ride along. At 11:45 p.m., Paul and Jackson went to a spacious room that had a sign saying 'Authorized Personal Only.' The coroner approached both crime investigators. She was a bewitching woman pushing her middle thirties. Her parents had emigrated from Ireland back in the 1960s. Her name was Tylor. She took care of herself even though she had a ten year old girl from a Polish pimp named Skubinsky. The father of Tylor's kid had never been around, which led Tylor to file for a divorce. Tylor hadn't known that Skubinsky was a pimp until she got pregnant. He lied to her saying that he was working as a construction contractor.

As she looked at Jackson, Tylor became sexually attracted to him. She admired the way he expressed himself. Tylor even fantasized that Jackson could be her new beau, but she didn't know that Jackson wasn't straight.

In the meantime, Rocky (Paul) was checking out the fanny of the female coroner. Tylor noticed how Paul was looking at her buttocks and that was why she avoided any eye contact with him.

"Ms. Tylor, what can you tell us about the victim's death?" Jackson asked the question that Paul thought of asking.

"Well, he took four bullets; two in the head and two in the heart. Whoever was the shooter, he was precise. I'm talking about someone who was either a Green Barret, Special Forces, or something…"

Paul asked, "So, you're sayin' it was a done by professionals?" without realizing how he had interrupted the coroner.

"Yes! I believe that was a setup, and the shooter was a professional hitman," Taylor said as she kept avoiding eye contact with Paul.

"Ms. Tylor, do you think it was only one shooter?" Jackson asked, portraying his insightful thoughts.

"Yes! I believe all of the bullets were shot by the same man. Smart thinking, Jackson. I admire that," Tylor was flirting with Jackson. The African-American smiled at her compliment, but he couldn't tell her about his sexual orientation. He had put a lot of effort into keeping his personal life private at work, feeling that disclosing his sexuality would be inappropriate and unprofessional.

"I'm trying to put two and two together," he announced. Paul and Tylor were staring at him, confounded. Jackson threw a glimpse at both and continued, "Here is the scenario; if it was a single shooter, he must have needed a few seconds to shoot all four bullets. That implies that someone saw him. We need to look around for any witnesses."

"Cripes! Attaboy!" Paul burst in enthusiastically, and Jackson gave him a look saying, *"Hold your horses. You frigging meatball."*

"There something else you should know," Tylor declared.

"Cripes! Go ahead," Paul interrupted Tylor for the second time.

"We couldn't identify the victim! I have no idea where this guy came from. Surely, he wasn't an American."

"What are you talking about? He can't just touch down from a spaceship! He was not an alien, right?" Paul asked, staring at Tylor, as if he was saying, *"Don't bullshit us!"*

"He was a hundred percent human being," Tylor declared.

"I'll have to talk with ICMP ,"† Jackson proclaimed and sighed.

"Cripes! I don't like it, Jackson. It doesn't sound good!" Paul complained, and Jackson gave him the look saying, *"What makes you think that I like what I've just said?"* Jackson and Paul exchanged pleasantries with Tylor. A second before they left, Tylor put a business card in Jackson's coat. She hugged him and whispered, "Call me if you need more information!" Tylor couldn't stop looking at Jackson as he walked out of the morgue. Paul saw the whole romantic scene, but he didn't say anything. Mancini knew that Jackson would be pissed if he asked about it. The homicide detectives left from Cook County, deeply buried in their thoughts.

---

† International Commission on Missing Persons

***

It was midnight when the black cargo van parked at the main entrance of an abandoned industrial building in Little Italy.

"Where is he?" Rocco asked, feeling frustrated. He hated waiting for people.

"Take a chill pill, Rocco. He will be here in a minute," Joe answered. He disliked waiting, too. He also knew that complaining wouldn't change anything.

Rocco and Joe used burner phones when they were working. People could take the battery out of a burner phone, but they could not take the battery out of an iPhone, unless they had a small screwdriver to remove the back panel. Even if someone turned his iPhone off, Apple still traced the serial number to each smartphone. Android and iPhone were not great at protecting the privacy of users. When the screen of the smartphone was dark, that didn't mean the smartphone wasn't working. After a notification popped up on a smartphone, the display turned ON, and that particular smartphone showed the notification, whether it was from Facebook or another app. How did that happen? Every smartphone was consistently linked to the closest cellular tower empowered by the source. People couldn't see the changes because the connection was made by frequency emissions. The nearest satellite recognized the IMSI (International mobile subscriber identity) of the smartphone and established a network. Wherever the person went with his smartphone and connected to WI-FI or a cellular network, that person was visible to the cellular tower. That cellular tower collected the data of each device at any time and place on earth. This data had been checked, and saved by the host or the source providing the network. That meant the mobile source knew the exact location and what process had been made by the owner's smartphone which had connected to the satellite. Mr. D had paid a lot of money to get that information from formal CIA agents. He held a large percentage of the assets of a certain cellular provider, and every employee had to use burner phones supplied by Mr. D. He had given orders to his employees to call if changes had been made, and the phone calls could be no longer than a minute.

Five minutes later, a black 2020 Lincoln Continental was slowly approaching as if it was a police patrol. Rocco and Joe stepped closer to the Lincoln. A window rolled down, and a husky voice echoed,

"Do you have anything interesting to tell me?" Rocco and Joe exchanged a glimpse, then Rocco said, "We did what you instructed us. We were waiting at the liquor store, and I shot the motherfucker."

"Rocco, how long did the shooting take?"

"I can't really tell, boss," Rocco shrugged. He went on, "Five to six seconds!" He had no idea why that was so important.

"That's too long! There must have been witnesses. Mr. D will be pissed," the voice from the Lincoln proclaimed. A few seconds passed, and the same voice continued.

"The other guy you shot is in the hospital. His name is James Dobrev, or something like that."

"Do you want us to take care of him?" Joe Smith blurted out.

"Nah! Joe, how many times do I have to tell you? You don't kill someone you don't know. That's the rule! Where are the Dodge's plates?"

"Here!" Joe pulled out a black plastic bag and handed it to the man in the Lincoln.

"Now, listen to me carefully. You guys go to your apartments. I will have to check who this James is, and we will go from there. Okay?" the man said. Rocco and Joe nodded almost rhythmically and walked back to the black cargo van. The man in the back seat of the Lincoln was Freddy Limo. They called him *Limo* because he was the first personal driver working for Mr. D, but that was many years ago. Freddy Limo was now Mr. D's lapdog and would do anything for him. He was humble in front of the employees, but he exposed his bossy attitude from time to time. Freddy was a hillbilly who had grown up in Denver, Colorado. He was abused by his father back in the early 1980s. He left for Chicago in 2001 and hadn't spoken to his family since. Freddy was an overweight man in his fifties. He loved to eat hot dogs and any fast food he could find. He had a big scar on his left cheek from a knife fight. He was being attacked by a Mexican gang when Mr. D saved his life. Since then, Freddy had dedicated his life to him. Freddy had short silver hair and a classic-style full beard. He was a charming man, but he could stab a person in the blink of an eye.

It was midnight when the cargo van and the Lincoln left in different directions.

3

When James woke up, the clock was ticking at 12:15 a.m. A charming Asian nurse in her early twenties came to check on him.

"Hello, Mr. Dobrev. I'm Lisa. How are you?" the nurse questioned.

"I'm fine. Which hospital is this?"

"You are at the emergency room in Illinois Masonic Medical Center. The EMT technicians brought you here twenty minutes ago. You've been shot in the arm. As the result of the gunshot, you lost consciousness. Your blood pressure was critical, and you had a high temperature. At this moment, your vitals are showing good results," she paused to take a deep breath and continued, "You have an interesting last name. Where are you from?"

"It's a long story. My father came from Bulgaria a long time ago, but I was born here in Illinois."

"Bulgaria! This is so cool!" the Asian nurse exclaimed. Lisa wanted to make an impression that she knew about Bulgaria, but the truth was she hadn't heard anything about the country before. As they talked more, Lisa liked James; she felt comfortable around him even though she had just met him.

"What do you do for a living, James?" Lisa was curious about her patient.

"I've published a few books," James answered humbly, trying to skip the nitty-gritty.

"Oh my God! You're a writer! This is so cool!" The Asian sounded exhilarated, and that made James feel awkward. He hated when people called him a writer, but that was unavoidable because he was writing books. An hour later, James was transported to the ICU unit. At 8 in the morning, a man in a white coat burst into the intensive care unit where James was seated.

"Hello, James. I'm Doctor Green. How are you feeling?"

"My arm hurts, other than that, I feel fine. What can you tell me about the gunshot, Doctor Green?"

"First and foremost, you are a lucky man. The gunshot went through the top muscle in your arm, called the 'Deltoid.' The X-rays showed that the bullet isn't in your body, and that's great news. Regardless, we must be sure that there isn't anything in your arm that may harm you in the future. We will schedule an MRI and CT scan just to confirm our assumptions. You will have to take an antibiotic to protect you from any bacterial infections. I think after two weeks, you will be good to go, then you have to attend physical therapy.

"Why am I feeling so drowsy?" James questioned.

"You're feeling drowsy because we gave you some sedative medications to numb the pain in your arm. The muscle inside was damaged. It will take a while before you can use your arm normally." Doctor Green spoke so fast that James could barely follow what the physician said.

"One more question I'd like to ask," Dr. Green proclaimed, and James nodded.

"Did you get your vaccination?"

"No, Sir! I have been busy lately." James was surprised by Dr. Green's question.

"I would strongly suggest having your vaccination while you're in the hospital. Zener is a dangerous virus. People are dying from Zener every day. Please, consider getting your shot soon before it's too late." The statement from Dr. Green was compelling or urging more than asking. James showed his thumbs up, and Dr. Green left the medical unit.

On Monday, around 2 o'clock, Michelle and her boyfriend Frank invaded the medical unit where James was killing some time by staring at his iPhone. Michelle was dressed slutty. She walked on high heels, wearing black leather leggings, and on top she had a white cross wrap cropped tank top. Michelle had long curly hair and a charming face. She looked sexy, and she weighed around 120 pounds. James' mom was pushing her mid-fifties but could still make young boys chase her and buy her gifts. She felt sexy and powerful, like a woman who could have any man she wanted. That was why James felt uncomfortable being around his mom. Michelle looked like an old prostitute, and she loved it. She persuaded Frank to finance breast implants. Her boobs were big enough to entice people into staring at them. Michelle had never worked for anyone except herself in her life, even before she married James' biological father. It was the same story when she met Frank. He was all over her. Frank was forced to buy a retail space, and he turned it into a hair salon. Michelle managed her salon, but she wasn't really doing anything. She used the hair salon as an excuse to spend time with her besties.

James looked at Frank, who was dressed as if he was broke and living on welfare. He had been wearing the same faded blue jeans which he had had for ten years. His pullover cost him 11 bucks, his hat was $5 plus tax from Walmart. Frank wore a black coat that used to be good back in the 2000s. He was pushing his sixties and wasn't interested in what he wore. Instead, he was proud of what he had, a house in Schaumburg and a beautiful woman. Although, he didn't know that Michelle gave blowjobs to male strippers at a women's party for her birthday five years ago.

"James, how are you feeling, dear?" Michelle said and approached the bed where her son was lying.

"Mom, I'm fine. I'll be okay." James felt unease when his mother started holding and kissing his forehead.

"What happened? What did the doctors say," Michelle asked. She cried and, at the same time, patted her son. James described his unpleasant experience at Jim's liquor.

"Oh my God! I'm sick and tired of this city. It isn't safe anymore. James, I want to ask you something, but you have to be honest with me," Michelle gave him a look saying, *"Don't lie to me, James!"*

"Yeah, sure, mom!"

"Have you ever been involved with drugs and gangs?" Hearing this question, the writer thought, *"I can't believe what she just asked me. My mother is a nutjob."*

"Mom, why would I do something stupid like that, jeopardizing my life? I told you already. I was at the wrong place at the wrong time," he replied, getting a bit jumpy when his mother underestimated him.

"Dear, I'm your mother, and I will always love you till I can't breathe. It was just a question. I'm concerned about your safety." James nodded. He hated when his mother was giving him a lecture for no reason.

"We'll come to see you on Thanksgiving. I'm… so…" Michelle couldn't control herself and burst into tears and leaned on Frank's shoulder. Devastated, Michelle couldn't look at how her baby lay on the medical bed and couldn't comprehend why someone had tried to assassinate her son. Michelle would die to save James' life. She would do anything to protect him, but at that moment, she felt helpless and horrible.

"Everything will be all right. God is with us," Frank was talking robotically. He tried to say something to look like he cared about James, hopping that James and Michelle wouldn't decipher that he actually didn't give a damn about James. But his plan failed because James knew how phony he was.

"I'm going to visit your son, Patrick. I will remind him how much we love him. Okay, dear," Michelle said and blew a kiss at James. Then she and Frank left the hospital room.

Patrick was eleven years old and was the only child that James had. He was at Northwestern hospital with a locked-in syndrome called 'Pseudocoma.' His body was completely paralyzed as a result of a brutal car accident that occurred in Boston two years ago. Rebecca, Patrick's mother and James' wife, was driving their Subaru Forester when a pickup truck ran a red light and rammed into the Subaru. At the moment of the car accident Rebecca was killed, and Patrick had had a locked-in syndrome since then. It was traumatic for James to accept the death of his wife and the fact that his son was anchored in a wheelchair.

The writer had to dwell with the feelings of the loss of his wife and his lifeless son.

***

On Monday, the next day, two strangers burst into the room where James was recuperating. One of them was an African-American man in his late thirties wearing a Gucci coat and a Banana Republic pullover. The other man was a white dude with a bald head and a grouchy face, saying, *"Don't bother me!"*

"Hello, James! How are you feeling? I'm Detective Jackson, and this is Detective Mancini. We'd like to ask you a couple of questions.

Do you mind if we talk for a second?" Jackson asked. James had an idea of what was going on, but he was still shocked by his unexpected visitors. He nodded in agreement.

"Great! Thank you! Sir, do you know this man?" Jackson asked, fumbling with a portrait photo of the man with unkempt hair that James had met at the liquor store. James looked at both homicide detectives and revealed how he had encountered the stranger in the photo.

"That's all I know," James wound up his narration, and the detectives nodded.

"Sir," Paul questioned, "have you had any clashes or altercations with any gangs before?

"Nah, I write books, and I'm fine with the royalties. It would be unwise for me to mess around with gangs."

"Did you write a book called *The Illusion of a Kiss*?" Jackson asked, he was deeply involved in the conversation.

"Yes! Have you read it?" James and Jackson were lost in an intense discussion about the book, and Paul was starting to feel bored. He contemplated stepping out for a quick cigarette but he remained in the room.

"I have a question," James announced, and Jackson gave him permission to proceed.

"Who is this guy anyway?" the writer asked. Jackson and Paul exchanged a look saying, *"Shall we tell him?"*

"At this moment, we are uncertain of who he was and what he did," Jackson declared.

"What we think is that this cold murder could be a set-up." This time Paul said.

"What do you mean?" James asked and made Paul frustrated.

"We called this case 'The Cold Murder' because it is mysterious and was committed ruthlessly during the winter," Paul answered, his anxiety was growing as he disliked being in hospitals.

"Thank you for your objectification!" James replied sarcastically, growing jumpy due to Paul's frustration.

"Paul, why don't you wait in the car? I'll see you in a minute," Jackson suggested.

"All right. See you later, James," Paul tried to sound nice, but he was a sketchy cop who hated to deal with civilians. Mancini stormed out of the room, and Jackson proceeded.

"I apologize for my partner's comportment. He is a nice guy, but he has a distinctive character to put up with," Jackson said while approaching James. The closing distance was making James nervous. "*Why is this guy talking so weird?*" he thought.

"Are you related to Ivan Dobrev?" Jackson said.

"Did you know my father?" James asked, mouth agape.

"Let's say I'm familiar with any case that has never been solved," Jackson's words astounded James.

"Do you think my father's death has anything to do with this murder?"

"It's hard to say. I mean, your father was killed back in 2001, and now it's 2021. Do you follow what I'm sayin'? Let me tell you something: here is my number. Call me if you find anything that could be helpful unravelling this 'Cold Murder.'"

"Sure, I will. Thank you, detective," James said. Jackson flashed his charismatic smile and left the hospital room.

On Wednesday, James was transferred to another medical department. He was sent to a non-intensive care room on the sixth floor. The room was spacious; it had a TV unit mounted on the wall facing the medical bed. There were neat cabinets filled with medical supplies on the right side of the bed. A few armchairs and a leather couch were placed on the left side of the bed. There was a huge window that looked onto the east side toward Lake Shore Drive.

Despite physicians' instructions not to walk in the room without assistance, James got up and wandered close to the window and stared at the sky. It was 5:30 p.m., but the night had already fallen onto the city of Chicago. James was mesmerized by the beauty of the Windy City. He had traveled all over the States and overseas to Europe and the Middle East, but he was infatuated with Chicago—a city he loved beyond measure. Two hours later, James was just about to close his eyes when his iPhone rumbled. It was a text message from his mother saying:

Dear, I forgot to ask; did you get your vaccination? Don't be upset; it's just a question. See you tomorrow. Love you.

James loved his mom, but he couldn't grasp her urge for getting that vaccination. He lived in a free-thinking world, which meant he held onto his belief in thinking like a free man. He felt suppressed when others tried to distract his mind by saying what was true and what was not. The thought of what he'd been told gave him the feeling that he was imprisoned in a different world: the one that the government instilled in him to think of what had been set to be true. He had heard of friends who had vaccinations and were still getting sick. It didn't make sense to him to get vaccinated if he could get sick again. "*What was the purpose of those vaccinations?*" Thinking of that was making him feel despondent. He decided to distract his mind and turned on the TV. On the news channel, they were talking and urging people to get vaccinated. James was sick and tired of listening to vaccination reports. He knew that the tabloids were exaggerating the situation for the sake of the society. They had some videos and interviews to confirm their statements, but not all of what they said was close to the truth. The media was a business. Sometimes, they needed to amend their stories to keep people interested. Otherwise, they would lose popularity. James was aware that the media was controlled by the government. He had seen some bloopers on YouTube when the newsreaders were reading absolutely ridiculous stories in which they were losing it and bursting into laughter. Some newscasters admitted and commented that those absurd stories were untrue. Pondering all this, James decided to take a nap and fell asleep around midnight. At five in the morning, he was aroused from a nightmare about the shooting at the liquor store.

***

On Thanksgiving, around noon, James had twelve visitors: a few uncles, cousins, and aunts from his mother's side came to see him. Michelle brought a lot of food that made James think that he was at a Chinese buffet. His room was filled with sounds with animated conversations that gave him a headache. Thirty minutes later, a nurse named Melissa came and walked out all of James' family. He gave her a look saying, "*Thank you.*" Melissa giggled and whispered. "I'll be back with you shortly." Hearing those words, James smiled and felt relieved that his room was his again.

Melissa came back a few minutes later. She was a breathtaking beauty in her twenties with a messy braid hairstyle, and her gymnastically toned body looked attractive. Melissa and James talked about his books. She was fascinated to meet a writer because she was an avid reader. She promised to check out his book '*The Sun in Darkness.*' Melissa left her phone number just before she left the hospital. She hoped to hear back from him, even though she was dating someone else. James didn't have problems getting along with chicks. He knew that Melisa was interested in his pogo stick. However, he disliked sleeping with other women as he felt like he was cheating on Rebecca, even though she went to be with God in 2016.

4

On the first Wednesday of December, a black Cadillac model Escalade 2020 was waiting at the main entrance of the Illinois Masonic Medical Center. The driver's window rolled down, and a cigarette smoke billowed out. That Cadillac was in outstanding condition. That vehicle shone as if had just come out of the dealership. A couple of minutes later, a nurse of Mexican descent pushed a wheelchair to the luxury Cadillac. James was sitting on that chair. The nurse politely asked if he needed help to stand up, but James refused. The writer was up on his feet in a second. He opened the door of the Cadillac, and the driver joyfully said,

"James! It's good to see ya, bud. How are you feeling?"

"Charles, you whackjob! I can't describe how happy I am to see you."

"C'mon, jump in," Charles said, and gave James a fist bump. He dropped his cigarette in a half-filled bottle of water. Charles thought it would be ruthless to smoke when his friend had just gotten out of the hospital.

"Man, this Cadillac is fire! I don't think I have seen it before." James was a happy camper; not about the Cadillac but because he was out of the hospital.

"What did the doctors tell you?" Charles asked.

"That I am a lucky man," the writer replied.

"I don't need a doctor to hear that. I know you're a lucky bastard. Why do you think I'm hanging out with you?" Charles smiled, showing his cocky behavior.

"Charles, don't be jealous!" James said.

"Jealous of what? That you've been shot in the arm?" Charles said, he had fun teasing his friend.

"Exactly! I'm a hero. The chicks in the hospital were checking me out. One of them took my phone number."

"Get out of here. Are you for real? She could lose her job because of that!"

"I'm not joking. It doesn't matter anyway, cuz I won't talk to her," James declared, and Charles thoughtfully nodded.

"What if she decides to contact you?"

"I don't know, man! That's the last thing I need to worry about," James said while looking out the window. Charles was interested in what his buddy was doing in the hospital as he admired that the writer was successful with women. Charles couldn't comprehend how the chicks were attracted to his friend. He thought that women's behavior was always mysterious, like the recipe for Coca-Cola. James didn't know that Charles was spending a lot of money hooking up with girls on the internet. The architect was paying them to do kinky stuff; for example, Dirty Sanchez and golden showers.

***

The night was so dark, as if the daylight didn't exist. It was dangerously cold in Chicago, and while most residents bundled up, some teenagers thought they were invincible. Despite the cold weather, James wore his light Prada coat and stretch Mugsy jeans. The first medical responders had to cut off his pullover to avoid moving his arm unnecessarily. Since he couldn't undress due to his injured arm, James wore the same hospital gown.

It was around 8:00 p.m. when the pristine Cadillac parked on the side street of James' dwelling. Stepping out of the Cadillac, James noticed that some of the street lights were blinking, but he didn't think much of it. He reminded himself that he had bigger things to worry about more rather than some malfunctioning lights.

The cold weather compelled Charles to talk because he was freezing, "You wanna go to *Pint* to grab a beer?" He offered while his eyes were scanning his friend. It took a second before James answered.

"I don't think it's wise to drink right after getting out of the hospital," Dobrev said. "But, I'll be glad to watch you getting hammered."

"Great! I have a chauffeur for the night!" Charles said, happy to tease his friend. James said nothing. They went upstairs. Charles followed the writer because he needed to urge his friend to get ready faster; otherwise, it could take forever. James unlocked the door. His condo looked like it had been abandoned for years. Everything was neatly placed as if were on the front cover of a home decor magazine.

"Charles, make yourself comfortable. I have to get rid of those clothes. I smell like a nasty raccoon."

"Are you taking a shower?" Charles asked.

"Partly, I can't expose the injured arm under the shower," James said.

"Okay!" Charles yelled from the kitchen. James went to the living room, and flicked the power switch. The light went on, and the writer froze. He was flummoxed, his eyes couldn't look away.

"Charles, come here! You have to see this," James yelled, still staring at the thing that had made him perplexed.

"What do you mean?" Charles' voice echoed from the kitchen. He walked into the living room, and his eyes widened. He couldn't believe what he saw.

"What the heck is that?" Charles asked, still frozen like James, both standing motionless like statues. Charles had goosebumps on his forearms. The terror crawled on his neck as if a giant tarantula was scurrying up his body. The writer and the architect were gazing at the gray wall on which were scrawled the words:

I KNOW WHO YOU ARE

Each word was written in capitals about a foot high. These words were painted in black on the gray wall which was opposite the balcony. Charles was petrified and James looked as if he was hypnotized. They exchanged a questioning look.

"I've got a big problem. They are watching me!" James declared. Charles wanted to say something but he realized that his words would be useless. James took a screenshot using his iPhone and forwarded it to detective Jackson. Then the writer shared with his friend the story of how the two homicide detectives had visited him in the hospital. While listening to his friend, Charles was thoughtfully gazing out of the window, purposely avoiding the message painted on the wall. The architect figured that with the light on, the message could be seen from the street.

A minute passed, and he asked, "What you are going to do, buddy?" Charles looked at his friend as if he was begging him for money. James was scratching his head.

"I don't know, man! I will have to speak with my tenants."

"The Mexicans!" Charles cried out, and James nodded. The annoying sound of an incoming call interrupted the conversation between them. It was James' iPhone. He gave the signal to Charles to keep it quiet during the call.

"Hello... Uh…Yeah… at 12! Okay, I'll be there!" James talked on the phone while he stared at Charles.

"Yeah, okay. See you tomorrow!" the writer said and hung up the phone.

"Who was it?" Charles grilled, pondering that his buddy was feeling angst about something.

"Jackson, the homicide detective. He wants me to meet him at Starbucks tomorrow, I guess," James declared. He was still rubbing his head, lost in deep thoughts like an ancient philosopher pondering the universe.

"Jackson said that we need to leave the condo and not touch anything. They will come tomorrow and check the entire place for fingerprints and whatever they do. They also want to ask the neighbors if they saw someone or anything unusual. It's a mess," James declared. He was about to lose his mind. His anger piled up, and he started to imagine how he was smashing his home.

"Where are you going to spend the night?" Charles asked, his compassion for his friend was palpable.

"I don't know, man. I'll probably go to some cheap hotel, or whatever. I have no idea. I don't want to bother my mother. She will freak out. You follow?"

"Yeah. You can stay in my apartment," Charles offered.

"Nah! I don't want to get you involved in this predicament. It's too much. You don't need this crap."

"James, are you serious? I'm your friend. Besides, I'm involved already. I'm a witness. You know that," Charles said. "Do you have any idea who could be messing with you?"

"Can't really tell. I mean, I don't know, man. Let's go to *Pint*. I need an Irish tea," James suggested.

"Okay, I'll be waiting in the car," Charles declared, and James gave him thumbs up. The writer went to the bathroom to splash his face with water. He didn't care if that amounted to destroying evidence. At that moment he flicked the switch in the bathroom, and the light started blinking. James stared up at the blinking light, thinking, "*What is going on with all these lights? Am I freaking out, or what?*" James didn't shower as he had planned. He wanted to take his laptop and leave the condo as soon as possible. Instantly, a voice that resembled Charles' rumbled from the street.

"You A-holes!" the voice yelled, and the sound of screeching tires blasted out loudly. James rushed down the stairs to see why his friend was screaming. "*I hope I won't see him lying on the ground, having been shot by some hoodrat,*" he thought. Dobrev sneaked through the main door of his townhouse and saw his friend cursing and waving his hands as if he was trying to warn everyone about an approaching meteoroid.

"Charles, what happened?" James asked, shocked to see his friend like that.

"Man! When I walked up to the Cadillac, I saw a black, I think it was a Ford Edge, parked on the other side of the street. As soon as the people in that vehicle saw me, they sped away out of sight. I couldn't take a picture of the plates," Charles complained, and that perturbed James.

"Let's get the hell out of here!" James said calmly, but his rage was about to explode any second. Charles looked at his friend, and gave him a look saying, "*That's what I'd like to hear, bud.*" Charles was worried about James. The thought that he could lose his friend made him uncomfortable. James and Charles drove to *Pint*, a typical Irish-American pub located in Wicker Park. The bar had a few pool tables and around 20 booths, and 100 TVs mounted to the walls. The pub had a 50 foot long bar, where a few bartenders served booze to the thirsty patrons. The center of the joint had space big enough to mingle and socialize. The writer and the architect burst in, and the people there greeted them as if they'd come to buy drinks for everyone. James and Charles pretended that nothing had happened and took a few shots of Russian vodka. They almost got into a fight arguing about where James should sleep. Despite Charles' protests, James decided to check-in at the Best Western hotel located at 3434 Broadway Street.

The next day, James was waiting for Jackson in Starbucks at the corner of Clark and Dickens Avenue. Dobrev grew impatient whenever he had to wait for someone and sat next to the window to distract himself by watching the passing vehicles. The writer was dressed in a brown leather jacket, a white Champion long sleeve shirt, and blue Tommy John pants. His swept-back hairstyle looked immaculate. Five minutes later, Jackson stepped into the Starbucks. He rushed past the stream of people who were waiting in line. Jackson wore a dark blue Kenneth Cole coat, a flannel shirt, and black Levi's jeans. He smiled charmingly at James and wanted to give him a hug, but instead, he shook James' hand like a businessman. The detective had a hot Blonde Roast, and the writer drank a London Fog Tea Latte. They exchanged polite howdies, and after a few minutes of casual chit-chat, Jackson cut to the chase by asking essential questions regarding the unpleasant message that James had found the night before.

"Do you have any surveillance in or around the building?" Jackson asked while jotting something in his notebook.

"Nah, I've never had anyone stealing from my property. Even the packages I get are untouched."

"I see," Chris Jackson nodded thoughtfully. After a few seconds he continued, "I'm trying to suss out how they got in. Did you see anything broken, like a door or a window?"

"Frankly, on the night when I went to the liquor store… I don't recall locking the doors to my place," James confessed.

"That means the thugs had an easy time sneaking into your condo, which makes it difficult for us to trace them. Have you noticed any of your belongings missing?" Chris continued, not averting his squinting eyes from James.

"Nah! Actually, everything seems to be where I've left it. After I spoke with you last night, I didn't touch anything, which means I'm not completely sure," Dobrev said. He sounded uncertain, but Jackson got his point. A few seconds later, Jackson avoided looking at James. His face was as if he was saying, "*I don't know how to tell you this.*"

"James, there is something that you need to know about your father's murder."

"Huh? What do you mean?" The writer looked flummoxed. He hadn't expected to talk about his father.

"I looked at the files of your father's investigation. There was a burning car around eight miles from the location where your father was gunned down, okay? Here is where the things get even creepier. The night of the shooting at the liquor store, we found a vehicle that was blazing around seven to eight miles away," Jackson explained.

"What! You've gotta be kidding!" James' eyes widened as if Jackson had just pulled out a gun and pointed it at him.

"I'm not joking. Listen, it could be just a coincidence, but I don't really believe in that. Besides, in both burned cars, the plates were missing." Listening to the homicide detective, James covered his face as if he had a sudden headache.

"I think you need to rest," Jackson asserted, and tapped James' arm. The writer looked at the detective as if to say, "*What the heck are you doing?*" Then Jackson stood up and said, "I have a lot of work to do. I'll drive to your house to interview your neighbors. Hopefully, I'll find something that will help with the investigation. Whoever killed the stranger and now is harassing you won't get away with it. Oh, there is one more thing. I would like to speak with your friend, Charles. Do you mind sending me his number?"

"Not at all. I'll forward it to you. Thank you for your time, Detective Jackson."

"My pleasure!" Jackson smiled and urgently left Starbucks as if he needed to drop number two. Jackson forgot to pay for his coffee, but that didn't matter because James had intended to pay the bill anyway. The conversation with the homicide detective made him feel simultaneously comfortable and awkward. The thought of his father's death reopened the old emotional wounds in James' heart. He could have physically broken the noses of many people, but he didn't know how to fight in this predicament. This only added to his headache which was already growing bigger. James took an Uber to his hotel and decided to take a nap, but he couldn't fall asleep. Dobrev opened his laptop and started typing in attempt to work on his book. He wasn't as productive as normally would be as his mind wasn't focused on writing.

***

Thirty minutes after the conversation in Starbucks, Jackson parked his Camaro on the side street next to James' dwelling. He hopped out of the car hastily as if he was pissed at someone who had just hit his bumper. The African-American detective surveyed the townhouses that looked like soldiers lined up at the funeral of a prominent general. Then he glanced up at the blue sky. There were no clouds; it looked like the weather was hot in the middle of June, but actually, it was freezing. The cold weather forced Jackson to scuttle by the gate door of the townhouse.

"Hey! Don't you dare to go a step further!" a voice rumbled behind Jackson's shoulders. The African-American detective turned around and saw his workmate, Paul, running toward him.

"Hi, Paul! Why are you running?"

"Cripes, because it's cold, and my wife told me that I need to exercise," Paul responded, and Jackson smiled. He always laughed at Paul's jokes, but this time Paul was serious, which made him sound even more hilarious. The Italian detective was talking while Jackson was opening the front door.

"I found the owner of the Dodge. I mean the car was registered to a guy named Collin Furlough. He lives in a small town called Hart, Michigan," Paul said.

"Michigan!" Jackson repeated, interrupting the Italian detective.

"Yes, Michigan. But there is more! So this guy, Collin, had claimed that his Dodge was carjacked two years ago. One particular day, Collin started his morning, he was thinking of going for a ride to a local coffee shop, but when he walked out his door, his car wasn't in the driveway. Then he called the police, and the car has been reported missing ever since. The police precinct in Hart told me that they never found the perpetrator."

"Hold on! Let me get this straight. You are saying that this man Collin woke up in the morning, and when he decided to go for a ride, his car wasn't there, and no one knew where that car could be?" Jackson asked, and Paul just nodded.

"That ain't good. Sounds like we are dealing with a big player," Jackson mumbled under his breath, and Paul nodded again. Both detectives walked up the staircase and walked into James' condo. They took pictures and left no stone unturned in their search. Jackson and Paul were strenuously looking for a DNA trace or anything that could lead to potential evidence. After two hours of painstaking work, the detectives were astounded. They didn't find anything. Jackson came up with the conclusion, that whoever had painted the wall, had brought their own paint, brush, and roller. He also guessed that the interloper had left the townhouse, covering his own tracks.

At 2:00 in the afternoon, Jackson and Paul left the condo. Jackson locked the door with the key that James had given him. Both detectives went to the first floor and knocked on the door where the Mexican family lived. A man in his early forties opened the door. His face looked perturbed, as if he was thinking, *"Oh, God! I hope they don't find the kilo of cocaine hidden in my mattress."* The man had a big mustache and curly hair, and his belly was a step ahead from his legs because he drank around fifty cans of beer a week. The Mexican said that his name was José. Jackson spoke Spanish, not fluently but enough to have a decent conversation. The interrogation was short, and José didn't reveal any useful information. Jackson was bummed out that the investigation wasn't progressing. He felt like a freshman who had just started studying criminal investigation. Jackson was grateful to have the chance to be a homicide detective. He had dreamed of becoming a detective ever since he was twelve. He dedicated his life to solving mysterious cases and incarcerating murderers. It was this sense of duty that drove Jackson to take his job seriously and work tirelessly to unravel the details of this nefarious assassination. Also, he felt sympathy for James, thinking that the writer shouldn't deal with those unfair circumstances. He believed that James had nothing to do with any gangs or drug dealers. Dobrev was a successful writer, even though, in his own eyes, he didn't feel that he was an accomplished one. Why would he be involved with criminal gangs? Jackson surmised that the writer had money, and he wasn't interested in a materialistic world, power or influence.

In a few minutes, Jackson and Paul walked to the red Camaro.

"Do you need a ride?" Jackson asked politely.

"Cripes! I'm good, though. I rented this white Ford Fusion parked over there! You charge too much," Mancini said, laughing.

"Kiss my black ass!" Jackson sounded offended, but actually, he was messing with Paul. Both detectives became silent as though they were two strangers who had not met before.

"What's the next step?" Paul asked, looking at his rental car for no reason.

"Have you seen the camera footage from the liquor store?" Jackson asked.

"Cripes! I don't know if they have any!" Paul automatically answered as if he was a robot.

"Sure they have! That's a liquor store, not a florist shop," Jackson pointed out. He was getting a bit frustrated that he had to say something that was obviously clear. Paul nodded and said, "Okay, we will go and check the cameras from the liquor store, and I will interview the residents in the area. Hopefully, they can give us some useful information."

"Listen. Paul, you are going to have to do it by yourself. I have to speak with a guy named Charles. He is James' closest friend. I think he can give me some information about this case," Jackson informed Paul and they split off in different directions like two rats scurrying in different streets. Paul headed to Jim's Liquor to speak with the owner. But it was a waste of time because none of the cameras from the liquor store were pointing into the streets. The owner explained that his cameras observed the inside of the store, not the outside. The owner refused to give any additional information. Paul bought a huge bottle of vodka and thanked the man for his time.

Jackson got in touch with Charles, and they made plans to meet at Charles' apartment on Friday.

***

Dobrev attended a private physical therapy clinic called *We Care* located on North Ashland Avenue. James knew that if a man didn't take care of himself, he would eventually end up in a hospital. That's why he visited the *We Care* clinic three times a week. In that clinic, everyone was cheerful and easy to talk with. The physician who took care of James was Olga, a girl in her early thirties with beautiful curly blond hair and glowing blue eyes, whose parents had come from Ukraine after the end of the cold war. Olga guided James in particular exercises to train his injured arm. After his first visit, he started feeling better.

***

On the first Friday of December 2021, James headed to Luigi Children's Hospital on Clark Street. The hospital was huge, and had cutting edge technology. The design of the building looked splendid, as if it were owned by a top airline company. Many well-known pediatricians from all over the world worked at that hospital, which was why the medical facility was ranked as one of the top hospitals in the country. James walked into the hospital wearing a gray North Face hat, a black leather Michael Kors jacket, and blue Banana Republic jeans. He was carrying an Amazon package and hurriedly paced through the hospital corridors. It was around 10:00 a.m. when James walked through the room where his son was seated. When he saw Patrick, tears fell from James' eyes, and at the same time, his smile was flashing because he was happy to see his son.

"How you doing, buddy? I have a present for you!" James stated exuberantly and started unwrapping the Amazon package.

Patrick couldn't talk normally. Although, he could hear the words from his father. James looked at his son. Patrick had beautiful brown hair that looked just like his father's, but his brown eyes and handsome face resembled his mother's. He was 5'5" tall, anchored in a wheelchair completely paralyzed except for his left eyeball. The other eye was partly closed. The writer hugged his son and sat on the chair next to him. He then pulled out a Bears cap and shirt. He asked the nurse to help him to put the new clothes on his son. James and Patrick used to watch the Bears playing in Soldier Field before Patrick became disabled.

The nurse left the room, and James pulled out a children's book from his plastic bag and started reading. James loved reading just as his father had. The writer remembered how his dad was always reading after he came home from work. Ivan Dobrev had worked seven days per week. He never took a day off, except Christmas. He wanted to make sure that James could attend college. Unfortunately, Ivan Dobrev was shot a few years before James went to DePaul University. Thinking about his father and his son, James felt heartbroken. He tried to look unflappable, but his tears were dropping onto the pages of the children's book.

"I'll be right back, buddy," James said to his son, and went to the lavatory. He cried there as if he was a coward bullied in school. Five minutes later, he washed his face and marched back to his son. He wrapped his arms around Patrick and kissed him goodbye.

"I'll be back soon, buddy!" the writer whispered to his son and left the hospital. James refused to accept Patrick's medical condition and was willing to do whatever it takes to find a cure, even if it meant putting his own life on the line. James couldn't understand why his son had to struggle in that way. He prayed to God for his son and craved to see him playing football with other kids.

An hour later, James left the hospital and went to another liquor store. He bought a bottle of Jameson and headed to his hotel room. He was gulping alcohol heavily as if he was participating in a drinking contest. He wanted to numb the pain that came from his heart, which wasn't going away on its own. Drinking alcohol was the only way to kill that pain. It was around 4 in the afternoon when his phone rang. James picked up.

"Hello!" the writer said, and the next second, his eyes widened. "You've got to be kidding me! Are you for real?"

***

At 10:00 a.m. on Friday, while James was at the hospital visiting his son, Jackson requested an Uber and headed to Charles' apartment.

Charles had invited Jackson to his place for a cup of tea. His apartment was in an upscale building located on 680 Inner Lake Shore Drive. Charles loved this apartment, and he was thinking of buying it. Many of his friends had stopped by his apartment for casual meetings. Also, he was doing late night gangbangs, splurging money to screw around with vicious chicks—it was something that he enjoyed doing, after his divorce.

At a quarter past ten, a white Toyota Camry pulled into the driveway of the building where Charles lived. The detective hopped out of the Camry and wandered to the front desk. The vestibule looked busy. Christmas was approaching, FedEx, UPS, and Amazon employees were bustling around, carrying huge packages. Jackson walked to the lobby and saw a white man in his late fifties who was working at the front desk. He was dressed in a suit bought in the 1990s. His hair resembled Hugh Grant's hairstyle. Jackson tried to speak with him, but the man looked busy and was multitasking. Jackson identified himself, and the man gave him permission to go upstairs without calling Charles.

Chris Jackson headed to the elevators. The elevator ride seemed to take forever because Charles lived on the 44th floor. As the detective walked to a door bearing the number 4451, he knocked on the door repeatedly.

"Charles! It's Jackson!" There was no answer. Jackson repeated Charles' name. And again, there was no answer. The detective looked around and grabbed the door handle. "*It's open! Why would he leave the door open? People living in those types of buildings keep their doors locked,*" he thought and opened the door prudently. The apartment was dead quiet.

"Charles! I'm Detective Jackson. Are you okay?" Jackson yelled respectfully. There was no answer. It was illegal in the state of Illinois to sneak into people's houses, but Jackson had been invited with a text message. The detective stepped inside. There was a lavish bathroom on the left side of the apartment. Jackson walked through the hallway and headed to a spacious living room where an expensive white couch was placed across the room. The living room was aesthetic. There were a few bookshelves, and the floor was covered with a pricey carpet. On the east side of that living room, there was a wall made of glass that faced Lake Michigan, providing a spectacular view. There were a bunch of fancy coffee tables and some art furniture spread around. Everything in the living room looked squeaky clean and untouched.

"Charles! Do you hear me?" Jackson raised his voice, feeling uncomfortable in the silent apartment. The door of the bedroom was ajar, and that tempted him to take a look. The detective felt weightless, stepping carefully on the carpet as if he was walking through an area filled with landmines. Jackson prudently opened the door of the bedroom, and his eyes widened. He looked like a frightened owl. The view in the bedroom made him queasy. Charles had been stabbed brutally on the left side of his neck. He lay on the bed with his eyes and mouth open.

"Holy Smokes! Who the heck would do something like that?" the detective exclaimed. Even though Jackson was a homicide detective, he avoided looking at the cadaver. At the next moment, the detective fumbled into his coat for his smartphone, and a noise of breaking a vase echoed from the other side of the apartment. Jackson turned around with lightning speed and glued his back to the wall. He fumbled out his firearm and bellowed, "Chicago P.D. Backup is on the way. There is no escape!" The African-American detective did as he said and called 911 for backup. He felt nervous like an animal cooped up in a cage. "*Stay cool, Jackson! They will be here any minute,*" Jackson thought to himself. However, he couldn't stay still anymore. He grabbed one of Charles' shoes and tossed it in the living room to distract whoever was there. He then popped out from the bedroom, pointing his firearm.

"Freeze! You mother…"

"Meow!" Charles' cat sounded irritated. The detective hadn't a clue that Charles had a pet. "*It was the cat!*" he pondered.

"Hey, buddy! You scared the shit out of me!" Jackson talked to the cat like Eddie Murphy talked to the animals in *Dr. Dolittle*. A few minutes later, the entire building on Inner Lake Shore Drive was filled with deputies, police officers, and the media. It was chaos. After an hour, Paul came over and quickly walked to Charles' apartment. Jackson called out his name, and together they interviewed every employee in the building. The man at the front desk explained that he had seen a Domino's driver who asked permission to go to Charles' apartment. The man at the front desk had called Charles and let the delivery driver upstairs, and that was the last time he had spoken with Charles. The delivery driver had left the building 30 minutes before Jackson's arrival.

"What did he look like?" Jackson quizzed. The man at the front desk described that the driver from Domino's was a white man, tall, and muscular. He wore a cap with a Domino's logo and sunglasses. The police called for a police sketch artist to draw a portrait of the Domino's delivery driver. Two murders, and all they had was a portrait of somebody who might not be even connected to the crime. Jackson felt embarrassed that he had so little that could help with the investigation. The building had cameras in the lobby but not in the residential units. The homicide detectives could assume that Charles voluntarily opened the door for the delivery. But they couldn't understand how the murderer got him onto the bed without leaving blood anywhere else. Besides, they couldn't find any weapon in the apartment, and that was driving the Chief of Police nuts. There were too many questions whose answers remained unanswered.

Two hours after Jackson had found Charles' body, the mayhem in the building cleared out, and he called James to notify him.

"You've gotta be kidding me! Are you for real?" the writer said in a state of absolute shock.

"It's not a joke. I need to talk to you," the homicide detective proclaimed.

"Sure! Uh… I'll meet you in the lobby of my hotel. Sounds good?" James offered. Fifteen minutes later, Jackson and James shook hands at the lobby of the Best Western.

"There is a restaurant at this hotel. The food is worth the money. Follow me," James said, and Jackson walked next to him. The restaurant was delightful and cozy. There were a hundred tables in that place, and half of them were occupied. The floor had glamorous pricey-looking tiles. On the right side, there were a couple of big windows that had been embellished with custom made drapes. Jackson and James took a table for two. The detective had a coffee, and the writer was rinsing his mouth with Bourbon.

"You drinking? It's 4 in the afternoon!" Jackson asked, confused. Dobrev decided to change the subject and talked about Patrick. Metaphorically speaking, he poured out his burden onto Jackson's shoulders. He then said, "Detective Jackson, have you found something about Charles' murderer?"

"So far, we have a sketch of a possible suspect. Here! Do you know this man?" Jackson showed the portrait of the delivery driver.

"I have no idea who that man is. Why would he kill Charles?" James asked.

"I was about to ask you the same question. There is something else you should know. Do you remember this guy?" Jackson handed a black and white photo to James. The writer glimpsed at the photo, and his eyes popped out as if he had just seen a ghost.

"Wait a minute. This is the mysterious stranger that was shot at the liquor store! The photo looks old, but he looked almost the same age. How is that possible?

"It's insane, right! We finally identified that man. His name was

Boris Gurmanov. Born and raised in Moscow. He owned an electrical company based in Moscow and mysteriously disappeared in June of 1966. The last time they saw him was when Boris left his apartment, and he had never come back since. That was what the National Guard of Russia told me," Jackson finished his monologue.

"Hold on for a second! This cannot be true. How old was Boris when he disappeared?"

"I believe he was around forty-five," Jackson answered.

"Naw, man. That cannot be true! Look at the picture. You're telling me that this man was forty-five in 1966. Today is December 15th, 2021. That means that Boris should be a 100-year old, and he didn't look like a 100-year man. He looked like a forty-five-year-old when I saw him at the liquor store. That's insane!"

"I couldn't agree with you more. That's why I wanted to talk with you…and"

"Are you sure this is the right guy?" James interrupted the homicide detective.

"Positive! We sent Boris' body back to Russia, and they confirmed his identity with a DNA test," Jackson announced, and that made James uncomfortable. The writer felt ignorant, like a man who couldn't understand the simplest thing.

"Let me get this straight. You're telling me someone wanted me dead because they saw me with this guy?" Dobrev asked.

"In many ways, yes. But I think if they wanted it, you'd be dead already. I think they are trying to scare you. Perhaps someone, like an oligarch, has been embroiled in something big. Whoever that guy is, he is mad at you. That's what I think," said Jackson, making a quick synopsis, and James nodded, indicating that he had nothing to say. It took a few minutes of awkward silence before James started speaking.

"Okay! I'm screwed. What should I do?" James asked, embarrassed by his poor language.

"I think you should leave the country for a while. Until we find the perpetrator."

"A vacation! That sounds wonderful! But what about the expenses, my son Patrick and this virus… uh… Zener?" James asked, indicating his reluctance towards the idea.

"Don't worry about Zener. Also, I'll arrange you to travel on a private jet no matter where you go. And I'll ensure your son is well taken care of. No one would know where you'll be flying to," Jackson sounded persuasive, but James didn't look convinced. He thought that he shouldn't go anywhere and believed that he needed to protect his family more than ever. Also, James didn't want to look like a coward by escaping from his hardships. There was a pause. The writer and the homicide detective were silent. Over the years, James had learned how to live in a state of compartmentalization. His faith had helped him to exist in resilience. Dobrev was certain that he had been living through difficulties in which the end would come soon. He believed that a trip to a different country wouldn't be a proper solution.

"So, what do you think?" Jackson went on. James didn't feel comfortable when someone pressured him, but after a few minutes, he responded.

"I need to think about it. Give me a couple of days. At this point, this is all I can tell you."

"Listen, I'm not pushing you anywhere. I just want to help prevent another murder. This is completely off the record. Normally, the police would not send you anywhere unless you are a witness to a brutal homicide. Not to mention, the police should keep you in the State until this case is closed. But this is not your case. I'm offering to help you prevent another murder and also because I sympathize with your hardship. Do you think it's easy for me to pull some strings and make it happen, sending people away?" Jackson asked, and James remained silent. But then, the writer asked, "Jackson, why are you helping me?" There was a pause because Jackson couldn't reveal the real reason why he wanted to help the writer. The detective liked James and took this case a little more personally than he should have.

"I've told you already. I don't want to find your body slashed at your apartment. That's all," Jackson declared. He was a cordial man, and James acknowledged his concern. Ten minutes later, they split in different directions. Jackson drove to the police department, and James went to his room to finish the bottle of Jameson. Around 11 in the evening, the writer lay on the floor in his hotel room. He had blacked out from the alcohol. The next morning, he had a bad hangover. Despite his wooziness, Dobrev went to the nearest liquor store, grabbed another Jameson and returned to his hotel room to get inebriated. The loss of his friend made him drink excessively. At the hotel room, he was bawling like a toddler who had lost his favorite toy. Pain struck his throat as if he had got a bone stuck in it. All of a sudden, the light in the bedroom was blinking rhythmically. James witnessed the blinking lights as if something bad was about to happen, but he ignored this fact. He was afraid to share that with other people, they would think of him as a nutcase.

At midnight, the writer collapsed on the ivory carpet in his hotel room. The whiskey knocked him out.

***

On Sunday, a week before Christmas, the sky was overcast, but the weather was surprisingly mild. The temperature was in the mid-forties as around twenty-five vehicles were rolling to a cemetery called *Eternity,* located in East Irving Park. Jackson felt remorse for the death of Charles, he was determined to prevent another murder. He was driving his Camaro and following the other vehicles, with James quietly seated in the passenger seat. It had been five hours since Dobrev had sobered up, and that made him feel parched. James was mournful and sad. He missed his buddy. He had reached out to Charles' parents and proposed to cover the bill for the coffin, but they politely refused.

Around 75 people came to Charles' funeral. Some of them were college friends and guys from his office. His parents flew from Arizona along with a bunch of cousins and aunts. A few friends of the family came as did two prostitutes who had known Charles for many years. Everybody encircled Charles' grave. A preacher from the local Catholic Church was reading out loud a verse from the Bible. The people at the funeral started sobbing and lamenting. It started to rain as if God himself was crying.

"A funeral is one of those events that no one likes to attend, but people have to be there to pay tribute to the one who has passed away, "Jackson thought while he was listening to the preacher.

The funeral was just about to end when Jackson's phone rang. He looked at the screen of his phone, and realized that he had to take that call. "Excuse me," he whispered to those near him. He stepped aside and answered.

"Hello! Yeah! Wait a minute. What! Oh no, no, no, no. I'll be there in a minute," Jackson enunciated and passed through the grieving crowd.

"I got to go! You will be fine, right!" Jackson whispered to James.

"Yeah! Is everything all right? the writer asked.

"I don't know yet!" Jackson murmured under his breath and left the funeral.

***

Jackson sped his Camaro as if he was being chased by a ruthless gang. He turned on his police lights and ran through every intersection on his way, trying to outrun the clock. After fifteen minutes of insane driving, Jackson parked his Camaro in the Northwestern Hospital parking garage. He then rushed to the ICU unit and couldn't believe his eyes. The picture was unpleasant.

"Oh, Lord!" he exclaimed, looking down and shaking his head in disbelief. His partner, Paul, lay lifeless on the medical bed. His eyes were closed, and his head was wrapped with a bandage. A woman in her early forties knelt next to him, tapping her forehead into Paul's chest. Her name was Teresa—Paul's wife. She had black curly hair and sexy lips. Her hourglass type of body gave her a feminine allure. She wore the pants in Paul's family. As a person, she was stubborn and adamant, but she was someone that Paul could trust. Teresa was dressed as if she was going on a date. She wore a caramel-colored corset over which she had a lapel neck double breasted trench coat. Her black leather legging pants displayed her stunning legs. Despite dressing like a single woman, Teresa loved her husband. She had never cheated on him, except one particular night when she went to a lady's night party and bumped into a friend from college. They both got hammered and started making out at the party. It was a mistake that she had made many years ago.

"What happened?" Jackson asked. The detective stepped closer and hugged Teresa. Paul's wife tried to look stoic, but she started crying.

"Here's what happened. Last night, Paul went to his cousin's in Wisconsin. A few hours later, when he didn't call I started getting worried. I was calling his phone, but nobody answered. I called his cousin and he said that Paul had left his house at 11:30 p.m. I was so tired that night that I fell asleep on the couch. This morning, I woke up with extreme pain in my back. I have allergies, and my nose was stuffy. I made my cappuccino, checked the kids, and then opened the front door to walk the dog. And then I saw... [Teresa was sobbing]. I saw Paul lying on the driveway, as if he was a homeless man. This is horrible! Who could possibly do this to him? He is a nice guy who didn't have enemies. Why did they have to beat up my husband?" Teresa was constantly crying, covering her face because her makeup was messed up and making her look like she was on the set of a zombie movie.

"Everything will be all right, honey. What did the doctor say?" Jackson grilled.

"They say that he has a severe concussion and his brain was damaged as a result of many punches to his head. He is in a coma. The doctors cannot tell how long he will be unconscious. His parents are flying in from Florida. What should I tell them?" Teresa paused and started crying again. Paul provided everything for his family, shelter, food, and paying the bills. Teresa was afraid that if she became a widow, it meant she would have to start working, something she had never done in her entire life.

Jackson grabbed Teresa's shoulders and declared, "Teresa, I need you to focus. I know this is a tragic moment for you and your family but I need to see your security recordings."

"I'm not sure how it works. Paul was playing around with those cameras. I've never been interested in them." Hearing her statement, Jackson remained silent. A minute later, they both jumped into the Camaro. Jackson gave her a ride to her house because he wanted to check those cameras. Twenty minutes later, the red Camaro pulled into the driveway of a fancy house in Lincolnwood. They hopped out of the vehicle and Jackson immediately searched for the cameras which were mounted outside of the house. The African-American detective was convinced that he could solved the puzzle if he watched the recorded tapes from the cameras. Jackson had a dexterous ability to work with modern technology. In no time, he watched the video from the surveillance cameras on Paul's iPad. The records showed that at 4:00 a.m., a black Ford van had stopped at the curb, and Paul was dumped on the driveway like an empty beer can. The people who had thrown him out were all dressed in black, wearing gloves and masks. The van drove away at a mild speed, resembling a USPS truck that appeared to have no license plates. Jackson had nothing. His intuition let him down. Even though that unpleasant situation was too difficult to deal with, he toughed it out and didn't lose his faith. He would do anything possible to catch these nefarious people. Jackson learned how to be stoic after his father left his mother for another woman. His mom lived in a studio, located a few blocks away from his condo in Hyde Park and he was taking care of her. Jackson wouldn't have become a homicide detective if his mother hadn't emboldened him to study hard. His brother, Prince, had been living in New York for fifteen years. Prince worked as a photographer at an eminent company and hadn't been back to Chicago since he moved out. His usual excuse when invited was, *"I'm too busy."* Prince sent money to his mom, but he never showed up for a visit, and that upset Jackson. He couldn't comprehend why his brother acted this way.

***

Over the course of a month, the police investigative report listed two murders, a homicide detective in a coma…and Jackson had nothing. His mind was stuck in a deadlock. The mayor was demanding more information, and Paul's family was getting on his nerves. The chief of the precinct was questioning his work. The pandemonium in his head was gradually increasing, and he felt like it was about to explode like a volcano. The stress from work made it difficult for him to sleep. Jackson was waking up in the middle of the night. It became a routine, which increased his anxiety. However a week later, the detective came up with an idea of what had to be his next step. The following morning, he rang James. They talked briefly. Jackson didn't reveal the reason why he called, but his statement was straight to the point.

"I need to talk with you! Meet me at the Sheraton's lobby on 301 E North Water Street at 11:00 a.m.," Jackson said and James reluctantly accepted the offer. The writer had been sober for three days, which was essential to him as he struggled with alcohol use.

As the writer went inside of the Sheraton, he looked around. The vestibule looked glamorous; everything was pristine. The lobby was gargantuan. The ceiling was over twenty feet high and the antechamber was immaculate, it resembled a painting worth a million dollars. The south side of the antechamber had an ethereal view, facing the river walk. Jackson and James occupied the seats that were next to the windows looking towards the river walk. Jackson preferred to stay away from other people because the conversation with the writer was confidential. At first, they discussed the unpredictable weather in Chicago, then Jackson cut to the chase and shared what had happened to Paul. James was shocked. He couldn't understand how people could be so ruthless.

"I believe you need to fly overseas. You have to leave the country for the sake of your family." Jackson declared. The writer sighed, rolling his eyes and remained silent. His facial expression displayed that he was thoughtfully trying to pick the correct words.

"Before we can move on, I need to ask you a question," James said, and Jackson nodded.

"Have you found out anything about Boris yet?"

"Listen, we've been brainstorming this ruthless crime, and I'm pretty sure that the answers will be revealed soon." It was a profound response that caught up James off guard.

"Jackson, I know you are a sagacious man who takes his job seriously. I'm not questioning your work, okay? I'm asking if you've made any progress with the investigation."

"We are looking at the data collected from both victims. A few detectives are coming from New York to work with us. At this point, that's all I can tell you."

"Jackson, your response is ambiguous. Please, just answer my question," James spoke respectfully.

"The answer is NO. I don't have anything. Not just yet. Are you happy? You think it's easy for me to be put in this position? The chief of police is in a state of slow burn. The mayor is getting on my nerves. I can barely sleep at night. I'm doing you a favor; you will travel for a few weeks. People splurge thousands of dollars on vacations, and you're receiving one for free, financed by the government, and I think…"

"Jackson, cool your jets. I'm not arguing with you. I apologize if I said something inappropriate. I'll do it, okay. I will take a trip far away from here, but you have to promise me that you'll keep an eye on my family, okay?"

"Absolutely! You have my word. I mean, your family will be under a witness protection program even if you don't have anything to testify. I will report to you daily. I'm on it," Jackson said and became silent. Then he went on, "Why do you writers have to be so stubborn?" James looked straight into Jackson's eyes and declared,

"I'm not a writer!" They both burst into laughter. Then Jackson asked his last question.

"Where would you like to go?"

"Bulgaria."

5

It was the second week of January 2022, James was escorted in a stretch limo to a private airport in Chicago. Jackson was driving behind that limo. He wanted to make sure that James wouldn't be assassinated by those who had been terrifying the entire city.

Patrick was transported to Schaumburg where Michelle and Frank were to take care of him. Police troopers would daily check on James' family. Michelle had agreed to collect the rent from the Mexican tenants who lived in James' property. The media wasn't allowed to broadcast anything about it. Jackson contacted the parliament of Bulgaria to make sure that James wouldn't be locked in the American embassy in Sofia because of misleading information. Also, he informed the Bulgarian prime minister about James' excursion. The homicide detective did an impeccable job by orchestrating safe transport. The trip was covert, only a few agents knew where Dobrev had been transported. The flight took around fourteen hours. James hated planes, he felt uncertain while traveling airborne.

During the flight, James was reading an autobiography of Mike

Tyson called *The Undisputed Truth*. That book was engrossing, but he only read it because he wanted to stay sober.

Uncertain thoughts clouded his mind, and he couldn't shake the uneasiness he felt about his son. As a father, he couldn't help but blame himself.

***

On January 15th, at 8:00 a.m., the private jet landed in Plovdiv, Bulgaria where the air was clean and easy to breathe. The twilight in the sky was as exquisite as if it was an artwork worth millions of dollars. The weather was cold but not as cold as Chicago.

It had been 15 minutes since James landed, and he was already mesmerized by the beauty of Plovdiv. Dobrev had always wanted to explore that city. He thought that Plovdiv was an appropriate hideaway and simultaneously a pleasant destination.

James was escorted in a new Mercedes by two Bulgarian authorities, Jack and Liam. Jack was in his early thirties (same age as James). He was 5'8", and his face resembled an owl's. His body looked like he hadn't been in a gym for the past ten years. Unlike Jack, Liam owned a sport center in Plovdiv where he was actively teaching Aikido. He was an expert in that martial arts with the ability to protect himself, and was followed by many peers. Liam was in athletic shape. He was 6'3" tall, within 190 pounds. He was devoted to work for the government as the minister of culture. The city of Plovdiv had a deep reverence for Liam, and he was proud to work for his hometown. Liam was in his fifties, but lived like a proactive man in his twenties. He ate healthy, and shagged his wife twice a day.

As they were driving to Plovdiv, Jack and Liam tried to speak English, but James preferred to use his Bulgarian. He wasn't fluent, but he could articulate a decent conversation. His father had taught him to speak Bulgarian.

***

The Bulgarian government arranged an Airbnb apartment in downtown Plovdiv and a car rental at the U.S. expense. Jack and Liam were assigned to keep an eye on James while he was staying in Bulgaria, but in reality, they wouldn't bother unless there was a significant threat to his safety or if he violated any laws.

***

James opened the door of the Airbnb apartment and looked around. It was a one-bedroom apartment on the third floor of a building that looked similar to a townhouse in Chicago. The apartment had been stylishly renovated. The bedroom had a king-size bed with painted walls in a light blue color. The living room had a huge TV attached to the wall, and a black leather couch was set against the wall. That couch had enough space for a family with six children. There were bookshelves that lined every wall. James felt like he was staying in a small library, and he loved it. His luggage wasn't big. He didn't bring many clothes because he had intentions to shop from the local stores. He only brought his computer and all of his drafts to finish his book, *The Cold Summer*. His book was going fine, but he struggled with the final chapters. James had been working on this title for about a year. He thought twelve months were probably enough to write a book. However, his drinking problem was slowing the process down. His agent, Carl, touched base with him once a month. Carl always encouraged James to finish his books. They had known each other for seven years. During that time, they only talked about business. Carl was interested in making money, and the more he had, the more insatiable he became.

At noon, James prepared his laptop and started to work. He opened the windows on the north side to let the breeze come into the apartment. He believed that writing came naturally when he had fresh air circulating around him. After three hours of writing, the lust for alcohol forced him to stop work. His hands started shaking as if he had Parkinson's. It wasn't bad enough to seek medical help, but enough to make his work awkward. He then made a quick phone call through the app named 'Viber' to get a brief report on his son from his mom. Then he dialed another number. A second later, a man's voice said.

"Hello!"

***

On Monday, James decided to explore Plovdiv, which was distinguished by the seven hills that rose throughout the entire city. The downtown area resembled the Old Town in Chicago. The streets there were overflowing with young people and there were a bunch of luxury restaurants with Mediterranean food that depicted the culture of Bulgaria. Many bars and jazz clubs were located close to each other, like tattoos on a man's back. Even though the temperature was below 30 F, the streets were crammed with people. It was around 6 in the afternoon when James was standing at a bar that had a funky name called 'Marmalad,' which, translated into English, was a subtle way of saying, "get hammered." The writer thought that was hilarious. He went through Marmalad's door, looking debonair, dressed in business casual and wore a black coat and black shoes, his khakis were gray, like the color of the foggy sky. Dobrev ambled to the countertop bar where a chubby chick with blue hair was checking her Instagram on her smartphone. James looked around. Marmalad had a proficient bar with variety of booze lined up behind the bar in a pyramid shape. The walls of the entire gin mill were built from solid bricks. On the walls hung a bunch of framed photos with some of the most prominent movie stars in Hollywood. *"Gosh! The owner must be a movie maniac,"* James thought. Half of the capacity of that bar had been occupied already, but Dobrev easily found an empty spot by the bar. He politely asked for the cheapest beer. The bartender with blue hair looked at him as if he had asked to see her naked. James felt uncomfortable drinking alone in a foreign country. Despite his discomfort, he tried to speak with the bartender with the blue colored hair, but she shunned him almost immediately. James shrugged off the rejection and drained his draft beer in less than four minutes. He then looked at his Tissot wrist watch. It was 6:30 p.m. A minute later, a man with a big beer gut went through the door.

"Hey, James! What are you doing here, Ballsack?" the man with the beer gut exclaimed.

"Big John! You asshole, where have you been?" James said. He used to call his friend *Big* John because he was a small kid in his freshman years. But over the years, John had become an insatiable eating machine and gained a lot of weight—over 250 pounds.

John and James had known each other for over twenty-five years. They both had grown up in Chicago as best friends. John was in his early thirties. He was 5'8", but his obese body made him look shorter. His nose looked more like the beak of an eagle. John was a prosperous entrepreneur. His truck company was doing well in the States and he was able to control his business remotely. He had moved from Chicago to Plovdiv around six years ago and bought a mansion that was a five-minute drive out of Plovdiv. John was married to a Bulgarian girl, and he was the happy father of two daughters.

James and John were having an elated conversation because they hadn't been seen each other in years. As they were talking, John asked, "James, are you here on vacation or for business?"

"Both!" James replied shortly. He couldn't reveal the real reason why he had had to travel to Bulgaria. Even though James put effort into camouflaging this information, John figured that something bad had already happened.

"How is Patrick?" John asked but the writer didn't answer. The questions about his son were making him uncomfortable. John nodded tacitly, understanding that he shouldn't ask and the reason was simple—Patrick' medical condition.

"How is your family, Big John?"

"My daughters grow faster than my hair! Kate is three, and Kimberly is five. They are adorable and I love them so much. Every time I see them, they melt my heart. They look so cute when they stare at me with their innocent eyes. As my wife… (Big John looked away as if he had already regretted mentioning his wife)… my wife, Amelia. Oh man, she is gorgeous. The most beautiful woman I've ever seen in my life."

"How did you meet her?" James questioned.

"Oh! That was easy. I went to a dive like this one. I sat by the bar close to the bartender and ordered a coffee. I was making a few phone calls regarding some expensive freight for my business. Then all of sudden, this gorgeous gal Amelia came to the bar, and we started chatting. I offered to buy her a drink, she accepted, and we didn't stop talking for the next three hours. We had a really good conversation. After that, I took her on a few dates, and… you know we've been together since then," Big John finished his prolonged monologue. The story of how he nailed Amelia made him proud of himself. The truth was; if Amelia hadn't sought his attention, Big John would have never been able to talk to her.

"That's cool, Big John. I'm happy for you. What does she do for a living?" James sounded interested, but he was just making a conversation with his old friend.

"She is a painter. I gave her a huge room, and now she uses it to do her crafts. She makes enough money to take care of herself," Big John said proudly. The truth was that Amelia wasn't making any profit from her paintings. She consistently asked John for money because he was the breadwinner, responsible for taking care of his family and ensuring that his wife was provided for. John was too proud of himself to reveal the truth about his wife. Although Dobrev figured that something was wrong with his friend.

"What's eating you, Big John?" James surprised his friend with this question.

"Nothing! What makes you think that something is bothering me?" Big John replied. His insecurities had kicked in.

"C'mon, John! I've known you since we were kids. What's the matter?" James asked, and Big John sighed.

"Okay, here is the thing! My wife spends 3-4 hours in the gym; she goes there five times a week. That's insane! She is not going to be a bodybuilder, so why does she need to spend so many hours there loafing around? Isn't it obvious? She is cheating on me!" Big John protested as if he was complaining to customer service about additional charges on his bills. James nodded and declared, "Has it ever crossed your mind that you may have misinterpreted her actions?" James pointed out. Big John looked at his friend as if a stranger was talking to him.

"Huh? What do you mean? I'm not following," Big John asked in a state of confusion.

"I think you are not giving enough attention to your wife, which may be why she's going to a place where others can admire her. I believe if you take her on dates and spend more time with her, she will open her heart to you. Of course, I could be wrong. I've never met your family. I'm just expressing my opinion. Does that make sense to you?" James grilled. Big John's eyes widened. He looked at James with confusion and then burst into laughter. His guffaw was so loud that others in the bar surveyed him with suspicion. It took a minute before Big John could talk.

"James, you are a nutcase! That doesn't make any sense to me. How can you come up with this crap?

"Let me ask you a question. How often do you take your wife on a date?" James made a good point. His straightforward question changed John's face.

"I don't know… once in every two weeks… I guess. That's not enough?" Big John asked, and James shook his head no.

"Okay! Next Saturday, you will have dinner with my family. I won't accept *"No"* for an answer," Big John announced.

"That would be lovely. I'm looking forward to meeting your family. Excuse me for a moment, I need to take a Mondo duke," James said.

"A Mondo what?" Big John asked.

"Mondo duke," James repeated. John looked at him, baffled.

"What's that?"

"A Mondo duke means the act of taking a massive bowel movement. I've learned if from *Impractical Jokers*," James happily stated. "Oh yeah, those guys are funny. A Mondo duke! You fucking meatball," Big John sniggered.

"I'm not an Italian!" James declared.

"Yes, but you are still a meatball. Go and take the Mondo… whatever you called it," Big John said, and James laughed out loud. He then politely asked the bartender where the restroom was and quickly ambled to the commode. The Bulgarians in the joint surveyed James because he looked different. The girls were enticed by his bravado, but the guys gave him unfriendly looks. James avoided getting into close contact with locals, especially, in bars because he knew that something could go wrong faster than the speed of a supersonic jet. A couple of minutes later, he came back from his mission, tapped the arm of his friend and sat adjacent to him. Big John gave his friend a smirk and placed a stein of draft beer in front of him.

"That's on me," Big John proudly stated as if he were handing James a check for $20,000. James gazed questioningly at his friend and said, "That's my last call. After this beer, I'm leaving this dive!"

"Yeah, whatever you say. Cheers!" The buddies who shared the same childhood were cheerfully gulping their beers. For the next couple of hours, James and Big John drained fourteen more draft beers. They left Marmalad with a tip of over 40%. The friends from Chicago (James and John) were inebriated. They tried to go to a strip club, but they couldn't enunciate the address to the cab driver. And so, John staggered to his mansion, and James wobbled to the Airbnb apartment.

The next day, James had to wrestle an obnoxious hangover. He drank numerous cups of tea and many glasses of orange juice but those methods didn't help him. *"No more drinking! That's it. I'm done!"* his inner voice exclaimed. James idled on his bed until noon before he began working on his novel. At 3 in the afternoon, he called his mom to hear updates about Patrick. He also spoke with Detective Jackson to get any updates about the Cold Murder. Jackson didn't have any new information or any forensic evidence regarding that case. They spoke for about ten minutes before James ended the call. He felt relieved, that nothing bad had happened. He tried not to think about the murder because it would make him uneasy. At 4:00 p.m., the writer concentrated on finishing his novel. James followed the advice of his father, Ivan Dobrev, who had taught him that a man needs to be disciplined and work every day to achieve something in life. The writer decided to create a new regime, a paradigm of lifestyle that he would follow during his vacation in Plovdiv. In the mornings, James had a quick breakfast (usually fruit), then started to work on his novel. In the afternoon, he would explore the city of Plovdiv for a few hours, then he had to come back home and do exercises for his arm. In the evening, he ate soup and read a book until he drifted off. The most important thing for James was to reduce his drinking, which meant avoiding bars, pubs, or any places that served alcohol.

***

Saturday, the first week of February, James was driving his rental car, a white 2018 Ford Fiesta. He rolled up to John's property. John kept his word and invited the writer to his mansion for dinner. Dobrev checked the GPS on his iPhone to make sure he wouldn't get lost. After thirty minutes of driving, he pulled the rental car over in front of a big archway bonded with two creepy-looking gates.

"Damn! That's a huge property!" James said to himself. He wasn't sure if he was at the correct address because there were no street numbers, so James rang John to make sure he wasn't lost.

"Hey, buddy! Where you at?" John asked.

"Can't really tell. I'm in front of a big archway and…"

"Yeah, you made it! Go to the gate and press the intercom button and I'll buzz you in," John stated. James did what his friend instructed him and the gate automatically opened. Dobrev hopped back into the rental Ford and rolled through the gate. It was 8 o'clock, and the darkness had already slunk over the sky. As he drove through, James surveyed the property. There were a few street lights that brightened the premises. Also, there was a topiary arrangement in which a few fountains were placed. On the right side was a modern gazebo, which looked as big as a house, surrounded by a bunch of ferns. There were many trees lined up around the mansion, making it look like a tropical rainforest. The entire property was encircled by a brick privacy wall that was ten feet high. The writer was flabbergasted; the mansion looked like it belonged to some Hollywood celebrity.

James drove through the paved driveway and kept exploring the property. He then saw two men dressed identically who were waiting for him at a circle drive. James stopped the car, and one of the valets opened the door for him. "*John has valet parking here!*" he thought.

"Good evening, señor, James. I'm Miguel. I will take you inside. Please, follow me," said the man who looked like a Spanish soccer player. He was dressed in a black jacket and black trousers.

"Yes, thank you! What about the car…?" James was in such shock that he almost stuttered and couldn't enunciate his words properly.

"This is Hugo! He will take care of the car. Please, follow me, sir!" Miguel said with a charming smile. James and Miguel ambled through a garden pathway that looked like was part of a fairy tale. The mansion where John lived had European architecture. There were a few columns at the front door that held a huge balcony above. The front door was so tall that even an elephant could easily sneak in. The mansion looked more like a British castle. There were two wings on each side that had an oval shape that reached up to the top floor. The mansion itself had been constructed using M-rock style stones. James was escorted to the den, where he gave John a brotherly hug. There was a pause. Then John introduced his wife, Amelia. James surveyed John's wife. She was a blond chick in her mid-twenties. Her strapless dress portrayed her figure as if she was a model posing for a magazine. Amelia had an enthralling face and sparkling blue eyes that looked like she could be Miley Cyrus' sister. John's wife spoke in Bulgarian because she wasn't interested in speaking English. Amelia wasn't interested in meeting James from the get go. She smiled at him, but her thoughts were, "*Okay, let's get over with it.*" She seemed to avoid talking and simply smiled as if she was a ring girl in a boxing fight. John presented his daughters, Kate and Kimberly, who looked like twins. John's daughters had hay-colored hair and blue eyes. They were adorable. Often, people commented on their beauty. Kate and Kimberly were fascinated by

James' floppy haircut and how he was dressed. They were constantly smiling at him.

They all sauntered to the dining room on the second floor, which had space for more than fifty guests. A massive gas fireplace was located on the north side of the room, while Amelia's paintings adorned the walls. They occupied the rectangular dinner table, which was made from African Blackwood, the most expensive wood in the world, and measured twenty-five feet in length. A massive chandelier glittered above the table, with a price tag that exceeded $25,000. The ceiling, which was over twenty feet high, embellished with more than one hundred embedded ceiling lights that made the dining room brighter than daylight. A 100-inch TV was attached to the wall on the south side of the room. As he walked in the dining room, James realized that the food had already been served on the table. There were oysters, lobsters, salmon, steaks, and all kinds of vegetables. The quality of the food was the highest, as if the president of the United States was dining there. To make that dinner, John had hired one of the best chefs that could be found in Plovdiv. James and John's family had an amazing dinner, all except Amelia. She wasn't in the mood. No one could fathom the reason why. Actually, John was forced to ask his wife if she was feeling sick but Amelia refused to talk. Her answers were short and apathetic. After dinner, John and James walked out to the 1600 square feet balcony. It was big enough to make a small wedding for thirty people. The view from the balcony was so picturesque that it seemed to mesmerize James. The entire city of Plovdiv and a few mountains could be seen from there.

"So what do you think?" John asked, staring at his friend.

"Man, your mansion is lavish. I've never been in a mansion like this before. It looks like Sylvester Stallone lives here!"

"Yeah, the mansion is fine, but I didn't mean that. I was asking about my wife. Did you see how weird she is?" John's eyes looked as if he was saying, *"James! Help me, dammit."*

"Yeah, I see what you're sayin'. Have you ever tried to talk to her?"

"What do you mean?" John looked puzzled.

"Okay. You have to find out what's bothering her. Obviously, she isn't happy with something, and your job as a husband is to acknowledge her frustration," James lectured his theory. John sighed, thinking about what he had just heard and then gently tapped the injured arm of his friend. "James, I've known you for twenty-five years, and I'm not buying any of your words. What are you trying to say?" Listening to John's proclamation, James burst into laughter. After a few seconds of guffawing, the writer went on.

"Take her to an expensive restaurant. Then, surprise her with flowers or a gift that would make her happy. When you both are sitting at the restaurant, talk to her. By *talk,* I mean listen to what she has to say. Do not interrupt her. You need to find out what pain is hiding behind her heart. Does that make sense to you?" James finished his speech. John was silent. He stared at his friend and snapped, "Hold on! How come you know so much about women?"

"John, my old buddy. Don't question my knowledge. You're the one asking for help. I have acquired this information from many books. I know you don't read, so there is no use referring you a book."

"Yeah! I heard, ya. Hold on. I'll be right back with, ya," John exclaimed and went inside. While John was inside, James stared at the picturesque view. He looked like a kid dreaming of being a movie star. Despite his gleeful expression, James was feeling perturbed as he worried about his family, especially Patrick. Around five minutes later, John came back holding a black box with an Arabic inscription.

"What is that box?" James grilled.

"I bought it when I traveled in India," John stated proudly. He opened the box and took a cheap cigar.

"They are watching you!" John quietly said as if he didn't want to be heard. Hearing this, James' eyes widened as if John just called him a lousy cocksucker. "*Wait, what? What is he talking about?*"

"Big John, what are you talking about?" James asked, and John looked around to make sure that no one was eavesdropping.

"Is that some kind of a joke? What are you saying, John?" James kept asking as he looked completely confused.

"No!" John mumbled, shaking his head no.

"Big John! Looked at me!" John stared at James. "What are you talking about, buddy? What do you know?" the writer asked in disbelief.

"I can't tell you more!" John said, his tone indicating that he regretted the conversation.

"What do you mean you can't tell me more? Spill the beans, dammit!"

"I would love to, but I can't," John was carefully picking his words.

"John, what do you mean *you can't*?" Dobrev was hell-bent on finding out what his friend knew.

"If I tell you more, they will kill my family!" John declared, and James became confused once again.

"What do you mean, *they*?" James asked. John shook his head, showing his unwillingness to speak.

"Okay, John. Thanks for the dinner! I'll talk with you later," James cried out, turned around, and headed out of the balcony.

"Be careful!" John said, and James showed his thumbs up without turning. Dobrev was imperturbable, but his mind was storming. He walked down the staircase that lead to the first floor of the mansion. Miguel stood by the front door, surprised that James was leaving so early. But Miguel wasn't a chump; he knew when he had to keep his mouth shut. He escorted James to the curved driveway, which surrounded perfectly trimmed bushes that resembled big mushrooms. The writer walked through the concrete paved driveway and waited for the valet. In no time, he hopped in the rental Ford and drove off from the property. Twenty minutes later, he rolled through one of the main boulevards of Plovdiv and noticed that a few street lights were blinking. "*Nah, man! Those lights, again! What the heck is happening with me?*" James thought. He felt disappointed and betrayed by his childhood friend. He couldn't understand why John had acted so weird. James and John had spent a lot of time together in their twenties. They had graduated college together and treated each other as brothers. Over that time, John started a business with big rigs and became very busy. In the meantime, James had been competing in a few boxing tournaments and had no time to fool around as well. From best buddies, they became strangers.

"*It is sad when life compartmentalizes people's friendships. Gee, I need a drink,*" James' inner voice whispered. He knew that In Bulgaria, people could buy alcohol at any time. Liquor stores were like casinos; they never closed their doors. For that reason, James went to the closest liquor store, bought a bottle of Jameson, and went to the library apartment to knock himself out. Dobrev was living in a dystopia, his fears of failing to be a father and a good person were chasing him perpetually.

6

The next day, Sunday, James had a horrendous hangover. He had drunk until 4 in the morning, and woke up at noon. The headache was making him nauseous, but he didn't throw up. Despite his headache, James was proactive. He rinsed his mouth and took a cold shower. After that, he started to clean the library apartment that looked like complete mess as if he had thrown a cocaine party with rock stars. James hated living in filthy places; his parents had nurtured him to keep his home squeaky clean, and they did a good job.

After an hour, the apartment looked immaculate, as if no one had lived there for years. At 1 o'clock, he called his mom. They talked for around fifteen minutes, which was just enough time to get a report of what was going on in Chicago. James missed his family, especially Patrick. He wasn't sure how long he had to stay in Bulgaria.

Later on, James started working on his novel. He considered writing as an ethereal endeavor that was bringing him eternal gratification. When James was writing fiction, he felt like the Creator of the Universe. In his novels, James created characters, places, relationships, unpleasant predicaments, and so on, just like God does in the real world. That was why Dobrev felt entitled and obsessed with his work.

At 6 in the afternoon, James got tired and stopped the work on his novel. His eyelids became heavy, and his mind was congested. The writer decided to refresh his mind and ordered a lobster bisque from a local restaurant that had many good reviews. Dobrev tried to eat healthy food to keep his body in functional shape. He had been a pescatarian for two years. He also avoided drinking milk and eating any type of fried food. The lobster bisque wasn't what he had expected, but at least filled his stomach. At seven in the evening, James thought about what he should do next. He couldn't sleep yet. His agenda was to do something entertaining or something that would sidetrack him from consuming alcohol.

"I got it!" James exclaimed aloud as if he was talking to somebody. He then opened his laptop and Googled information about cinemas around the area. The title '*The Father Who Moves Mountains*' grabbed his attention, and without wasting a second, the writer bought a ticket for a cinema called 'Stare' from their website. An hour later, he took his seat at the movie theater. The houselights in the cinema were still on, and the big screen was off. James surveyed the audience as if he was looking for someone he might know. The movie theater was occupied to half capacity. There were many guys with their girlfriends or entire families with bunches of kids but there weren't many single guys like him. All of a sudden, the writer turned around as if someone had called out his name and saw a big man who sat alone about four rows behind him. The man looked like a biker in his late forties. He was bald, wearing a leather jacket and dark sunglasses. "*Who the heck is wearing sunglasses in a cinema?*" James' inner voice proclaimed. "*Well, there are many different people around the globe!*" he thought and shrugged. The writer turned back to the big screen. The movie lasted about two hours. James liked that movie. It gave him hope that he may be a good father one day.

When James walked through the lobby, something in his peripheral vision forced him to turn around. The same man that looked like a biker was now about ten feet behind him. He was still alone. He looked at James as if he had to tell him something, but he remained speechless. That biker was a big and tall man, resembled the WWE superstar, 'Big Show.' He was wearing the same glasses as earlier; it looked like they were glued to his face

"Excuse me! Can I help you with somethin'?" James asked, feeling uncomfortable. The biker didn't flinch. He acted as if he was deaf. James couldn't tell if the biker was looking at him because he was wearing those foolish sunglasses. He decided not to interact with the stranger and scuttled to the exit. The writer hopped in the rental Ford and roared out from the parking lot. Holding the steering wheel, James looked at the rearview mirror and noticed that a black Mercedes was driving behind, which made him restless. Immediately, James veered off to a gas station and observed how the Mercedes passed him. "*Were they following me?*" he thought, unsure of what to do. "*Maybe, I'm barking up the wrong tree!*" Dobrev considered the possibility that he might be misinterpreting the whole situation. He even thought about contacting the two Bulgarians who had helped him when he first arrived in the country, but ultimately decided against it.

Later the same night, James parked the rental Ford at a prepaid garage and walked to the Airbnb apartment. That night, he remained sober as he had planned and crawled into his bed to get some rest. He couldn't sleep; his agitated mind wouldn't allow him to. Thoughts about his family overtook him, along with the fact that there might be people watching him. James wasn't convinced that staying in Bulgaria was a good idea. His intentions were simple: to return to

Chicago. *"My time here is over!"* That was his last thought before he dozed off.

***

Monday, the next day, James awoke around 10:00 a.m. He hadn't slept well, but felt relieved that he didn't drink the night before. Dobrev couldn't have coffee; it made him sick. Instead, he loved tea; it stimulated his bowel movement. After he finished his business in the bathroom, James phoned the homicide detective, Chris Jackson.

"Hi! How you doin,' Jackson?" James was perked up to speak with the detective.

"I'm fine. How is your vacation? Do you like spending time in Bulgaria?" the detective asked. They talked more casually as they had known each other for a while. After exchanging a few common phrases, James asked, "What can you tell me about my family? Do you think that they're safe?"

"Absolutely, I send a patrol twice a day to check them out. Nothing has changed since you've left. We're tracking the traces to find anything that connects the Cold Murder and the killing of your friend, Charles," Jackson reported.

"And have you found anything?" James chimed in.

"Unfortunately, nothing yet but we are working on it." Jackson was getting agitated, talking about the same subject over and over again. He was feeling overworked, handling two homicides and the assault on his partner Paul, who had been in a coma since.

"Jackson, I'm thinking to hop on a plane and fly back to Chicago. I shouldn't be here," James announced, sounding as if he had been thinking about his speech for a while.

"No…no…no. James, listen to me carefully. I went to a lot of trouble to ensconce you in Bulgaria. You can't just fly back to Chicago. I need more time. I'm telling you. It's gonna be just fine. I mean…

Is there a problem there? Do you have something to tell me?" Jackson asked, making James feel anxious. The writer wasn't sure if he should inform Jackson about his bizarre encounter at the cinema.

"James, are you there?" Jackson asked. It took a few seconds before James could answer.

"Yeah, yeah. I'm okay. I'm getting a little homesick, that's all," James replied, using a roundabout answer, which didn't surprise Jackson. They spoke a little more over the phone. After they wound up the phone call, James stared at the laminated floor, thinking about what he could do for the rest of the day. He went to the bathroom and gazed at the mirror. *"Gosh, I need a haircut,"* his inner voice protested. James became uncomfortable when his hair got longer. He googled a few local barbershops and peeked through the window to determine the weather. The sky was overcast; the temperature was in the mid-forties. *"Screw it! I'm taking a ride to a barbershop,"* James thought. In a blur, he put on gray denim trousers, a black Gucci pullover, and on top a dark blue colored coat. The writer drove the rental Ford to a barber shop called 'Buzz the Fuzz.' He chose this barber shop because it had a humorous name and many good reviews. It was 10:30 a.m. when James went into Buzz the Fuzz. The barbershop had an appealing design and upscale equipment, but it wasn't spacious. Dobrev was thrilled to explore the place. However, he had a hard time explaining what he wanted. The only employee at the barbershop was a gypsy guy with a buzz cut and a perpetually puzzled expression who didn't speak English at all.

At noon, James left the barbershop, unsure if the gypsy guy had done a good job on his hair. Dobrev hopped into the rental Ford and drove to the mall to buy some clothes and something for his son. Not that James needed any clothes but he wanted to kill some time. As he waited leisurely for a green light at an intersection that wasn't jammed with many vehicles, then *BOOM!* All of a sudden, the rental Ford wiggled as if there was an earthquake. Something had hit James' rental from behind. *"Damn! What the heck was that?"* James cried out silently. He glanced at the rearview mirror and noticed another vehicle behind him. Dobrev grabbed his iPhone and pressed on the hazard lights. Then hopped out of the car to make sure that the other vehicle wouldn't drive away. As he approached the other vehicle, a person hopped out of the other car, causing James to freeze as if he saw an extraterrestrial creature that had just walked out of a spacecraft.

"I'm so sorry! I don't know what is going on with me. I spilled a bottle of water on the car seat and got distracted. Are you okay? I hope you are," a woman in her mid-twenties blurted out.

"I'm fine, thanks. Are you injured?" James asked, not taking his eyes off the woman.

"No! Thank God!" the chick said. She paused for a second and went on. "My name is Anna. What's yours?" she introduced herself politely and they both became lost in an engaging conversation. While they were talking, James and Anna couldn't take their eyes off one another. For a moment, they forgot that they were involved in a car accident. Anna looked luscious, wearing high heels, with her muscular legs reminiscent of a swimming champion, and her figure resembling that of the gorgeous actress Maia Mitchell. Her eyes were hypnotic. Her skin color was bronze and her brunette hair was as good as it would have if she had been an actress shooting commercials for hair products. She was ostentatiously attractive; when Anna walked down the sidewalk, people did double-takes. She was also sexy, well-dressed, intelligent, and confident.

In what seemed to be only a minute later, James and Anna parked their cars on a side street out of the traffic. It was a minor car accident and both vehicles were drivable. Anna told him that she would take care of everything. Staring at her, James looked deadpan, but his heart was racing. The writer had interacted with over a hundred chicks, but he had never seen such a sultry girl like her.

"Where are you from?" Anna asked.

"I was born and raised in Chicago," James replied, showing a poker face, yet he was excited.

"Oh my God! That is so cool! I love Chicago. I've been there multiple times," she exclaimed happily. Up until that moment, they were communicating in Bulgarian. After James revealed that he was from Chicago, they switched to English.

"Are you traveling for fun, or are you on a business trip?" Anna inquired.

"Actually, both. I'm trying to finish my book!" he stated, and Anna lifted her eyebrows.

"You're a writer!" Anna squawked. James hated when people called him a *writer*, but he couldn't be mad at Anna because it was his own weirdness about what people called him.

"I would say that I'm a guy who writes books," James stated with a smirk on his face. Anna gave him a look as if he had just insulted her.

"What is the difference," the gorgeous chick asked.

"I don't know. It's just the way I am," James sounded like Eminem in one of his songs. Regardless of his weird articulations, Anna kept asking him questions. Dobrev knew that if a girl talked to him that meant she liked him.

A few minutes later, a policeman arrived on the scene and scrutinized the damage by snapping pictures of the vehicles before filing a report. Both vehicles had minor damage, and the police officer finished his report, quicker than James expected.

After the police officer left, James asked, "What do you do for a living?" Then Anna burst into laughter. She laughed so hard that James had the impression that he had asked the wrong question.

"I'm an injury lawyer! Are you injured? Do you need a lawyer?" Anna laughed at her own sarcastic question, revealing her attraction to him. James and Anna talked for a few minutes more. Then the writer stated "Anna, it was lovely chatting with you. Unfortunately, I have to go, but I think we should get together later this week."

"Oh my God! I was just about to say that!" Anna emphasized. That was her way of saying, *"I was hoping that you'd say that."*

"Mantastic! I'll talk to you later!" James said. He pretended that he had something urgent to do. The truth was that he was doing it on purpose. That was his gimmick that he used to entice chicks. "Mantastic! What do you mean?" Anna asked. Her English was fluent, although, she had never heard that phrase before.

"I believe the word *Mantastic* is slang. It means a man who is feeling fantastic. Are you asking because you are impressed with my English?" He asked. James sounded a bit cocky. That was his way of saying, *"I want to talk with you."* Anna didn't answer. She was thinking and surveying the man in front of her.

"Okay, I really have to go! I'll talk with ya later," James blurted out and hopped in his rental Ford. Anna couldn't understand why James was in such a rush. Usually, men were all over her like bees on flowers, but James was different. He was mysterious, and that made her interested.

An hour later, James stepped into the library apartment. He had to start working on his novel but couldn't stop thinking about Anna. He wasn't sure what he should do. Dobrev was overexcited like a kid falling in love for the first time. He hadn't felt like that since he met his wife, Rebecca. Thinking about it, he concluded that Anna wasn't a good influence on him, so he made a conscious effort to focus on other things. *"What shall I do?"* his inner voice asked. Then an idea came to his mind. James searched through his luggage and pulled out a book called TREJO — the autobiography of the actor Danny Trejo. James was interested in Danny's stories and began reading from the paperback. An hour later, his iPhone rang. It was Big John.

"Yeah!"

"Hey, James! How you doin'?

"Not much, John. Reading a book. What are you up to?" the writer asked while looking at his Tissot watch—it was half past six in the evening.

"A book! That sounds boring! Let's get together. I'll buy you a drink," John proposed. There was a pause. At first, James wasn't sure what to say. He then declared, "I don't know, Big John… I had a bizarre day."

"Great! We can talk about it at the bar. I'll be waiting at the G's bar," Big John proclaimed.

"Are you there already?"

"Nah, but I'm on my way. I'll see you soon!" Big John said and hung up the phone.

G's bar was in downtown Plovdiv, which was a five-minute walk from James' place. G's was a typical sports bar that looked the same as others in the area. It had a countertop bar at the center. There were booths spread on each side, except at the entrance. Also, there was a staircase that led to the basement. In that basement was the entertainment area filled dartboards, pool tables, and a few foosball tables. It was 7:30 in the evening when James burst into the bar. He was dressed in business casual as though he were attending a huge convention center. James stepped inside and looked around. G's Bar wasn't busy and had plenty of space, but Big John wasn't there. "*That mother flower lied to me!*" he thought, and sat on a stool by the bar and ordered a Jameson. Dobrev was quiet, but that didn't mean he was calm. He disliked when people acted tricky, like John. Around ten minutes later, Big John came over and gave James a brother hug.

"I thought you were here, liar!" James protested. He looked like he was frustrated, but actually, he was happy to see his friend.

"I told you, I was on my way here!" Big John replied.

"Look at you! What are you wearing? Is that a tracksuit? You look like a retired truck driver living on a pension," James pointed out.

"Listen, I'm a multimillionaire. You know that. Why would I borrow trouble and wear clothes worth 10Gs? I don't need attention. I'm street smart and prefer to keep it low key. Look at you! You look flashy as if you are dating a highly paid actress from Hollywood," Big John said, smiling at his friend, but his thoughts were serious.

"Well, I work hard to make money, and I like to dress in nice clothes. Besides, I may get lucky tonight. You never know," James responded, and Big John shot him a frowny poker face.

"You've been lucky since you were born," Big John pointed out, and both laughed out loud.

"There is something you need to know," Big John went on. "I have a few buddies who work for the Bulgarian government. They told me that someone has been asking about you."

"Who?" James butted in.

"I don't have any idea. That's all I know. I was worried about revealing those details. That's why I told you that they could kill my family. I apologize for being such a jerk. I didn't mean to sound like an A-hole."

"That's fine. I don't hold any grudges, and I'm not mad at ya. I thought you said that you're buying me a beer?" James blurted out with a smirk on his face.

"How much can you drink?" Big John tantalized the writer. "No… no…no…no! Don't say it. We don't play this game. Just buy me a beer," James declared, and Big John bought six beers for the writer to drain.

"James, where have you been? I haven't heard from you for a couple of days" Big John asked while draining another draft beer. Dobrev looked away as if he was ashamed of the question. He then explained the story of how he had met Anna.

"She is the most sensuous and erudite chick I've ever seen," James announced, sounding hyperventilated like a boy having his first touch with a girl.

"Show me her Facebook or Instagram," John requested.

"Nah, I don't operate like that."

"What do you mean?" John asked, astounded.

"Here's the thing: social media ruins the whole mystery between people who have just met. It exposes pictures, places where people have been, and so on. We should be able to engage in conversations about knowing everything about the other person. But instead, all the answers are already laid out on social media. It kills the vibe. Let's assume that I had her Facebook profile, and I knew what she does and what she likes. Then what have I got to talk about when we get together? Does that make any sense?" the writer asked.

"James, you are a weirdo. I have no idea how you come up with those theories. Just have a beer, and stop dreaming," Big John suggested, and they both laughed. Staring at his friend, James made a look saying, *"I know what I'm doing, and I don't need to prove a point to anyone."*

"What happened with your wife? Have you talked to her?" James questioned.

"I don't know, man! I'm trying to talk to her, but she pretends that she is extremely busy. I think I will take her on vacation to Greece or Turkey."

"John, that's a great idea! That's an opportunity in which both of you can relax. Then she can talk to you about her feelings and emotions.

"Yeah, yeah. I guess that may work. I got a funny story for you," John declared.

"Go ahead!"

"So, a week ago, my wife and I had a shower together. We weren't doing anything particular, just taking a shower, okay? So, I accidently passed gas, then my wife asked, *'Why do you always fart on me?'* Then I replied, *'Well, honey, I don't want to hide anything from ya.'*

I was just being funny, and Boom! She flipped out and started accusing of being a jerk and blah-blah."

Hearing this, James was laughing so hard that he almost collapsed on the floor.

"Finish your beer! We need to go," John said. He went on, "There is a place that I want to show you."

"No… no. I'm good. John, I know what you are trying to do. I'm not going anywhere," James declared, shaking his head in disapproval. For the following minutes they debated whether to leave or stay at G's. However, at 10:00 p.m., James decided to roll the dice and agreed to go with John. The friends from Chicago cruised to a spacious storage place that looked like a rickety building. They sneaked in through the black door with no signs. They had to pass through multiple entrances, guarded by several bouncers. The corridors were built from cement and had a few cheap lights hanging on the walls. It felt like entering a highly secured penitentiary, with the length of the corridors adding to this impression.

"Where are we goin'? John, you know that I don't like surprises." James ran out of patience and that made him nervous.

"Don't worry. It is not what it looks like. Trust me!" Big John answered. As they approached, the sound of hip hop music grew louder from below. Hearing the music, James had already guessed where there were heading. After around five minutes of walking through the empty corridors, James and John stopped at a big door covered by a couple of bodybuilders. The bodybuilders searched them for hidden weapons and checked their identification. Then James and John burst in. They saw a huge strip club where a few naked chicks were twerking on dancing poles, which lined the center of the club. Two long-stretched bars were positioned from each side of the entrance. The strip club was about 140 feet long, and had more than 100 tables spread out like a Dalmatian's dots. The second floor was designed with a myriad of booths for lap dances. The strip club was lightened with a mixture of blue and red colors. The music was blasting so loud that the glasses on the tables were shaking to the beat. The design of the place resembled a basement where adult films were shot. The club had no signs because it was illegal—the owner was a former mayor who had been making deals with the current government. The same owner was paying money to the police to leave him alone and not bother him. The loud music didn't disturb any residents because the whole club was on the ground floor, and the walls had sound isolation.

"What's the name of this club?" James screamed in John's ears.

"I think they call it *The Line*," John yelled back.

"How the heck did you find this place?" the writer asked.

"James, who are you, chief of the police? Stop asking annoying questions. C'mon let's have a beer and sit out there," John suggested, and both walked to a booth next to the dancing poles. James was smart enough to understand how stupid he was to be in that club as he knew that it was pointless to stay there.

"Big John, get me a beer. I'll be right back. I have to drain the lizard," James cried out, and went looking for a restroom. He asked the security where the washroom was, and headed toward a black door. The hallway was so dark that James couldn't find the door handle. The restroom was old, and filthy. It looked like it hadn't been cleaned in weeks. "*I guess the Health Department hasn't been here yet*," he thought, relieved that he was alone in that restroom. After finishing urinating, he went to wash his hands when unexpectedly, the light above him started blinking.

"Those frigging lights! What now!" Dobrev spoke out loud as if he was talking to someone. He then left the restroom without turning off the lights. He was disgusted to touch anything there. When James was gone, the light that was blinking stopped as if had never blinked before. The writer returned to the booth and saw John chatting with a naked stripper. She was stellar with a muscular body that looked as if she was a martial artist; her curly blonde hair looked stunning. Big John was mesmerized by her boobs. He didn't mind visiting strip clubs while he was married. Being the breadwinner, he believed that he deserved to have fun. However, John was mistaken in his belief. Even though he was taking care of his family, his behavior was wrong.

"Hey, Ballsack! What took you so long? That's Bunny. She's a friend of mine," John introduced the stripper to the writer. James wasn't interested in Bunny, even though, he was physically attracted to her. His mind was occupied by thoughts about those blinking lights. Ever since he got embroiled in the Cold Murder, he saw blinking lights wherever he went—it started getting annoying. James couldn't reveal that to anyone. He thought that people would think of him as a man who was losing his mind. "*Am I getting crazy? Do I need to see a psychiatrist?*" he thought.

"Hey, Buddy! What is it? Are you okay?" John asked as he noticed that his friend stared thoughtfully.

"Yeah, I'm fine," James replied with an expression that seemed to say, "*Dude! Are you kidding me? Why are you asking those questions?*"

"Listen, I'll leave you alone for a couple of minutes. Bunny and I …"

"Don't worry. Go!" James interrupted him. John took Bunny to the second floor, and they headed to a private room. In the room, Bunny started dancing, but John wasn't interested in her dancing skills. He gave her extra cash, and Bunny started doing lollipops. John disliked making love with other women, but he liked painting chick's faces with his sperm. While John were having fun, James got disinterested, which was a bad sign. When James got bored, his vices started to kick in. He called the waitress and ordered two beers which he downed in less than two minutes. The alcohol was making him dizzy. In a little while, James felt disgusted by the strip club and didn't want to stay a minute longer there. As James looked around, suddenly, his eyes froze. He saw the biker that he had encountered at the cinema. The biker wore the same clothes but this time his glasses were off. He had an expression of an angry man who had lost a lot of money on gambling. "*Who is this guy? Why is he watching me? I better slide off, but I can't leave without John. Where is he? Dammit!*" James' inner voice echoed in his eardrums. An ominous feeling made him unsafe. James wouldn't start a fight in that strip club, but he had the feeling that others would. He knew that staying any longer could lead to trouble, and he didn't want to take any chances. "*Come on, John! Get your fat ass back here!*" Dobrev grew impatient and dialed John's number. Five minutes later, John came over.

"James! What's going on, buddy? Why have you been calling me?" John asked. He then turned around and nicely kicked out Bunny.

"We need to go as soon as possible!" James talked with consideration as if he had just admitted a brutal transgression.

"Why? What had happened?" John asked, his expression making it seem as if he was asking, "*Man! What have you done?*" James knew that he was too anxious about leaving. Although he always claimed that patience was his best friend, but not this time. The situation was urgent, as if someone had been shot. John wasn't ignorant. He knew that people could get dicey in that illicit strip club.

"Okay! Let me cover the tab," John said while looking for his billfold.

"It's taken care of. Let's bounce!" James declared and briskly checked his pockets to make sure he had everything. Just before he was about to leave, James looked at the bald biker. They were making eye contact as if both questioned, "*Who the fuck are you?*" The next moment, James and John stormed off through the corridors as if someone had offended them.

"What's all this about?" John asked out of breath. "Stop. Dammit!" he snapped, annoyed by his friend.

"They are watching us! Or at least me," the writer said over his shoulder without slowing his pace.

"James!" John raised his voice and grabbed his friend's shoulders. "James, is there something you need to tell me?"

"Let's go to my apartment, and I'll explain. I'll call an Uber."

"Uber?" John repeated as if he didn't hear.

"Yeah, Uber or Lyft. Whatever they have," James cried out. Chuckling, John declared, "Rideshare platforms don't exist in Bulgaria."

Ten minutes later, the friends from Chicago sat in a cab. They were quiet, as if they didn't know each other. The cab rolled towards downtown Plovdiv at a moderate speed. While he looked out the cab's windows, James recalled what his father used to say, *"Time is a power that cannot be controlled by humans."* Thinking about time, James was restraining himself from doing something foolish and believed that the time of his predicament was over. He also put faith in God and prayed for brighter days. Praying made James feel homesick and he constantly thought about his family.

"Do you have any booze in that apartment?" John asked, disturbing James' thoughts.

"Yeah! Trust me, I need a drink too!" James said, confidently. The cab parked at the Airbnb address, and the friends from Chicago immediately went to the library apartment. As they went inside, James narrated the story about the shooting in front of the liquor store and the murders of Boris and Charles.

"Hold on a second! You're telling me that this guy Boris is a time-traveler?" John asked, cringing as if he was groundhogging on the toilet.

"I have no idea what he is. All I know is that Boris looked the same as he did sixty years ago. He was a Russian refugee, and his name was enmeshed in something big. So now, some crazyhead is killing people, and my family and I are in great danger. That's why the Chicago cops had put me in witness protection and sent me here," James stated.

"Everything will be fine, buddy. You have no guilt whatsoever," John tried to cheer his friend up, even though, he had no idea what James was talking about. An hour later, John left the apartment, and James continued drinking on his own till the early hours of the next day.

***

The following day the hangover made James nauseous. He hadn't slept well. The trepidation was making him restless and limited his ability to sleep. James sauntered into the library apartment and did his morning routine. Then he made a tea and squeezed two lemons, just enough to make his face frown. At 3:00 p.m., (which was 8:00 a.m. in Chicago), James called Jackson to hear the updates about his family.

"We found Charles' murderer," Jackson announced quietly.

"Splendid! Good job, Jackson. That's a huge step. Do you think he will talk?" James asked. He was overexcited upon hearing the information about murderer. He thought that Jackson was a step closer to unraveling Boris' murder.

"He is dead," Jackson pointed out with the dispirited voice.

"What? Are you kidding me? Hold on! How come? Who killed him?" James couldn't believe what he had just heard. His elated spirit turned into a huge disappointment.

"His name was Kevin Mills. He was forty years old. No kids, no wife. His body was gorgeous and muscular, though. Anyway, he was murdered with the same weapon that he had used to kill Charles. We found him lying on the bed in his apartment in the Humboldt

Park area. However, we'll trace his tracks, and I'll learn everything about Kevin. Where he went, where he farted and brushed his teeth—everything," Jackson spoke with hope as if he knew where this case would take him.

"Okay. That's something," James said and asked, "How is Paul?"

"Same. Bedridden, in a coma since day one. The good news is that nothing worse has transpired so far. I mean, his medical condition is not deteriorating. That's what the doctors reported. How is your arm?" the detective asked.

"Better. I think I will start going to the gym, just some light training. Nothing too crazy," James replied.

"That's good, though. Keep your body in good shape. That's my motto," Jackson laughed at his wisecracking remark. "Oh, I almost forgot. I spoke with the patrol officer, and he reported that your family is fine. Listen, I got to go. I'm running late for a meeting. I'll keep you posted. Talk with ya later," the detective said and hung up the phone. James was speechless, staring at one spot, and pondering about his conversation with Jackson. "*Am I making a mistake? Why didn't I inform him about the people who were watching me? Actually, who is watching me?*" he asked himself.

Dobrev spoke with his mom, then he called Big John to make sure he was still alive. After ending the phone calls the writer thought for a moment, "*What can I do now? It's too late to work on my book. Isn't it? I guess I can text Anna.*" He was following *the three day no contact rule,* which he had read in books designated to guide people's dating life. As James thought about her, he texted Anna. She didn't respond until the next day when they exchanged a few text messages. After that, James wanted to speak with her.

"Hey, Anna. It's good to hear your voice again. How's everything goin," James said in an exhilarated voice.

"Oh my God! I was about to say the same thing. How is your

book going?" Anna spoke fast, as if her phone was about to die at any moment.

"My book it's not important right now. The more important is your health. How are you feeling after the fender bender?" the writer asked, scoring points with every word he was saying. He knew that these points could escalate his chances of hooking up with her.

"Speaking of health, I had some obnoxious pain in my left hand, and I went to see my family doctor, just to ensure that I am okay. The doctor said that my hand is fine. Anyway, I am worried about you. Are you having any pain?"

"Why? Are you saying that you will take care of me?" James asked playfully.

"I'm not a doctor. I thought you knew that already," Anna said while she laughed.

"Oh, yeah. I think I hurt my elbow. I thought of speaking with an injury lawyer."

"Oh, really! I can help you," Anna blurted out in a playful way. It was clear she was interested in him. Although, the ball was in his court. James had to lead the type of dance they were trying to get into.

"Yeah. I have an idea. Let's get together. Can you meet me at the parking lot of the Mall Plovdiv?" James asked.

"What are we doing? Are you taking me to a restaurant?"

"No! I can't tell you. It's a secret. I have a great idea, trust me!" James enunciated. He wanted to emphasize the word '*trust* because many chicks were feeling iffy about meeting strangers on a first date. Actually, the word '*trust*' made Anna uncomfortable. Her mind was saying, "*Why did he have to use this word? What's on his mind?*"

"Unfortunately, I won't be able to make it today. I have to work late, and most likely, I will be exhausted. Sorry." Anna decided to pull the hand brake and blew him off. She did it because she was uncertain of his intentions. Anna had met many assholes and flamboyant douchebags that were trying to impress her with how much money they had and what position they were in on the totem pole. But James was different. He joked with her like they were childhood friends, and that gave Anna the impression that they might have fun hanging out. James seemed cool to her. He didn't sound like an idiot or some kind of weirdo, but Anna needed more time.

"Yeah, well, how about this Friday?" James threw his last chance for the moment. There was a pause. Anna was hesitant. She didn't want to make him feel like a loser or chopped liver.

"Friday! I guess I will be free. But I'm not absolutely sure yet. I can get in touch with you on Thursday," Anna made an effort to say something that sounded positive.

"That's fine. I'd better get back to work. I'll talk with you later," James said and hung up the phone. He stared at the freshly painted wall in the library apartment, thinking, "*Something is going on with this chick! I have to find out how she feels about meeting me.*" James sank into a deep abyss of thoughts. He knew that Anna was a woman who could date six guys in a week. He also knew that his only chance was if she really wanted to meet him. The writer tried to understand something that could not be understood. As James thought about her a little more, he realized that dwelling on her was pointless and decided to shift his focus to something else. The writer was levelheaded man, and merging his thought onto something different wasn't a big problem for him. He had been in many difficult situations in which he had sorted out what was best for him and others. He kept recalling the loss of Rebecca, and his son's disease. Dobrev wanted to refresh his mind. He needed something that would make him feel better. And so, the writer decided to go to the nearest gym called '*Olympia*.' James wasn't into lifting weights. He was taking it easy and ran on the treadmill, wearing wireless headphones glued to his ears. The muscular people who trained there sized him up, giving him the look as if they were saying, *"Who the heck are you?"* James wasn't worried about those people. Even though he was retired from boxing, James was still a dangerous fighter.

It had been an hour since he started working out, and his legs were feeling pain. As James watched the mirror's reflections, his eyes suddenly widened. *"What the heck!"* he thought.

The writer saw the same bald biker who he had encountered at the strip club and the cinema. That biker was working out on a Seated Lat Pulldown machine, which was a couple of feet behind the writer. The biker's presence made James disturbed but he pretended that he didn't see him. James didn't look for trouble, and for that reason his mind urged him to leave. He scurried to the locker room and dressed without taking a shower. Then he walked out to the parking lot, looking around to check if someone was following him. *"I made it. No one is behind me!"* That was what he thought.

***

On Friday, James parked his rental vehicle at the parking lot of Mall Plovdiv. The rental company had replaced the damaged vehicle with a Ford Fusion. That didn't make any difference to him. He wasn't interested in what car he was driving. The clock on his iPhone was displaying 6:30 p.m. James was waiting for Anna. She had kept her word and got back to him the day before. Anna was running late because she wanted to look appealing. She had a difficult time dressing because she didn't have any idea of what they were doing or where they were going. Ten minutes later, Anna parked her Hyundai Elantra next to James' vehicle. The writer hopped out of the rental Ford, and his face froze. He hadn't seen anything like that before. Anna looked sensuous, like a highly paid star in Hollywood. Her beauty resembled the Mexican actress, Eiza González. Anna wore a gray Astro type dress; her black high heels matched her coat. Anna was a naturally beautiful woman. She didn't need any makeup or eyeliner. Walking toward James, she was smiling at him, thinking, *"Am I beautiful? I hope my hair looks fine!"* The writer was shocked. He tried to conceal his excitement and pull himself together. At first, James felt awkward and wasn't' quite sure if he had to hug her or give her a formal handshake. *"Screw it!"* he thought and spread his arms to embrace the gorgeous injury lawyer. She felt a little awkward, but she liked that he wanted to hug her.

"Hello, Anna! It's lovely to see you again. You are bodacious," James stated with elated voice.

"Thank you! What do you mean bodacious?" Anna asked a bit confused.

"In this case, I meant that you're looking gorgeous and attractive," James answered. His smile was sealed on his face like an American flag sewn on a naval uniform.

"Thanks. You're looking good as well. Where are we going?" Anna was eager to find out what his plans were.

"Your dress is magnificent! Are you trying to impress me?" James teased her. There was a pause. Anna cracked up in a loud guffaw. After a few seconds, she got it together and said, "It's not anything special. I didn't know how to dress because you didn't say where we are going."

"Actually, it doesn't matter because where we are going you'll have to take your clothes off," James stated with a smile on his face that seemed to say, *"You know I'm perfect for you."*

"What! What are you talking about? Where are you taking me?" Anna blurted out. She was dead serious. Her expression looked like she was about to flip off.

"You'll see," the writer said playfully.

"No! I am not moving until you're telling me where we are going," Anna was obstinate. That was how she became successful in her job.

She didn't like the idea of meeting someone without any plan of where they would be going. She liked James, but if he was going to act like a total weirdo, Anna would give him the cold shoulder.

"Do you trust me?" James asked, staring at her.

"Trust you? I don't even know you," Anna responded.

"Yeah. But you've already come here, without having a clue where are we going, right?" James declared with a facial expression as if to say, "*I got this!*"

"So! What is your point?"

"Since you've come here, that tells me that you have already trusted me a bit. Then why don't you come with me and see what my plan is? And if you don't like it, you can leave anytime. What do you think?" James finished his speech by shooting a playful yet serious facial expression. Anna's face changed. No one had ever talked to her like that. But somehow, she felt more comfortable listening to what James said. He was a man who knew what he wanted, and that was why she became more attracted to him.

"Okay! But if It's something foolish, I'll leave," Anna pointed out, and James nodded as if he was expecting this answer.

They took the elevator down to the first floor and walked through a big door that led to main entrance. Mall Plovdiv was in a gargantuan building. It had three levels, each of them usually took 15 minutes to be explored. On that day, the mall was packed as if they were giving out free food. There were a bunch of restaurants, many retail shops, a cinema, and even a supermarket. There were many fast food chains and fashion outlets that made Dobrev feel dizzy. James and Anna talked about how big Mall Plovdiv was while they were walking through the crowd. They stopped at a bowling lounge called 'Hit the Strike.'

"Oh! That was your plan. Was that all you meant with the chatter about taking my clothes off?" Anna asked, almost giggling.

"I was messing around with ya. C'mon, let's bowl. You said that you're good at bowling, right?" James asked, relieved that Anna liked his plan.

"You wanna bet?" Anna offered.

"I don't gamble," James answered.

"Me neither!" Anna said, and they both laughed happily, as if they were getting married.

James and Anna had a lot of fun during the bowling game. The writer was astounded because Anna outclassed him. She was making four or five strikes per game, and that confused him.

"Damn! You're a phenomenal player. Do you sleep here?" James asked while watching the scoreboard on the TV screen that was attached to the wall.

"You can't mess with me. I told you," Anna talked over her shoulder while she bowled another strike. As they played, James made Anna laugh and she enjoyed hanging out with him. She needed to take it easy after a stressful day at work, and James was the man who made her feel comfortable. They ordered juicy pizza sprinkled with vegetables and sausages.

"Do you want to drink something? A beer?" James asked politely.

"Naw. Beer makes me burb. That's gross. I'll have a martini. What about you?"

"I like drinking beer but I also enjoy tasting good whiskey," James stated. Hearing his own words, Dobrev reminded himself that he shouldn't drink in front of Anna because when he got drunk, he could transform into a piece of shit. Under the influence of alcohol, he might get pugnacious, and his behavior might become rude and pathetic. After two hours of being embarrassed, James got bored with bowling. Anna stepped close to him and whispered in his ear, "There is a place I want to show you. Let's cover the tab." James nodded. He called the waitress over and pulled out his billfold. Anna rummaged in her purse, too.

"Anna, I'm taking care of the bill," James stated but Anna shook her head in disapproval. She was obstinate, especially when it comes to finances. Over the last five years, Anna had had offers from lots of pushovers. Guys holding political influence tended to relinquish everything possible to allure her. However, Anna cut them off. She didn't need a powerful man; she wanted someone that she could feel comfortable with.

James and Anna debated about the tab for a few minutes more, but eventually, they peacefully consented to split the check. Anna suggested that James should leave his vehicle at the Mall's parking so she could drive him to the place she had mentioned earlier. At first, James wasn't sure if that was a good idea. But then he changed his mind, and both jumped into her Hyundai.

"Your car has been repaired already?" James asked, puzzled.

"Yeah, I have some friends. They take care of me," Anna said without looking at him. The ride took about 10 minutes. Anna drove on a paved road toward the foothills. The end of the road led to the highest point of the hill. She parked her car where the road ended. They both hopped out of the vehicle and took the stairs that led to a big monument that was erected above the city. From the monument, they could observe the entire city. The view was breathtaking, portraying the beauty of Plovdiv, which drew James' attention. He had never seen something so beautiful and had no idea that Eastern Europe could be so enthralling.

"It's beautiful. Isn't it?" Anna asked as she stepped close to him.

"Yeah, I mean it looks like a picturesque creation made by the nature. This beautiful city makes me speechless," James said without taking his eyes off the sightseeing view.

"It's cold," Anna whispered. The wind was playing with her curly hair, creating an unforgettable scene. Anna didn't mean that she was cold. That was her subtle way of saying, *"Hug me, please!"* What she didn't know was that James had studied how women's brains functioned by reading many self-help books.

"Come here!" James said and wrapped his arms around her shoulders. Anna was amazed. She hugged him like he was her father. She felt comfortable and secure being around him because he listened to her and emphasized with her feelings. But there was something that Anna was afraid of. *"He is too guarded!"* she thought. James didn't talk about his life as if he was hiding something. This brought up the question that Anna couldn't wait to ask.

"James, are you married?" Anna whispered as if she had already regretted her question. There was a pause.

"I was," James' answer was short, as if he was ashamed to talk about his marriage.

"Uh, so are you divorced?" Anna asked in confusion.

"Not really," James continued with his short answers.

"What do you mean? What are you hiding?" Anna was interrogating him as if she was asking a client about his injuries at work. James sighed. He knew that he had to tell her the truth and revealed the story of how his wife died and the medical condition of his son, Patrick.

"Oh my God! That's awful. I'm so sorry. I didn't mean to…" Anna started sobbing. She got emotional when she heard about disabled kids. Anna loved kids, and hoped that she would be a great mother one day, just as great as her mom was. Anna grew up in a loving family. Her father cherished and worshipped her. She had an older sister who lived in Switzerland with her husband and daughter. Anna had donated money to entities and organizations that worked with bedridden kids. She had always felt rectitude when she helped kids. The gorgeous lawyer felt horrible about pushing James to talk about the tragedy in his family.

"I'm really sorry! Is there anything I can help you with?" Anna said in tears, holding James tightly.

"Actually, there is one thing you can contribute," James stated, looking at her eyes.

"What. Tell me!"

"Just be my friend," James spoke softly as his words came with confidence. Although, he thought that the word 'friend', wasn't quite right.

"Let's go. It's cold," he went on, and Anna nodded as if she was saying, *"Thank you!"* There was some chemistry between them, but both felt uncertain of what would be right, and what wouldn't. James thought that it would be wrong if he exposed his feelings too early because he cared about her. The only thing he had on mind was to act normally and communicate through actions, rather than words.

A few minutes later, Anna dropped James at his rental vehicle. She hugged him as if she wouldn't see him again. Then she screeched the tires of her car and stormed off as if she was offended. James stared at her vehicle until it was lost out of sight. He was confused but also convinced that Anna liked him. However, there was something that didn't make sense to him. Anna seemed to be happy with him, but then she would urgently leave as if a family member was dying in the hospital. Anna never explained why she was always in such a rush.

It was 10:00 p.m. when James burst into the library apartment. He thought about having a glass of whiskey, but he ended up brushing his teeth in the bathroom. Suddenly, the light fixture above him started blinking. James looked up as if Jesus was calling his name. *"What is happening in my life? Why are these lights blinking?"* The frustration in his mind was making him uneasy. Since the shooting in the liquor store, he had been in a predicament that challenged his common sense. James was looking for answers, but he didn't know who could help him out. The writer was certain that if he told someone that the lights were blinking wherever he went, people would assume that he was freaking out. *"Maybe I should see a psychiatrist who would listen to my bizarre story? YES! I got it. There is only one person crazy enough to hear my abnormal narration, and that person is my mother."* The clock on his phone displayed 10:30 p.m., but Chicago was 8 hours behind, which meant it was 2:30 in the afternoon there.

"Hello, James! How are you, darling?" His mother blurted out, her voice was distorted by the blaring hairdryer at the salon, which sounded like background noise in a song. It was difficult for James to hear.

"Mom! I'd like to talk to you for a second," he almost yelled.

"What! Honey, I cannot hear you. Can you call back later?" Michelle replied. The background sound at the hair salon annoyed James. He sighed and said, "Okay," before hanging up the phone. He decided to bottle up his anxiety and not call his mother back. Instead, he hopped onto the bed and closed his eyes, but he couldn't fall asleep. His consternation was making him restless. Hours later, he finally sank into a deep slumber until the early hours of the next day.

7

It was March 5th, 2022, and the cold weather did not discourage the people of Chicago from walking the streets and having fun. The mayor had organized a parade that occupied the entire downtown area, and on that day, the streets were filled with thousands of pedestrians but no vehicles (except for police patrols). It was a memorable day for Chi-Town and the entire globe. On this day, political leaders in every state announced that Zener was tolerable and no longer lethal for humans. The government repealed the mandates, and the director of the National Institutes of Health declared that there was no reason for people to be intimidated anymore. However, people were still being encouraged to get vaccinated to protect themselves from the annoying virus (Zener). Grant Park in downtown Chicago was crowded with over 100,000 people in celebration of this commemorative day. A music event was held in the park and there was a big stage where a myriad of musical stars performed their hit songs.

Jackson, the homicide detective, was watching the parade from a police patrol. He was dressed business casual as always, but he wasn't there to celebrate. He decried the idea of having such a huge ceremony while there was a serial killer who could easily assassinate another victim. Harry Burns, the lieutenant of the police department, approached the police patrol where Jackson was grimacing.

"The mayor must be crazy!" Burns said.

"Yeah, I told him that he shouldn't allow this spectacle. Not until we have more information about the Cold Murder," Jackson declared.

"And what was his political statement?" Harry asked, looking straight into Jackson's eyes. The detective looked at Harry and said, "He is adamant! He proclaimed that the City of Chicago needs money and Chicagoans need entertainment."

"What about the governor?" Harry questioned.

"I haven't spoken with him yet. Although, I know that he had approved this event and demanded more security to protect the civilians."

"That makes sense, though. How is Paul?" Harry asked.

"Same! The doctors cannot predict when he could wake up," Jackson answered with an agitated tone because he carried the guilt of Paul's assault.

"Don't blame yourself," Harry said, and Jackson shook his head in disapproval.

***

Rocco was putting his jeans on. He wasn't rushing, but he had to leave in a few minutes. Joe Smith had to meet Rocco at a bar called *Seekers* located in Bucktown. Rocco had no idea why Joe had called him. Although, he knew that they wouldn't screw around by drinking. There was something that bothered Rocco—he didn't sleep well last night because he had snorted cocaine with some junkies the night before. In the past few months, Rocco did coke quite often and the dope made him irresponsible

"I'm late. Dammit!" Rocco said out loud as if he was talking to someone, while trying to outrun the clock. He knew that everything related to his job had to be done on time. Rocco was reclusive. He lived alone in his apartment in Little Village, but often he invited junkies and crack bitches. Even though he was hanging out with many people, Rocco had never told anyone what kind of job he worked. Also, he was aware that leaking any kind of information would earn him a spot in the cemetery. Rocco was also a stalwart man. He vowed to be loyal in his job. At 9:30 p.m., Rocco called a Lyft driver. He hated to drive in the city of Chicago because he was too impatient and couldn't tolerate the annoying Chi-drivers. One day, Rocco was involved in a minor car accident. He stormed out of the car and beat the shit out of the other driver. After that, he was arrested but later was bailed out because there were no charges and not enough evidence.

The Lyft driver came by with a white Nissan Rogue. When Rocco opened the door of the rideshare vehicle, the light flashed inside like a spotlight. His eyes widened as if he had never seen anything like that before. There were food leftovers, thrown on the floor mats. It looked like the Lyft driver had had a buffet before he came.

"Hey, man! Have you seen that mess on the rear side of your car?" Rocco protested. The Lyft driver spoke something gibberish in Spanish. Rocco was unfamiliar with foreign languages, but the driver kept talking to him as if he could understand Spanish.

"Vamos! Andale, Andale," Rocco pontificated. Those were the only two words that he knew. Hearing those words, the Lyft driver stopped yapping, and sped off. The ride took around 20 minutes. Rocco hopped out of the Lyft vehicle and stepped to the front door of *Seekers*. The security guy that guarded the bar looked small compared to him. Without saying a word, security let him go in as if Rocco owned the bar. *Seekers* was a typical Irish pub. The countertop bar was built in the shape of the letter "V" and was 15 footsteps from the front door. That night, *Seekers* was packed. The space around the countertop was narrow, and people had to squeeze past each other to move forward. People were celebrating as if a man had stepped on Mars.

"Hey, Rocco! Good to see ya. Come over, I'll buy you a drink," someone shouted through the loud crowd, where people were screaming to hear each other. Rocco waved negatively, showing that he wasn't interested in drinking. He was looking for Joe.

"Hey, Mack! Where's Joe?" Rocco shouted to the bartender who had a curly hair and the nose of a pig.

"He is in the back!" Mack responded. By "back" the bartender meant the basement. Rocco nodded and went through a door where a few Mexican migos were cooking food. He then passed the kitchen and opened a door that led to the basement, which like any other in the industry, had the smell of fermented alcohol and had rats that crisscrossed hurriedly like little ambulances. A few cheap light bulbs were hanging from the ceiling like terrifying bats. At the corner of the east side was a small bar built from several wine barrels and a sink as big as a chicken. A sixteen year-old boy was working at that bar. His name was Geovanni. He was an orphan who had escaped from a foster home a year ago. The owner of *Seekers* had found him loitering at the alley of the bar and offered him a job. Geovanni was a quiet kid and never asked unnecessary questions. "Hey, Geo! How you doin,' bud?" Rocco greeted the boy. He liked Geovanni. The boy reminded him of his childhood.

"I'm cool. How can I help you?" Geovanni asked politely.

"Give me water!" Rocco said, and Geovanni nodded. He pulled an Ice Mountain bottle from a small portable cooler and handed it to Rocco.

"Thanks, kid!" Rocco mumbled and walked to the other end of

the basement where a few guys were playing Texas Hold 'em. A dealer shuffled the cards on the poker table. This dealer was a divorced lady in her fifties who wore tons of makeup that made her look like an old whore. Her body looked like she visited the gym a few times a week. Her name was Kate. Joe kept staring at her from across the table. He was wearing a tracksuit and a Kangol flat cap, the same cap that Samuel L. Jackson had. The other players were businessmen from New York who had recently increased their investments in the stock market and had decided to play some poker. The poker players smoked stogies even though there was a sign on the wall saying: Smoking Prohibited! Joe played as aggressively as he did in real life. He hated when he was losing in poker, and that transpired too often.

"Hey, Joe!" Rocco shouted from a fifteen-foot distance. He knew that poker games shouldn't be disturbed unless something essential came up.

"In a minute! We are about to have a fifteen-minute break," Joe said while gazing at the other players. Kate shuffled the cards for the last hand. Joe was the Big Blind this time. He prudently flipped the top side of his cards; he had aces high. His face was expressionless. He then looked at the guy who sat next to Kate. His name was Thomas the Daggers, aka Thomas, The Fucker. They called him, The Fucker because he was so obese that he couldn't have normal intercourse, only lollipops. In the pre-flop, Thomas checked his cards and looked around the table. The others were waiting for his call. Thomas raised the pot with $500. The other players didn't call on Thomas' raise, and they threw their cards out. It was Joe's turn. He sized Thomas up. Dead silence floated over the poker table. Joe's expression was saying, *Do you want to fuck with me?* Thomas the Daggers, looked at Joe as if he was saying, *Give me your best shot!*

"I'll call your $500 and raise with $250," Joe announced calmly, and Thomas agreed to call on the bet. They both wanted to see the flop. So Kate laid out the cards, which were a King, 2, and Queen. Thomas raised the pot with $1000, and Joe bet $3000. Thomas called, and Joe raised more aggressively. The total amount of money collected in the pot was $10,000. Joe's heart was pounding as if he was about to jump in the ring and beat the hell out of Thomas.

Kate dealt the last community card, the River. Thomas exposed his cards; he had a pair of kings.

"Fuck!" Joe shouted bitterly and flung his aces high on the table.

Thomas won the pot with three Kings.

"Today is your lucky day, Sucka!" Joe yelled. He stood up and left the table. Thomas would have been happy to shoot him in the head. In these games, the players weren't allowed to carry their guns. Otherwise, it would have been like the Wild West. Joe stood up from the poker table and approached Rocco.

"You have a cigarette?" Joe grumbled under his breath. He looked like an angry bull that had smoke coming out of his ears. Rocco pulled out a pack of American Spirits and handed it over.

"You know what Eminem said?" Joe asked.

"What?"

"There is something inside me that is a little more happy when I'm angry," Joe quoted, and Rocco looked confused.

"I don't get it!" Rocco said quietly. Joe sighed. He gazed at Rocco as if he was saying, "*Really?*"

"This means that I would be happy to put the head of this fat ass in the toilet. Does that fry your chicken?" Joe elucidated.

"Hey, man! It's not my fault that you lost money on poker!" Rocco protested. "*Damn! He is right!*" Joe thought, but he didn't address it out loud. A minute later, Rocco and Joe went to a room where the booze was stored, 'The Booze Room' as they called it. Joe locked the door and said, "We have another job. Mr. D wants us to go to this place." He pulled out a piece of paper and continued the pep talk. They talk for about 10 minutes.

"Time!" Someone shouted beyond the door.

"Okay, I got to go," Joe proclaimed and ambled to unlock the door.

"You still playin'?" Rocco asked.

"Hell, yeah! I was up with 17Gs, and now I've lost $10,000. I need to get my money back! I'll see you tomorrow," Joe adlibbed. Rocco skedaddled from *Seekers*, and Joe returned to the poker table. Three hours later, Joe lost another $20,000. As the game ended, the players left the table. Joe stormed out of the bar without saying a word. Thomas was joyful. He carefully collected the $50,000 that he had just won. He wasn't in a rush. Why should he? Kate gave him a salacious look as if she was saying, *"I can give you a blowjob in the booze room."* Thomas understood the subtle invitation. He leaned close to her and whispered "Come with me to the booze room. I need to show you somethin'!"

"Ookay!" Kate said and smiled. She licked her lips, imagining what she was about to do in the following minutes. Thomas wasn't an attractive man, but his money enticed her and she expected a good tip. They went to the booze room. Kate hunkered down and unzipped Thomas' pants. His *thing* was so small that she actually had to search for it. Thomas' *thing* was dead, and Kate had to put some extra work to awaken it. The process took about ten minutes. Thomas had to make sure that Kate wouldn't rob him. He gave her $50 bucks. It wasn't a good tip. Thomas was a stingy scalawag; he wouldn't even give money to his mother.

It was midnight when Thomas ambled happily over to the parking space where he had left his Cadillac. *"50k and a blowjob. Yeah, today is my lucky day,"* he thought and hopped into his vehicle. He turned the ignition switch, and the car exploded in a blaze. Car pieces spread all around. Security alarms of the other vehicles shrieked noisily. It had been a setup. Joe was playing with counterfeit money. He lost on purpose to make sure that Thomas would be the winner. Those were the orders. Thomas was a tattler. He had talked about Boris with an undercover FBI agent a few weeks ago. Anyone who snitched in this business was brutally punished, and Thomas wasn't an exception.

***

Jackson's iPhone rang at 12:05 a.m., and he knew the reason for the call even before opening his eyes—phone calls after midnight meant that someone was being killed, hospitalized, or arrested.

"Yeah, I'm coming," Jackson mumbled somnolently. Fifteen minutes later, he was on the elevator that rolled down to the garage level. *"Prince was right! I should have become a doctor or lawyer!"* he thought. Jackson fired up the engine, and the Camaro snarled like a hungry lion. At 12:25, he parked his Camaro near to the parking space where the firefighters had extinguished the flaming Cadillac. The picture didn't look good. It was like a rat exploded in a microwave.

"Jackson!" Harry Burns shouted. He waved at him even though he knew that Jackson had already seen him.

"What do we have here?" Jackson said, grimacing at the burned Cadillac. Harry look at him and said, "At this point, we've found a dead body on the driver's seat. We…"

"The body will be taken for an autopsy. We have to identify the victim," a voice, familiar to Jackson, chimed in. Jackson turned around to survey the person.

"Lawrence! How you doing, babe!" Jackson greeted. Lawrence Fisher was superintendent of the Chicago police. He was an African-American, born and raised in the south side of Chicago. Lawrence had served in the police department for over thirty years. He had multiple awards given by the mayor of Chicago and the president of the USA. Fisher was the most prominent chief of police in the history of Windy City. He looked wholesome and in good training shape despite his age of sixty.

"I thought you were on vacation in Florida with your wife and the kids?" Jackson gave a pound to Lawrence.

"I was…. I flew back last night," Lawrence replied and looked around as if he had lost his kid in the mall. Jackson and Harry were silent as if they had messed up something really bad.

"The crime in Chicago has gone up 4% since Thanksgiving! I want to increase the number of the police patrols. Tomorrow I'll have a meeting with the mayor. Any witnesses?" Lawrence asked. Jackson and Harry shook their heads no.

"Okay! Keep your eyes open. Jackson, come to the City Hall tomorrow," Lawrence said. He looked pissed, but he restrained his anger and remained respectful by acting professionally.

It had been a long and busy night in Chicago.

***

It was March 31st, and at a quarter to eight in the morning, James headed to a modern coffee shop located in downtown Plovdiv, where getting around was easy. While walking to the coffee shop, James passed fountains, buildings, retail shops, etc. He was amazed at how bewitching this city could be. Plovdiv literally had foothills in the city—he had never thought that it could be possible. This city depicted so much history that James thought he walked into a living encyclopedia. He entered the coffee shop with a sign that read: Bulgaricano. It was a weird name, but James liked it. Inside the shop, the employees greeted him cordially. They had grown accustomed to him as he had been visiting Bulgaricano for the last couple of weeks.

"The usual?" One of the girls that worked behind the coffee machine asked.

"Yes, thank you." James drank a small espresso that was so strong it made his eyeballs feel heavy. He was quiet that morning, having a feeling that something ominous was about to happen, or had already happened. James pulled out his iPhone and checked the latest updates. His eyes widened when he read an article about a horrendous car exposition in Bucktown in Chicago. James felt sick to his stomach. He immediately dialed Jackson. They chatted for a bit, then James cut to the chase and asked.

"What happened last night? I read about an explosion in Bucktown."

"Yeah, it was an ugly picture. We identified the victim, though. His name was Thomas Macintosh, aka Thomas the Daggers; he was an eminent entrepreneur who lived in New York. The IRS told us that he had holdings in Amazon, Tesla, and Google. Also, he traded gold and petrol. A big fish. The bomb squad confirmed that there had been explosives in the car. At this point, we tend to believe that it could be a sign of a war between some big wigs."

"It's getting worse!" the writer exclaimed. He went on, "Do you think that Boris had anything to do with the assassination of Thomas?"

"Honestly, it could be Boris, or even you. At this point, I can't really tell." There was a pause. James didn't like having his name enmeshed in that crime. The problem was that his name had been implicated already whether he liked it or not. Jackson decided to change the subject and asked, "Have you spoken to your family?"

"Yeah, this morning. They are fine. At least that's what mom told me," James confessed.

"Okay, baby. Take care of yourself. I'll keep you posted," Jackson announced and hung up the phone. James was stuck in a state of heebie-jeebies. He wasn't sure what he should do. The detective advised him to stay in Bulgaria, but that didn't make any sense to him. He missed his family, especially Patrick. Flashbacks with Patrick and him spending time together popped up in his mind. Those memories made James feel sad and a little bitter. "*No parent should see his child suffering,*" he thought. An hour later, James had a long conversation with Carl, his book agent. The 'delivery date' was approaching. He had to complete the manuscript and send it for editing. James insisted on working with specific editors—he got pissed when others were amending his work.

"James! I need the manuscript by the end of this week. You're almost done, right?" Carl asked. He had never read the manuscript of any author. Even though he was a book agent, Carl hated reading. He was only interested in closing more deals. More deals meant more money, which Carl used for lecherous activities such as splurging in gentlemen's clubs and buying property.

"I'll send you the manuscript by Friday," James said, and Carl happily ended the conversation.

***

At 3 in the afternoon, James ambled with Anna to a bunch of museums such as the Art Gallery Philippopolis, the Museum of Natural Sciences, and the Historical Museum of Plovdiv. The gorgeous lawyer looked spiffy, as if she had just flown in from Hawaii. She wore a tropical dress and Wedge shoes. Despite it being only April, the weather was so warm and pleasant that it felt like it was August. Anna was over the moon; her smile portrayed the exquisite lines of her face. She talked about the history of Plovdiv and James was flabbergasted. They saw the reputed treasure of Panagyurishte, which was considered one of the most valuable treasures in Europe.

"Let's get a drink! I feel hot. I need something cold," Anna proposed, and James nodded.

"Do you have anything in mind?"

"Come with me," Anna stated. They went to the strip in downtown Plovdiv and sat in a coffee shop that looked like an Italian cafeteria.

"I've started reading your book!" Anna announced happily.

"Which one?"

"*The Lost Love*. I'm fascinated by your writing. I wish I could write like you," Anna said, looking sad for a moment.

"Don't be discouraged. Actually, it has been scientifically proven that women are better writers because they can naturally portray their emotional and spiritual thoughts. Does that make any sense?"

"I guess so. I think people would be impassive if they read my verse. I write emails for work from time to time, and it sounds awful to me," Anna said, her expression filled with discouragement.

"Yeah, because you're writing something that didn't make you feel compassionate enough!" James pointed out, but Anna refused to listen. She remembered her law school years, during which she had graduated with the highest grades. However, her colleagues had begrudged and mocked her for her success.

"You become dubious when people around you are questioning your work," James declared. Anna didn't answer, as if the writer hadn't said anything. "*She is uncomfortable!*" he thought. Anna changed the subject by talking about travel and vacations. She chatted about going to France. As she kept talking about this country, James interrupted her.

"Sounds like you want to take me on vacation to France," James was playful and Anna's face lit up with excitement, as if it were Christmas morning.

They talked a little more, then Dobrev suggested, "Let's go to the fountain over there." Anna nodded cheerfully. The fountain wasn't huge, but it was big enough to wash an elephant. Its beauty was spellbinding, as people sat on the ledge and stared at it. The waterfall from the fountain was illuminated by a bunch of lights, which attracted even more people.

It was 8 in the evening, the nightfall enhanced the picturesque view of Plovdiv. While James admired the city, Anna was staring at him as if she had to discuss something essential.

"How did you start writing books? What's your inspiration?" Anna asked, intrigued. *"Inspiration! That's a good word,"* James thought. He was surprised at how eloquent Anna was.

"Good question! My father, Ivan Dobrev, wrote short stories. I was always fascinated by his writing proficiency—I cannot explain why. One night he went to a birthday party and never came back. The police found him dead in the parking lot of a casino," James said in a low voice.

"Oh my God! He was murdered!" Anna exclaimed in terror.

"Yes, that was a long time ago. The police never found the perpetrator. I miss him a lot. Thinking about him and his poetry, I started writing my own stories. The answer to your latter question is simple: my father and my son motivated me to write," James finished his monologue, and Anna nodded. Tears were falling from her eyelashes. James felt guilty for making Anna sad and gave her a hug. At the next moment, Anna stared at James' lips. In a second, they started making out. The fountain behind them made a perfect view of pure romance. It was as if they were filming a scene from a rom-com movie. They both had been waiting for that moment. Anna's heart was screaming, *"Don't stop!"* And James was pondering, *"What am I doing?"*

"My place!" Anna said breathlessly. James thought for a moment. It could be a huge mistake if he came with her. He didn't want to embroil her in his difficult situation.

"I'll give you a ride to your place and then I'll drive to mine. I think that works for both," James carefully chose his words. He knew that Anna had taken a cab earlier because she left her vehicle at her residence. Anna gave him a thoughtful and perhaps confusing look.

"And...uh. You don't want to come over?"

"I don't think it would be a good idea," James said, and Anna nodded. It was hard for him to say *"No"* to the girl with whom he had a crush on, but he couldn't just spend the night with her because he feared the consequences of their relationship.

The ride took about ten minutes. James parked the rental Ford at the designated parking area. They started heavy petting in the car. James couldn't restrain his erotic desire any longer and Anna walked with him to her condo. She had a two bedroom apartment in a nice neighborhood. Her place was stylish and pristine as if it was featured on the cover of a real estate magazine. Their love making was beyond any description. Ineffable. Anna felt loved, and all of her sexual needs were fulfilled. The way James touched her made Anna feel like she was special. On other the hand, James felt horrible. Not because of Anna, but for the sake of his ex-wife, Rebecca. *"Rebecca wouldn't commit adultery, even if I was dead!"* he thought. Pushed by his thoughts, James skedaddled Anna's condo, leaving her in a thoughtful confusion. James was eager to get into the Airbnb apartment but he couldn't drift off until the morning hours.

***

April 1st was a rainy day in Chicago. The sky was overcast as if it was mad at someone or something. However, the weather didn't bother Joe Smith who was puffing a cigarette in his blue 2020 BMW 4 series. He didn't hold the vehicle's title, but he acted like he owned that car— Freddy Limo had given it to him for work. Joe was anxious because he had to wait for Rocco who was running late. Joe hated waiting. He looked at his wrist watch. It was 8:30 in the evening. The BMW was parked at a shady spot close to a storage building in Little Village.

"What the fuck is he doing? He's supposed to be here already, dammit!" Joe said aloud. He pulled out his personal smartphone and watched the third fight between Deontay Wilder and Tyson Fury. Joe was picturing how he would fight against Tyson Fury. "*Body, body! I'd break his ribs, and then when he drops his hands down… I'd go for 1-2 or mix. I'd confuse him with power and speed,*" Joe pictured. He had been craving a fight in the ring, but Mr. D wouldn't allow it.

A few minutes later, Joe checked his work phone. It was a cheap burner. Everyone who worked for Mr. D had been using burner phones since Boris' assassination. And every two months, they had to get new phones. Those were the orders. That way the FBI and CIA wouldn't be able to trace the phone calls. At 8:42, Rocco parked his VW Beetle next to the BMW. Joe was always amazed at how such a big man could drive a small VW Beetle. Immediately after stopping, Rocco hopped out from the bug-car and sat on the passenger seat of the BMW.

"Where have you been? I've been sitting here like an ignorant wacko waiting for you." Joe looked pissed. But actually, he was happy to see his workmate.

"I couldn't find my work phone!" Rocco looked for an appropriate excuse.

"Get your phone and shove it up your ass!" Joe exclaimed with a face that looked like he was about to burst into laughter.

"That's impossible!" Rocco protested.

"Everything is possible," Joe teased him.

"No fucking way!" Rocco was getting irked.

"Okay, then! What happened? Did you talk to your girlfriend?" Joe asked.

"She is not my girlfriend. We are friends with benefits. Joe, I'm a dog. You know that," Rocco said, giving Joe the stinky eye. Joe loved teasing Rocco, which brought him a lot of joy.

"Hey, I heard that this guy, uh…what's his name? The writer, who was next to Boris on the night of the shooting. What's his name? Dammit!"

"Huh! Uh-uh, you mean James?" Joe suggested.

"Yeah, that's right! James. I heard that James has been hiding in Bulgaria since February."

"So! Of course, he is hiding; he is a rat. That's what rats would do. What's your point?" Joe asked, appearing jumpy.

"I heard that he is a good boxer," Rocco said.

"Let me tell you something. I don't care if he is the WBC heavy weight champion. I'll crack his head! You understand me? He is a bum! I'll fight him anytime and anywhere. I'll do it for free!" Joe said aggressively.

"Okay. I'm just sayin' what I've heard," Rocco said, his face was dead serious, but it was also his turn to tease Joe.

"Yeah, whatever! Here is the target," Joe said and handed a photo to Rocco.

"Aha, that's interesting!" Rocco's eyes lit up like a huge spotlight.

"When?" Rocco asked, still looking at the photo.

"Soon!" Joe said, and both smiled hellishly.

8

"Done!" James said and punched the "enter" button on the keyboard. It was Friday at 3 in the afternoon when James closed his laptop. He felt exhilarated that the manuscript of his novel *The Cold Summer* was finished. He sent the draft via email to his agent and explained his work in a few words. The writer had come up with an inspiring idea of how to end his novel. His work didn't impress him, although he was happy with the plot.

James had been doing online therapy via Zoom since he had landed in Bulgaria with his therapist and was strictly following up every session. It had been five months since the gunshot, and the physical therapist continually encouraged him to do exercises to improve the muscle in his arm. His injured arm still gave him discomfort, but it was less painful. After finishing his exercises, Dobrev looked around the Airbnb apartment with thoughtful eyes as if to say, *"I need a drink."* He then decided to contact Anna and share the news about his novel. He texted her:

Hey, how's work? I need to talk with you.

Anna didn't reply, which made James concerned. "*It would be inappropriate if I text her again,*" he thought. Two hours passed, and still, there was no answer from her. And so, James decided to get in touch with his buddy, Big John, but just a moment before he grabbed his phone to dial his friend, Anna called him.

"Hey, Anna! How's your day goin'?" James said, his voice sounded humble.

"Hi, James! There is something that I need to share with you. Where can I meet you?" Anna announced. She was about to shriek from euphoria. "Are you for real? I was just about to say the same thing! Okay… uh… I'll meet you at 6 in Marmalad. It's that okay?" James offered.

"I have some work to do. Let's make it 7?" She said.

"That works for me too! See you there," James exclaimed and hung up the phone, wondering what she had to tell him. In a few minutes later, James hopped in the shower and dressed in his business casual clothes. He locked the door of the library apartment and left the building. He forgot to turn off the light in his bathroom, and that light blinked eerily.

***

At a quarter to 7, James stepped into Marmalad which was starting to fill with more people. The writer sat by the bar. The bartender was a peachy girl who smiled warmly at him. He smiled back and ordered Jameson on rocks. James promised himself to stay sober that night. The voice in his head reiterated how bad he looked when he was drunk. James struggled with an alcohol problem and didn't hide the fact that he needed help. He reminded himself to visit AA meetings when he returned to Chicago.

Half an hour later, Anna walked through the door, carrying herself with bravado and composure. She passed a few guys who stared at her lecherously as if they were prisoners that hadn't seen a chick for years. Her black ruched side wrap lounge dress accentuated her athletic figure. Her boobs weren't big but still bounced playfully as she walked. James was watching her with a smile on his face, almost as if he was saying, *"I'm fucked up! I need another drink!"*

"Hi, James! Are you waiting for someone?" Anna said teasingly.

"Yeah, I'm waiting for a gorgeous chick that said she had something to share with me!" James replied and they hugged, as if that would be the last time seeing each other.

"I don't have any idea of what you're talking about!" she playfully responded before ordering a dry Martini. Anna talked to James with excitement, sharing some stories with him about her job.

"James, listen. I need to tell you something!" Anna was dead serious. Dobrev had no idea what she was talking about.

"Please, go on!" He gave her a sign to continue.

"Next month, I'll be on the cover of *Attorneys* magazine, which is the biggest in Europe! Isn't that cool?" Anna asked, while James remained speechless.

"Wow, Anna! That's awesome! I'm so happy for you."

"Thank you! I am ranked as the most successful attorney in the country. The writers working for that magazine will interview me. I'll talk about the secret of my success and my life in general."

"I have to tell you. I'm impressed," James stated and gave her another hug.

"So, what do you want to tell me? Hold on! Let me guess; you finished the book!" Anna's eyes widened in a moment of anticipation.

"Nailed it!" James said quietly, and Anna shrieked in awe.

"That's awesome! When can I read it?" Anna asked.

"You have to wait, though. When you finish writing a book, you're not really done with it. We will need a couple of rounds of editing.

Then I will be able to look at the manuscript and approve the work. After that, we have to do the book formatting and the cover design and yada-yada," James explained while beaming his thoughtful smile.

"You suck!" Anna stated cheerfully. She had a great sense of humor and that was what James liked in her.

"I know! It's not exciting when you're a writer whose books are collecting dust," James pointed out.

"I didn't mean that. I was just…"

"I know. Relax, I'm just messing with you!" James interrupted her and Anna kissed him with passion, displaying her desire to be with him. It wasn't a secret that she wanted to be close to him and that made James nervous because he was uncertain about his future. He didn't want to involve Anna in the trouble that he had already been through. At that moment, James wasn't sure what was good and what was bad. However, he was certain of one thing: he didn't want to put Anna's life in danger. He was infatuated with her just as much as Bruce Wayne was with Vicky Vale. As James and Anna chatted animatedly, a voice interrupted them.

"Hey! The writing guy! I've heard that you finished your book! Is that right, or are you shitting me?" Big John's voice echoed from a few feet away.

"Big John! Come here, you lying bastard!" James yelled and gave his friend a brotherly hug. Then he introduced Anna to Big John. Anna shot her professional look at James' friend, surveying him from toe to head. This time, Big john was properly dressed as if he was going on a date with a beautiful woman.

"Where is your wife?" James asked John.

"I have no idea," John said, and the three of them burst into laughter.

"What do you mean you have no idea? She's your wife!" Anna asked, looking confused. She couldn't tell if Big John was joking or being serious.

"I mean, she is busy with her crap. I asked her to come, but she refused, giving me all the excuses that she could possibly think of," John responded. The three of them talked for hours. Anna restrained herself from drinking alcohol and only had a single cocktail. On the other hand, James and John were guzzling booze as if they were at a bachelor's party. At a quarter to 10, John looked nervously at his watch wrapped on his left wrist. He looked as if he was expecting something to happen at any minute.

"Excuse me, guys. I need to drop a Mondo duke!" John announced.

"What's a Mondo duke?" Anna asked, perplexed. James and John cackled as if they were watching the movie, *The Hangover*.

"Mondo duke is…" James started.

"Taking a big shit!" John chimed in, feeling elated to have the chance to express his knowledge.

"What! Are you for real?" Anna asked as she burst into laughter.

"Yeah, I've heard that he had cracked the rat!" James declared with a mischievous grin.

"What?" Anna asked.

"What?" John repeated after her.

"The expression *'crack the rat'* means the process of flatulence. Okay, enough with the English lessons! Cheers!" James asserted, and the three of them clanged their glasses. As they were drinking, Anna began talking about crocodiles, expressing her admiration with how these carnivores lived. She enjoyed watching documentary movies about wild animals, particularly crocodiles and alligators. James and John exchanged a questioning look as if they were asking themselves, *"What is she talking about?"* Then John looked at his watch.

"Speaking of crocodiles, I need to call my wife! Excuse me for a second," he announced. James and Anna laughed so loud that the others sitting close gave them unfriendly looks. James and Anna continued chatting. Five minutes later, John scuttled over and said, "I gotta go, guys! Anna, it was nice to meet you!"

"Are you okay?" James asked, trying to read his buddy's expression.

"Yeah, the crocodile needs some attention! Don't worry. It's nothing unusual," Big John said and skedaddled.

"What's up with your fella?" Anna grilled.

"A-aaa… not sure. He has some family issues. He'll be fine," James said. The writer and the injury lawyer spent an hour more at Marmalad. Just before they leave, Anna gave him a carnal signal that even a ten-year-old would recognize.

"Let's bounce," James suggested.

"Wait! You're not going to show me where you live?" Anna asked. There was a pause. James sank into deep thought. "*What now! She wants to know where I'm staying! What should I say?*" he asked himself as if he was questioning someone else.

"You really don't want to show me your place! James, what are you hiding? Are you scared?" Anna went on.

"I'm not scared! Let's cover the tab, and we'll go," James said, frowning. The alcohol was shaking his vision off. Not much, but enough for him to know that he was done drinking. James and Anna walked for about five minutes. She had to hold him because he was wobbling, just a tad. In what seemed to be fifteen minutes later, they burst inside of the Airbnb apartment, and Anna was in awe.

"I love this apartment! Who's the owner?"

"Abraham Lincoln," James replied.

"What?" Anna asked.

"I'm joking. I found it on the internet. I haven't even met the owner!" James lied. He didn't feel comfortable talking about his business in Bulgaria, especially when he was inebriated. Although, he felt like a jerk for not telling her the truth.

"Do you need a drink?" Dobrev asked kindly.

"Nah, I'm good. I've had enough for the night. You'll drink more?"

Anna was stunned by his drinking zest. James said nothing, but it was clear that he had issues with alcohol, even though he didn't appear frustrated that night. Anna did a quick tour of the library apartment. She then found James sprawled on the king-sized bed.

"I'm done drinking," James said out loud with a joyful expression. He lay on the bed as if he had been shot in the head, motionless. Anna joined him, and they started making out. Unlike a week ago, this time the wild mambo was quick, James was done in a couple of minutes. But it was enough to satisfy Anna's enthusiasm. She liked being next to him because she felt secure. At 3:00 a.m., Anna slipped out of the bed and whispered.

"James. Hey, James!"

"Uh," he grunted sleepily.

"I have to go! I'll talk to you later," Anna said quietly.

"Aaa… Okaay!" James mumbled under his breath.

"Nighty, night, sleepyhead!" Anna mouthed and smiled at James who looked like he was doing a sleeping impression on SNL. But James wasn't acting. He was tired as if he had shoveled for many hours in construction. At 5:00 a.m., his iPhone rang. "*Who is it? No, I'm not answering!*" his inner voice whispered. But his phone wouldn't stop ringing; it was becoming obnoxious. *Who the fuck is bothering me!* James was annoyed. The iPhone kept ringing disturbingly. It seemed like whoever was calling would not stop. James was rolling his body on the bed. His mind was hesitating, "*Should I take the call or not!*" After a minute of hesitation, he threw a glimpse at his phone. It was Big John. "*Okay, fuck it. I'll take the call!*"

"Hello!" Dobrev said sleepily.

"James! Thank God! I'm at The Police Department. I was arrested last night!"

***

Half an hour later, James hopped in his rental car and took off. He didn't speed, but he was in a rush. The streets in Plovdiv were deserted, with only a few cab drivers rolling around. James was looking constantly at his GPS, as he had no idea where the police department was. Twenty minutes later, he saw Big John waving as if he had been on a boat stranded at sea for hours and hollering, *Mayday! Mayday!* The writer parked the rental vehicle, and in the blink of an eye, Big John jumped into the car.

"What happened?" James asked, bewildered.

"Those bastards! Mother flowers," John said under his breath.

"Who? John, what are you talking about? You're not making any sense. Take a deep breath and tell me what happened?"

"Man! These people are insane! They arrested me!" Big John snapped, his face was fuming.

"Well, I can see that! You wouldn't chill out at the police department at five in the morning," James said.

"So, here is what happened. I came back home last night, and my wife was furious. I mean, she was shrewish, screaming some pointless accusations. I said, 'Calm down! Why are you screaming like that?' She kept mumbling in gibberish, something like, 'You messed up my life, and I'm so depressed.' She was saying that it was my fault and that I ruined her life. Then, I asked, 'How am I ruining your life? I provide a home for our kids. Furthermore, you have all the freedom to do whatever you want.'"

"Right!" James snapped.

"Yeah, so she was saying that I didn't acknowledge her creativity and I didn't support her career as an artist, and that was making her very upset. I tried to hug her, and you know, to cool her off. She yelled, 'Don't touch me!' Then she slipped, and we both fell on the floor. As we were getting up, she cried out, 'I'm calling the cops!' I said, 'Don't you dare!' But she took a few steps away and called the police. In a minute, the sirens blared beyond the door. The cops burst into my property and handcuffed me. There were…gosh, I don't remember… 5 or 6 guys. I mean, everything happened so fast that I didn't realize how I ended up in the police patrol."

"What the heck! I mean why! That's so weird!" James commented.

"Yeah, right! And the funny thing is that the police didn't allow me to take my wallet. I didn't have money to grab a taxi. That's why I called you. I mean that's asinine."

"And now what?" James asked.

"They released me on a bail bond. I've been charged with a misdemeanor for assaulting my wife! Can you believe this crap?"

"That's a big trouble. What are you going to do? Do you have a good lawyer?" James asked.

"Yeah. I spoke with my attorney. The court will give me something like a restraining order. That means I cannot be close to my wife for the next 72 hours. I have to be in court after two weeks."

"Do you think your wife will press charges?" James spoke in a low voice, empathizing with his friend.

"That's the most essential part. I don't know. I have to bet on my lawyer. I mean, I don't know how the law works here in this country."

"Yeah, I see. Where do you want to go? You can sleep in my apartment. There is plenty of space even for a big fat ass like you," James tried to sound funny, but Big John wasn't smiling.

"Yeah! Take me to your place. I'll chill out for a few hours there. Then, I'll call my butler to bring some of my belongings, and then I'll go to a cheap hotel."

"Are you sure!" James' voice echoed as if he was saying, *"I'm here to help you."*

"Yeah, don't worry about it. I'll be fine," Big John said, but his face looked as if he was asking himself the question, *"Am I going to be okay?"*

James drove to the library apartment. At 10: 00 a.m., Miguel, the butler, pulled up in one of Big John's Mercedes.

"That's my ride. I'm out of here," John exclaimed, and James nodded. "Call me if you need something," James said and gave a brother hug to John. Big John walked to the door, a second before he grabbed the knob, he turned to James and said, "Thanks for picking up the frigging call this morning. You know, I would do the same for you." That was a lie. John wouldn't pick up the phone early in the morning, and James knew that.

"I know," James stated. He remembered years ago asking John for a small loan. That was when his father was murdered, and James needed some cash. Big John refused to help, giving excuses that he was broke when he had hundreds of dollars in his bank account. That was fine. James knew that his friend wouldn't help him when he needed it.

At noon, the writer called his mom and asked about Patrick. He missed his son. James couldn't describe with a few words the love he felt for his son. He prayed daily for him. Patrick had done nothing wrong to be in that medical condition and that was making James upset. *Sometimes life can be unfair to innocent people, and no one can explain why,* Dobrev thought. He couldn't deny his urge to go back to Chicago and tried to reach Detective Jackson, but his line was busy, so James left a voicemail. Jackson was the one who sent him to Bulgaria, and he was the one that had to bring the writer back to Chicago. Flying back to Chicago was complicated, but that didn't discourage James. He wasn't a tourist; he was sent to Bulgaria for his own protection. The Bulgarian government had allowed James to stay in Bulgaria. In this scenario, James couldn't just buy a ticket and hop on the next business flight as the Bulgarian border protection would stop him at the terminal and report him to the government. An hour later, Jackson called back.

"Can't stay here any longer. Jackson, you have to bring me back home!"

"Why? Is there something that I need to know, baby?" Jackson said in a low and calm voice.

"I'm getting head over heels into a Bulgarian chick!" James announced as if he was complaining.

"Ha-ha-ha. That's a good one," the homicide detective pointed out.

"No! That's not a joke. I'm absolutely serious. You have to bring me back home. Jackson, I need to see my family. It's been three months since I left Chicago, and I really need to get back."

"What about this chick? You can't just leave her," Jackson made a wise remark.

"True! I'll take care of that later. Don't worry about it. What's going on in Chicago? Anything new?" James asked the question he should have asked a minute ago.

"After Thomas' murder, nothing has been reported. The media is quiet too. They don't talk about the murder, as if it never happened," Jackson said.

"What do you mean? I'm confused," James declared.

"Can't really speak on behalf of the media. We don't usually work with tabloids, unless we need some information. Listen, I'll make a few phone calls, and I'll touch base with ya next week. Okay?"

"Gotcha," James answered and hung up the phone. "*That's weird. Why doesn't the media talk about the murders?*" the writer asked himself. He then decided to check his social media and look for anything useful about the recent murder in Chicago. The newscasters reported on another surge of the dangerous virus named Zener, advising people to be extremely cautious and get vaccinated due to the stronger and more lethal variant. James was growing skeptical as he read through the articles. The news about Zener was making him feel dispirited, and he needed to focus on something else. Anna. James didn't remember when she had left the Airbnb apartment.

He felt inclined to tell her the truth about why he came to Bulgaria and why he had to leave. He texted her:

Hey, gorgeous! Last night was wonderful. How's it goin'?

James had never called her *gorgeous* before. That word came in his mind as a playful way to get in touch with her. There was no response. "*It's Saturday! She must be busy with somethin'. I'll wait,*" James thought. Hours had passed, and Anna did not answer. *Something is going on here!* the inner voice of James spoke. He felt annoyed when people didn't respond to his questions, but he didn't mind it if it was someone unimportant. However, Anna was a person he cared about, so he was frustrated when she didn't reply. Finally, the next day, she texted him:

I need to talk with you! Call or text?

Her text shocked him, like Chris Rock was when he got smacked by Will Smith. James thought for a second, "*Anna is acting as if she's upset or maybe I misinterpreted her behavior. What should I do?* "*Screw it! Let's see what she's up to.*" In no time, Dobrev dialed her phone number, and she picked it up almost immediately.

"You lied to me! My friends told me that you are under witness protection regarding the shooting in Chicago on Thanksgiving! Why didn't you tell me? Don't you think I should know? Or maybe I'm not that important to you. Don't you realize how you're hurting me and besmirching my reputation as a successful attorney?" Anna spoke in a low voice, but she was ready to scream at any second.

"Anna! Listen, I can explain. I needed time to tell you the truth. I wasn't lying you. I just didn't tell you the truth at that time. I need to go back to Chicago, and I was about to tell you…"

"Oh! So, now you're leaving the country? You asshole! Who the heck do you think you are? Banging me twice and now pulling the shit and leaving. And on top of that, you're lying to me. I got to go, bye!"

"Anna, Anna. I care about you, and I was trying to handle…" James realized that he was talking to himself. Anna had ended the phone call. She didn't give him a chance to talk. Her "*bye*" sounded more like "*go fuck yourself!*" The injury lawyer was pissed and she had the right to be, but James needed a second to tell her how much he cared and that he was about to take her to dinner and surprise her with flowers. He wanted to explain everything by making a romantic gesture, but his misgivings made him uncertain. "Stupid! How could I be so blind?" James asked himself. He tried everything he could to avoid Anna and an hour later, he found himself trudging to Marlamad, where he sat at the bar, and started drinking aggressively as if he was at a wedding party. He couldn't restrain himself. There was a lot of heat that floated over his head. The cloud of problems masked his common sense and put him into a tough predicament. His mind was blindfolded, and that made him thirsty—thirsty for alcohol. James didn't realize that it was still Saturday until he burst into the bar. Hip-hop and RnB music blasted out loud, and the people were boisterous, but that didn't bother him. He was draining Jameson excessively. "Hey, what are you drinking?" a female voice echoed behind the writer. He turned to survey the person who talked to him and saw a young girl, perhaps in her adolescent years. The teen girl looked attractive and bodacious. Her body was skinny, even a bit scrawny. The writer didn't understand the question, because she used Bulgarian words that he had never heard before.

"Do you speak English, because I didn't understand what you were askin'," James declared.

"Oh, yeah! I was wondering what you were drinking," the teen said in a loud voice.

"An Irish Whiskey. What about you?"

"I drink Vodka. Cheers!" the teen girl shouted, and they clinked their glasses.

"What's your name?" James interrogated her.

"Call me Kristina! And what's yours?" The teen smiled at him and James surveyed her. Kristina looked like she was a sophomore in high school. Her boobs were small because her body was still developing. Kristina was dressed in light blue jeans, of an undefined brand, and on top, she had a sexy A-shirt that portrayed her athletic figure. Kristina had an enthralling smile, her face looked like that of a top notch model.

"How old are you?" James asked, feeling old next to the teen girl.

"I'm eighteen," Kristina smiled at James as if she was in love with him.

"Stop bullshitting me! You look fifteen or sixteen!" James said in a loud but playful voice.

"I'm not! Here is my ID," Kristina protested and gave him the plastic identification card. James took her ID and squinted. Usually, he didn't wear glasses in public, especially when he was boozing. *Damn! She's not lying! How that could be true? It could be a fake ID. But that's not my problem,"* the writer thought.

"You see! I'm not lying," Kristina said, and James nodded.

"So, where you from?" Kristina asked, clearly interested in him as she flirted openly.

"I was born and raised in Chicago, but my father was Bulgarian," James stated.

"America! That's cool. I have never been to the USA," Kristina exclaimed, looking ecstatic. She kept talking and asking him questions. James was sexually attracted to her, but he had no intentions of having any hunga-bunga with her. However, he didn't mind her company. It was actually fun listening to her stories.

"So… What do you do for a living?" Kristina asked. James talked about his books in a very humble and genteel way.

"You are a writer!" Kristina exclaimed in euphoria.

"I'm just a guy who writes books," James said.

"What's the difference?" Kristina looked confused.

"I'm not a reputed author like Stephen King for example. I'm not selling millions of copies worldwide. However, I do make a living from my books," James had to be candid. He didn't want to lie to Kristina, even if he had just met her.

"So, you're a writer!" She proclaimed while having fun with him. She found James humorous and entertaining.

"I guess you can put it in that way. Your English is proficient. Where did you learn to speak like that?"

"Oh! My parents sent me to an American school in Sofia" Kristina shrugged.

"Okay. Are you here by yourself?"

"Uh… I have friends that work here. This bar is like my second home. You know what I'm saying." Kristina was charismatic. She observed how James finished his drink and said, "The next is on me."

"You're buying me a drink?" James asked, puzzled.

"Yeah, what's wrong with that?" Kristina frowned for a second as if she was offended.

"I don't know. It's kind of unusual for a girl to buy me a drink."

"I don't know how it works in the USA, but here that's normal. So shut the fuck up and let me get you a drink," she said playfully. Katrina was messing around with him, but she was serious about buying him a drink. Hearing this, James recoiled as if someone had punch him in the face.

"Okay then. I'll have Jameson on the rocks! Excuse me; I need to drain the lizard," he said.

"Drain the lizard? What are you talking about?"

"I need to use the restroom," James said, omitting the proper definition of that phrase.

"Sure, I'll be here," Kristina said. A couple of minutes later, James came back and started gulping his drink. Then, in what seemed to be a few moments later, the writer fainted and collapsed on the floor. That was his last drink.

***

"Wake up!" a hoarse voice of a middle-aged man with a Russian accent bellowed in English. "Wake up! I said," the same voice blasted in James' ear. The writer stirred around.

Where am I? What the fuck happened? his inner voice asked. "What the fuck! Who are you?" James asked aloud. His eyes were covered with a bandana. James tried to move his body but he was tied to an office chair.

"Where the heck am I? Untie me? I haven't done anything wrong," James yelled.

"Stay still!" the same male voice commanded.

"Take off the blindfold rag or whatever you put on my eyes!" James almost screamed in shock. He couldn't comprehend why he was tied up.

"What do you know about Boris?" the man with a Russian accent asked. It was the same bald man with the beard who had followed James at the cinema and the gentleman's club.

"Why should I tell you? I don't know you. I can't even see you," James laughed on his last sentence.

"I'll repeat. What do you know about Boris?"

"Fuck off, Nimrod!" James said.

"Wrong answer," another man said. He also had a Russian accent, but his voice sounded louder. His name was Anton. He was the captain of the Russian mafia, called 'очистить,' which in English meant 'clean up the garbage.' Anton had many businesses based in Russia and Bulgaria. He made billions from crypto-currency and flipping real estate. He also, owned a few strip clubs, including the one that John took James to a few weeks ago.

"Who the fuck are you? Unwrap whatever you put on my eyes. Let me see your ugly face," James ranted.

"Ha-Ha-Ha. You're a funny guy, James," Anton said.

"Fuck…" Bzzzzzzz. A crackling sound echoed. The big bald man used a zap stick on James' testicles.

"Ugh… You motherfucker!" James screamed.

"Again! Wrong answer!" Anton gave a nod to the big bald man and he used the zap stick on James' crotch once again. Bzzzzzzz. James moaned again as if he was about to die. He stood up against a few more hits, but then his muscles became impotent. At that moment, James looked like Jesus Christ when he was crucified. The bald man stared at Anton as if he was asking, *"Shall I do more, boss?"* Anton gave him a sign to wait. He walked nervously through what appeared to be an office room, anxiously checking his watch. It read 8 o'clock in the morning.

"James, let me tell you something. I'm a very rich man, okay?" Anton said. "I have access to your personal files. I know everything about you. I have information about your father, Ivan Dobrev, your mother, and Patrick. Also, I know how your wife passed away. I know your social security number, where you live, and what kind of car you drive. I even know when you take a shit. I'm not your enemy, okay? All I need is… What do you know about Boris?" There was a pause. James needed a second to take a deep breath.

"I met him at the liquor store. On the way out, I opened the door, and he stepped out, then I walked behind him. At the next second, someone shot us. That's all I know. I didn't know his name until the police told me," James finished his short speech. Anton walked around, buried in deep thoughts.

"Okay! I don't believe you, but that's fine. Did you talk to him?"

"Not really. I just let him go in front of me. That was all."

"Do you know who killed him?" Anton asked. *"That's the dumbest question that I've heard,"* James thought.

"Not a clue. But I'd like to find out too. What's all this about this guy, Boris? Why is everyone asking about him? What did he do?" James interrogated as if he was a detective.

"I'm the one asking the questions here. Besides, if I tell you, then I'd have to kill you," Anton declared. James was just about to say, *"Go ahead!"* But then he reminded himself that he needed to stay alive for the sake of his son.

"Who are you, and what's your name?" James asked, even though he knew that his question wouldn't be answered.

"I'm a ghost. You know, like Casper in the movies. At one point, I'm here, and the next second I can disappear. Call me Anton or Anthony," the Russian mob boss asserted. James remembered that Kristina said her name using the same phrase. *"Call me Kristina!"*

"Ooh, so Kristina works for you. I got that," James finished his thoughts aloud.

"Huh? I don't know what you are talking about," Anton lied. *"Kristina did a fine job by putting a Mickey in James' drink. She is a good girl. A cunt, but a good girl. I guess she is a good cunt,"* Anton laughed at his own thoughts. James laughed back maniacally as if he was saying, *"You motherfucker!"* There was a clumsy pause as Anton looked at the ceiling thoughtfully.

"Okay, I'll let you go," Anton stated, his voice cold and threatening. "But keep in mind that we're watching you. And don't talk to the police about our encounter. We have people working in positions in many American police departments. Don't underestimate my power, okay?" Anton finished and waved at a girl who approached him, holding a syringe filled with a sedative substance. The girl injected James, and he trailed off at once. Anton snapped a finger, and three big guys came over. They shoved James into a huge garbage bag and took him to a loading dock where a black van was waiting. In no time, James was tossed in the back of the van as if he was trash.

***

"Where the fuck am I," James thought. It took him a few seconds to figure out that he was in a huge garbage bag. He hopped out of the bag, feeling embarrassed and looked around to survey where he was. There were a few gigantic factories around him. It looked like he was in some industrial area. He was dumbstruck. There were no words that he could find to describe his bizarre situation. His vocabulary failed as if he was an illiterate man who had dropped out of high school twenty years ago. After James checked his jeans, he was amazed to find that all of his belongings were still there. *"Thank God!"* he thought. Dobrev then took his iPhone and opened an app called 'Find my taxi' and requested a pick up. The ride took about 30 minutes. It was around 10:30 a.m. when he came to the library apartment. Despite his beaten-up body, he felt a sense of relief after the peculiar night he had experienced. *"I need a nap!"* his inner voice exclaimed. After 30 minutes of clenching his eyelids, James grasped the fact that he couldn't doze off. His mind was filled with dark thoughts. A lot was going on in his mind, and on top of that, his headache made him sick. He thought about Anna and how he had messed up his relationship with her. He knew that he wouldn't see her ever again, and that made him feel blue. James wanted to leave the country and never come back. He felt it was time to turn the page on his old life and start a new chapter, focusing on his family, and especially on Patrick.

An hour later, he tried to reach Jackson, but the detective wasn't available. He had to wait for a callback. In the meantime, he went to the nearest liquor store and bought a bottle of Jameson. After draining a few glasses, the writer thought to himself, *"Sometimes people find themselves infatuated with someone, but the relationship needs to be ended because of the negative consequences that result from it and the problems that arise. In those rare cases, people need to move on."*

***

While James was gulping alcohol and nursing his wounds, Jackson had to call a Lyft driver to make sure he was on time. The homicide detective was dressed spiffily; he had a gray Gucci coat and black athletic stretch fit slacks. His wing tip shoes looked spectacular. Jackson had a reservation at Michel Jordan's steak house on Michigan Avenue. It was 4 in the afternoon, and the gridlock looked bad in the city of Chicago. The ride took about 30 minutes, Jackson wasn't happy about being late, but he was buoyant to eat at his favorite restaurant. He sat at a black leathered booth and waited for his guest. At 5:00 p.m., Lawrence Fisher approached the booth where Jackson sat.

"Good to see ya, Chief. Please have a seat," Jackson was exhilarated to meet the legend of the Chicago Police.

"Look at you, Jackson! You look good. Does your coat come from custom branding or what?" The Chief of Police joked with Jackson, clearly delighted to be talking with the homicide detective. They talked about what was happening in Chicago, then Lawrence asked, "What's happening with the writer… what was his name?"

"James Dobrev. He wants to come back to his family. I guess he is homesick or something," Jackson replied.

"I don't think this is a wise decision, but if he wants to come back so be it. What about Boris? What do you know about this Russian… refugee?" Lawrence asked, his expression looked like a man who had had a bad day.

"I know that Boris was part of a project financed by the Russian government. I have a report that Interpol was looking for him two months before he was killed. The Russian ambassador equivocated and didn't give me much information."

"They are hiding something!" Lawrence Fisher added.

"Yeah! That's what I'm thinking. Whatever Boris had been involved in, it must have been something big."

"Someone fucked up!" Lawrence exclaimed.

"Yeah! That's right," Jackson nodded.

"You mentioned that Interpol was searching for Boris, why?" the Chief of the Police asked.

"After Boris disappeared in 1966, the Russian government sent what they called a *'Red Notice'* to Interpol for robbery. The funny thing is that there wasn't any robbery reported by the Russian government," Jackson stated.

"Let's take a break here. You are telling me that this dude, Boris disappeared in 1966. He hasn't been seen since, and all of a sudden, he was shot at some Chicago liquor store in 2021, and his face looked the same as it was in 1966. That's insane!"

"Yeah, that's how crazy it is," Jackson said.

"What about the media? Why don't they reveal Boris' past?"

"They say it sounds bogus and refuse to talk about it," Jackson reported.

"Yeah, whatever. If the media wants to stay silent, so be it. I have more importing things to do," Lawrence declared. "Oh, and by the way, how is the guy that used to work with you? What's his name…?" Lawrence went on.

"You mean Paul?" Jackson stated, and Lawrence nodded. "He has been in a coma since February. Doctors don't give much hope," Jackson claimed, and Lawrence nodded again. The Chief of Police and the homicide detective talked about the trending news for the following hour, then they split up, going in different directions.

***

"Where are we going?" Kristina asked Anton, the Russian mob boss, but he ignored her question, seeming preoccupied with his own thoughts. Kristina, Anton, and his hardball security were traveling west on the main boulevard in Plovdiv. They sat on the rear seats in a transportation van that had a sign that read *'Cleaners.'*

"We are going to spend a weekend at a hotel in Sofia, honey!" Anton replied with a smirk on his face. The Russian mob boss was a small and short guy, but his influence over people was gargantuan.

"I have a job for you, sweetheart," he went on.

"What job?" Kristina snapped.

"I need you to take care of an important man!"

"For how long?"

"Just for the night, sweetheart!"

"How much?" Kristina asked. Over the past two years, Kristina had done five jobs for Anton. She knew that he would provide security, but the money was short.

"$5,000 in cash. Are you interested? If you're not, I can contact another girl. I have many girlfriends, you know that. Anyway, I think you should take the job. I mean that's $5,000 for one night." Anton was persuasive, and the money was good. Kristina was quiet as she was thinking about the offer.

"Who is the client, and why me?" Kristina asked, and Anton disdainfully rolled his eyes.

"The client is an important man that has an essential spot in the Bulgarian parliament. He likes your pictures and insists on having your company. That's all you need to know. Are you taking the job?"

"I dunno, I mean, the money is good, but this client makes me feel uncomfortable and you know…" Kristina protested. Anton got pissed. "Stop the car!" he yelled. "You, open the door!" Anton commanded one of his guards. The door of the van opened, but Kristina didn't move.

"Are you taking the job or not? Come on, I don't have the entire night to waste," Anton said in a low yet malicious voice. A few seconds of silence filled the van as everyone was staring at Kristina. She had to decide immediately.

"Okay! Don't get mad on me! I need the money. I was just asking questions," Kristina said.

"I know, honey. You are a good girl," Anton said, mentally correcting himself. "*A good cunt.*" The van rolled for half an hour out of town. It was around midnight when the van stopped in the middle of nowhere.

"Why are we stopping?" Kristina asked in confusion. Those were her last words. The big bald man shot her in the head with a silencer. There was no client and no $5,000. Anton made up the whole story. He knew that Kristina was greedy enough to agree to his proposal. Her body was buried a few feet under the ground. No one would search for her—not when the cops get paid to stay silent. Anton had to wipe her out because she was the only person that could connect him with James. However, James couldn't provide any information to the police because he hadn't seen the faces of Anton and his guards. Besides, the police in Bulgaria were financed and controlled by the government and the mafia, so Anton had no choice but to get rid of Kristina. He cleaned the rats. That was how it worked.

***

A week later, James was watching the news at the Airbnb apartment. The newscasters talked about a girl that was missing. A photo of Kristina appeared on the TV screen. James was baffled. "*You motherfucker! Kristina was 18 years old, she was just a kid,*" his inner voice echoed. Disturbed by the news, Dobrev got angry and changed the channel. He then reached out to Big John to see how he was doing.

"Hello!"

"Big John! How you doing?"

"James! I'm glad to hear your voice, buddy. Listen, why don't you stop by for a drink? I'll text you the address," Big John said, sounding elated. James could tell that his friend was already drunk—the whiskey language was familiar to him.

"Okay, I'll swing by," James replied, worried about John.

"Great, buddy!" John almost chanted.

It was a Friday night, the 11th of April. The sky was covered with clouds, but it wasn't cold and James took a cab to the address that Big John had given him. The taxi driver took him to a hotel at the end of the city called *Peacock*. It wasn't the cheapest hotel, but it wasn't the most luxurious either. The employee working at the lobby sent him to the 10th floor. Upon exiting the elevator, James noticed two burly men standing by the door of suite number 1007. The guards asked James for identification and let him go in. James passed through the door, and his eyes widened. The hotel room looked like a gangster party. It was filled with a dozen call girls who were drinking cocktails and chatting with a few guys. These girls were half naked— some of them were braless. The guys were wearing eccentric clothes, and the writer wondered if it was because they were pimps. Hip-hop music was playing, but it wasn't loud. A fat fella was chilling on a couch and preparing cocaine on a coffee table. Everyone in the room came to that fat fella and snorted the coke. James surveyed the room and looked for his friend, but there was no sign of Big John. "Hey, how is the party goin'? Where is John?" James asked a girl that was staring at him.

"I don't know, baby, I think he is in the bedroom. You wanna drink?" the chick asked him.

"Naw, I'm cool. I'll see you in a minute," James spoke in Bulgarian and look for Big John. He found his friend talking to a guy on the balcony.

"Hey, James! Come over, buddy!" Big John exclaimed, exhilarated. He was smiling and having a good time, but that was just how he looked. The truth was that Big John was depressed, throwing a party to mask his problems.

"Let me talk to you for a second," James said to his friend.

"Okay, cool," John said and gave a sign to the other guy that seemed to say, "*Fuck off!*"

"What's going on, John? What is this party?"

"I'm chillin'. I need to cheer up a little. I'm in a very dark… you know how it is." Big John said.

"How are your kids?" James asked.

"I guess they are fine," John said, and then baam! James slapped him.

"Yo, what the fuck! Are you nuts? Do it one more time and I'll fuck you up," Big John yelled angrily.

"What in the name of God are you doing here? Fooling around with those junkies instead of trying to reconcile with your wife and save your marriage. Is that what you want?" There was a pause.

"Man! Why are you bustin' my chops? Is that why you came here? To pretend to be my father and preach about marriage. If so, get the hell out of here!" Big John raised his voice and covered his face as if he was ashamed of what he was doing. James gave him a brotherly hug.

"I'm sorry. Your marriage is not my business. You're mature enough to do what you think is best," James said.

"I know you're trying to help! Come here, let's have a drink!" John suggested, and James nodded.

"I'm just curious. Where did you find those crackheads?" the writer asked.

"Oh, man! That's easy. You call a pimp and say: *bring me some girls, and I'll buy booze and dope.* That's all you need to say. I've never seen those people, and it doesn't matter. They can talk to me as if we have known each other for years, and once the dope is over, they will skedaddle in a second." Big John said, and Dobrev agreed. James and John consumed alcohol only. The drugs were for the junkies.

"You want a girl?" John asked.

"Naw, I'm good. I'll take a hike soon," James politely refused.

"It's your call. Are you in love with that lawyer?"

"Not really. I have a good time with her, but she's too… uh…" James looked for the correct word.

"Intense!"

"Yeah. You can say that. She is a very successful lawyer, and I wish her all the best. But I had more important stuff to do." James replied.

"Are you going back to Chicago?"

"Yeah, soon I'll fly back to the Windy City. I need to take care of my son. I haven't seen him for almost three months," James replied. He didn't do much in the hotel room except for having a few drinks with John and a hooker, whose name remained unclear, who was giving him lollipops in the bathroom. At midnight, James hopped out of a taxi and wobbled to the library apartment. He chugged a few more glasses of Jameson before collapsing onto the bed like a dead animal.

9

It was the last Friday in April and James was a happy camper as he packed his luggage. The following day, he would fly back to Chicago. He couldn't mask his happiness; the fact that he was about to see his family made him cheerful. On Saturday, Jack and Liam drove by to pick James up. The government in Bulgaria had to make sure he would be escorted by official authorities. James left the Airbnb apartment and glimpsed at his escort. Jack and Liam were dressed in corporate suits; they looked like they owned assets worth millions of dollars. They exchanged polite phrases as if they were neighbors that hadn't seen each other for a while. James was escorted in a black AMG Mercedes model 2020, but the vehicle itself didn't matter to him. He wouldn't have cared if he had been driven to the airport in a John Deere tractor.

Two hours later, James was chilling out on a seat in a private jet. He took a deep breath; it would be a long flight.

***

While James slept on the plane to O'Hare, Big John was drinking Scotch in his black Audi. He parked his vehicle on the shoulder of a rural road a few miles out of Plovdiv. Big John turned his phone off. He didn't want to be disturbed. He was alone in the car, staring at the beautiful view. Big John was drinking alcohol straight from the bottle. In his left hand, he held a photo of himself and his family.

Staring at the photo, Big John didn't have resilience. His mind was too weak to endure the pressure. He listened to the demonic voice that was hovering in his head saying, *"You're a piece of shit!"* Big John had loved his wife, but he couldn't accept the truth that his wife wasn't being totally faithful. He found out that Amelia had crossed the line by committing adultery and had had a covert relationship with an 18-year-old boy who happened to have a huge shaft. Big John couldn't accept this story. A few seconds later, he placed the photo on the dashboard. He grabbed a Glock 17, closed his eyes, and shot himself in the head. The gunshot blasted like thunderstruck. Birds fluttered in different directions, startled by the gunfire. Big John committed one of the worst sins by killing himself and leaving his daughters fatherless.

It is sad when people make decisions based on initial impulses rather than taking a break and counting their blessings.

***

James scuttled through the international terminal at O'Hare. He dragged his luggage, passing through the gates of the airport. It was ten in the evening, and the airport was empty as if there had been a government order compelling Chicagoans to stay at home due to a destructive virus. James had requested a rideshare service, but his driver wasn't there. He looked at his phone and saw a few missed calls from Frank. There was also a text from him saying:

CALL ME ASAP. IT'S IMPORTANT!

"Hi, Frank, what's going on?" James asked, concerned.

"James! Thank God! It's about your mother!"

***

James was in a state of uncontrolled panic as he sat quietly on the rear seat of the Lyft vehicle, but his mind was about to flip out. The Lyft driver was Eastern-European, silent because he couldn't speak English. The rideshare vehicle headed to Schaumburg. James' mother had been missing for six hours. James didn't know what to do. He contacted Jackson and asked if he had any information about Michelle. Jackson promised to check the salon on the following day and interrogate everyone who had been in the salon. Her phone hadn't been in service since noon. Frank said that she had left her salon, but no one could tell anything more. There was a police patrol guarding the house in Schaumburg, but there wasn't any police surveillance at Michelle's salon.

At a quarter to eleven, the Lyft driver pulled his vehicle into the driveway of the house in Schaumburg. James stormed out of the car and briskly took his luggage. Frank came out of the house and gave him a hug. It became awkward. James and Frank had never hugged before.

"James! I'm so happy to see you. Let me take your luggage," Frank said jovially.

"Forget about the luggage. Give me the VIN of my mother's car. The police need it to trace the vehicle," James stated.

"Sure! James, I'm so sorry. I don't know what to tell you…"

"Just… Don't say a word. Where is Patrick?" James asked while entering the house. Frank took him to the room where Patrick sat in the wheelchair. James wrapped his arms around his son and started telling him how much he loved him. Tears dropped from James' eyelashes. He missed his son, a lot. James couldn't imagine what would happen if Patrick disappeared like Michelle.

"Look, buddy! I bought you clothes. I flew back from Bulgaria. It was an interesting trip, though," James was excitedly talking to Patrick. His son could only move his left eyeball, but James hoped that Patrick could hear him, even if he didn't respond. A few minutes later, James went in the kitchen to speak with Frank.

"Are you hungry?" Frank asked. James snubbed his question and respectfully asked, "Frank, is there something that happened between you and mom? Don't lie to me. Be honest."

"No! Absolutely not. I swear to God. We haven't had any altercations or bickering. James, I swear to God," Frank confessed. Dobrev believed him because Frank was a henpecked man; he would do anything to please Michelle.

"Okay, did she say anything that struck you as unusual? Anything that sounded weird?" Dobrev asked.

"Not that I'm aware of," Frank blurted out.

"Did she act strange or nervous for some reason?"

"No, James! Nothing unusual," Frank said.

"All right, I spoke with Jackson. He said that the police will start searching for her vehicle. They have to find it. She drives a frigging 4Runner, not a bicycle for Christ's sake! The detective also said that if Michelle doesn't show up in the next 48 hours, the media will announce her missing on TV," James finished his monologue, perturbed about his mother. Although his relationship with Michelle wasn't the greatest, he still loved his mother.

The next morning, James met Jackson at Michelle's salon. Her salon had 5,000 square feet of retail space, and it was located a 60-minute drive westbound from Chicago. The name of the salon was '*Top Models*.' It was the most well-known beauty salon in the area. Michelle had been managing her business for five years. *Top*

Models had cosmopolitan furniture and high tech equipment. Also, it had a 4.9 rating and over 500 reviews on Google. Michelle spent more than her annual profit to keep her reputation high. *Top Models* was a busy salon, but there was no security. Usually, beauty salons don't need security, and *Top Models* was no exception.

Jackson interrogated the workers and some of the customers of the beauty salon. Michelle had more than thirty employees, and no one could think of a bad word to say about her. The clients complimented Michelle and described her as a prosperous and cordial woman. Jackson couldn't find anything that could be helpful. Michelle had left the salon happily at noon on the day of her disappearance, and none of her clients could recall anything unusual.

"What do you think?" James asked Jackson. The homicide detective was tangled in his own thoughts, but his words came with confidence.

"I need to find her vehicle! That's the key."

"Do you think Frank has anything to do with her loss?" James asked, growing nervous as the questions about his missing mother started to pile up. It took a minute before Jackson could answer.

"Could be anything. Are they legally married?" Jackson managed to ask.

"Yeah, the reception was in Hawaii three years ago. But, as far as I know, Frank wanted to get hitched secretly. However, mom was over the moon about the wedding."

"That doesn't mean anything. Sometimes what we know doesn't necessarily lead to the truth. Does that make any sense?" Jackson asked politely.

"Absolutely!"

"All right then. Listen, go home and rest. I'll keep you posted," the detective suggested, and the writer nodded.

***

At three in the afternoon, James visited a private physical therapist located in Lincoln Park. His injured arm wasn't bothering him, but he still wanted to follow up on the healing process. The therapists there were gentle and friendly with him, but James didn't pay attention to the staff at the therapy clinic. He couldn't stop thinking about the fact that his stepfather might be involved in Michelle's disappearance. The physical therapy was done by 4:00 p.m., and James left the building smiling, yet his mind was filled with thoughts about his mother. As he walked to his vehicle, James glanced at his iPhone. The writer checked the Bulgarian newsfeed, and his eyes widened, as he saw the headline about the death of Big John. The article described that the police in Bulgaria had found him in his car shot with a gun that had been registered under his name. James covered his face with his hands as if he was ashamed of something.

"Oh, John! What have you done! How could you do something so stupid?" he thought. His mind was jammed with images displaying memories of John and himself. James was at the edge of a panic attack. He stood on Belmont Street, covering his face. People who passed him thought that he was a total weirdo. James had never faced so many troubles at the same time. He felt that whatever he did or wherever went, people around him would suffer as a result of his jinx. *"Gosh, I hope Anna is fine!"* his mind whispered. James decided to check his social media, he was interested to learn any updates regarding the injury lawyer. Then James became shocked because he couldn't believe what he was seeing. Anna had unfriended him on Facebook and Instagram. *"Whoa! Okay, I guess we are not friends anymore!"* he thought, feeling a bit sad that his relationship with Anna had been destroyed.

"That's the ugly face of life. Sometimes people who we care about leave us for reasons that don't make any sense. That is an ordeal that we need to learn to live with," James whispered to himself. He parked his Hyundai Accent on a side street a few blocks away and sat in his car for a while without moving. He just sat there, lost in thought about his tangled life.

"Gosh, I need a drink! But first, I need to do something!" With these words, he fired up the engine of his car and headed to his home in the city to collect the rent from the Mexican family. The tenants were paying in cash, and that was fine with James. It was Thursday, around three in the afternoon and the gridlock in Chicago wasn't looking good. It took him half an hour to get to his home. James parked his Hyundai on the side street close to his townhouse and went inside his building. He then stepped into the basement and unlocked a door that had the sign that read '*Office*,' which was a small room similar to the size of a master bathroom. James pulled out stainless steel security safe box and punched his combination on the keypad to unlock it. The safe box had a bunch of documents and a couple of keys. He took the keys, left the office, and walked to another box that had a label saying 'Letters.' That box was cemented to the floor in case someone tried to steal it. There's an empty slot on the box where the Mexicans had been instructed to drop the money for the rent. Using this method, the tenants and the landlord didn't have to see each other. James opened the Letters box and took out an envelope bulked with cash. He took the money and walked upstairs to his apartment. Even though Jackson had advised him to stay away from his property until Chicago PD found who was responsible for drawing the message on the wall, James decided to check the condo. He hadn't been in his place since he had left the country. The writer grabbed the doorknob and tried to unlock it. He then realized that the door was open. "*There is someone in my condo!*" he thought. James wasn't a pussy. He was ready to give up on his life to protect his home. He burst into the room swiftly and surveyed the premises.

"Who's there? Get out of my property, or I'm calling the cops!" he yelled. Instantly the noise of moving a chair screeched from the living room and James ran through the hallway to find out who was in there.

"Don't call the cops! Please, don't call the cops!" a male's voice shrieked in a state of terror.

***

"Who the fuck are you?" James said in a low but aggressive tone, holding the neck of a white man in his late twenties. That man had a buzz haircut and a slender body with a nose as big as a large spoon, his clothes looked like he worked as a manager in a classy restaurant.

"Talk! What are you doing in my property? Talk now!" James commanded.

"My name is Jake Kohen! I can explain. Please, take your hands off me. I need to breathe," the young man said.

"Do you have any weapons?" James asked.

"No, sir. I didn't come here to cause problems. Please, take your hands off me. I can't breathe." He went on, "I'll explain." The man, who said his name was Jake, declared. There was a pause, and James needed a second to think about what he should do.

"Okay, let me search you first. Turn around." James said and acted like a cop. Jake did whatever James asked without protesting. Dobrev opened Jake's shirt to see if there were hidden knives, wires, or guns. Jake was as clean as he had said.

"Talk, you dipshit! What the fuck are you doing in my property?" James ordered, he was on the verge of turning berserk.

"I worked for the guy who wants to kill you. And I'm here to reveal information that no one else can tell you. I'm running from my employer," Jake said, still scared.

"What?" What are you talking about?" James asked. Jake gingerly lifted his hands and sat on a chair that was adjacent to him.

"I'll explain. I work, or probably I should say I used to work, for a very bad guy. I'm not sure what his real name is, but everybody called him Mr. D. Here's the thing. I worked with computers. I studied cyber security, but I dropped out of high school because it was kind of boring and I was the most skilled kid in class. Anyway, I started a job as a database analyst in a company called 'Solution Creativity Inc.'"

"And this guy, Mr. D, is the owner of that company," James interrupted his unwelcomed guest.

"Not really. Mr. D worked with Solution Creativity. Basically, the company provides him with employees, and he pays them a large amount of money. Mr. D has access to every employee hired by Solution Creativity. In other words, Mr. D has employees through Solution Creativity. Officially, on paper, I work for Solution Creativity, but actually, I work for Mr. D. The paychecks come from him," Jake was talking so fast that James barely could catch his words.

"Okay. What's Mr. D's business structure? What does he do?" James asked, surprised by Jake's revelation.

"Mr. D has many businesses. I can't tell how many precisely. He holds 90% assets of a pharmaceutical company that creates medications, such as Adderall, Fentanyl, Xanax, etc. He had more than 20 enormous factories all across the states, distributing medications across the country and worldwide. Bottom Line, Mr. D is a very rich man. I'm talking about billions of dollars. Also, the Zener virus was developed in his laboratories."

"Are you for real?" James chimed in, unable to contain his surprise.

"I swear to God! There is more! Mr. D created the Zener vaccine and sold it to the government. I mean we are talking about trillions of dollars."

"Wait a minute. The vaccinations are free for everyone. How does the government make a profit? I wouldn't believe that the government would buy something without anything coming in. Where is the turnover?" James asked, astounded by Jake's words.

"Here is the catch! Have you noticed that the prices of everything had been rising?" Jake asked.

"Yeah!" James agreed.

"Here's the answer: it's inflation. The government had an excuse to raise taxes, gas prices, real estate, etc. And the most absurd part is that the media doesn't talk about inflation because of the Zener. They focus on the virus, and issues with inflation became petty. Does that make sense?"

"That's a good point. Let me ask you something; how do you know that?"

"I work or I used to work in databases, collecting all the data from Mr. D's pharmaceutical business. I'm a computer genius or computer nerd, as they say. I hacked one of the government websites and the information leaked there. May I have a bottle of water, please? I'm thirsty!" Jake asked.

"Okay. Come, I'll show you where the water is," James declared. As they walked into the kitchen, James kept a close eye on Jake. The unwelcomed guest looked innocuous, but that didn't mean he wasn't dangerous. James thought that Jake was a piece of shit. But a valuable piece of shit. He handed a bottle of water to Jake, and the computer nerd drank half of it. James was eyeballing him and asked, "Why would you hack the government?"

"Mr. D required information," Jake answered almost automatically.

"Okay, and this guy, Mr. D. What does he look like?"

"I have never seen him in person. No photos or anything like that. Mr. D stays anonymous," Jake finished his thoughts, and James asked his next question.

"Where is my mother? Do you know anything about her? She was kidnapped two days ago." James became bitter talking about the disappearance of his mom.

"I have no idea what are you talking about. This is something that cannot be found in the computers. I have no idea where your mother could be. I swear to God!" Jake confessed, his hands shaking from terror.

"Okay, let's say I believe you. What about Boris?" the writer asked, thinking. *"It's interesting when people often talk about a man who has recently passed away. It's like they bring him back to life."* There was a pause. Jake looked like he was hesitating about his answer.

"Boris was a part of a top-secret project. The Russians were doing a bunch of scientific experiments. They made him live longer but not continue to age."

"You mean like he was immortal?" James asked with wide open eyes.

"Not immortal because he is dead already. I think they call it 'The Rejuvenation Order.' That's what was written in the lab reports."

"That's insane! How's that possible?" James asked, so confused that he lost his diction for a second.

"Money! Money… Money! Mr. D wants to live forever. He has invested billions of dollars to live longer and he's a very powerful man," Jake said.

"Okay. Why would you come into my house? Did you write the sign on the wall that says: *I KNOW WHO YOU ARE?*

"I did not, but I gave them information on how to do it."

"Huh? You gave information to whom?" James asked.

"I don't know. I work from home. I've never seen anyone. Everything was being done through computers; paychecks, communication, and work in general," Jake finished his speech. He wasn't lying. Ever since he started working for Mr. D, Jake never left his apartment. He ordered food from Uber eats and Doordash. He was 27 years old, single, and had never been married. He usually left his apartment on Saturdays to get bongoed in some strip clubs. Other than that, Jake had instructions to stay at home and never share his job paradigm with others, even his family.

"So, how did you know that I was coming to my apartment at that particular hour?" James asked.

"You should get another car!" Jake shortly answered, and James looked surprised.

"Hold on for a minute," James said. He closed his eyes for a moment to analyze the situation. "So, why are you here? Why are you telling me all this classified information? Is there a gang that's waiting to ambush me downstairs, or what the hell are you up to?" James asked and Jake took a deep breath.

"A few days ago, I puzzled out that Mr. D wants to kill me because I know too much about his business. I have to run for my life. I just wanted to give you some info before it would be too late. Also, I need to ask you a favor." Jake said, his face exposed fear and consternation.

"A favor? What kind of favor?"

"Please, don't talk about us having this chat in person. Don't tell the police what I look like. You've never seen me. You can talk about our conversation because I want Mr. D to be sentenced for life in jail. We need to stop him."

"You got it! Is there anything else I can help you with," James said politely. He wasn't sure if he could trust Jake, but what options did he have? Jake didn't want anything from him, except to keep the information about him confidential.

"Gotta tell ya. You're a ballsy man to show up at my apartment just like that," James said.

"I don't know how I didn't pee in my pants," Jake confessed, and they both laughed.

"What are you going to do now? What's on your mind?" the writer questioned.

"I'm leaving the country early tomorrow," Jake revealed.

"Where are you going?"

"Can't tell you," Jake said with a smile and requested a Lyft driver.

"How can I be in touch with you?"

"I'll contact you!" Jake said. They wished each other good luck. A few minutes later, the Lyft driver came, and Jake left the apartment. James sank into a sea of thoughts, not believing what he had heard. He sat on a chair in the kitchen, took a piece of paper, and jotted down what he had to do. "*Tomorrow would be a long day,*" he thought.

***

It was Wednesday, the end of April. The weather in the Windy City was overcast and rainy, but it wasn't cold. Jackson decided to drive to Chipotle for lunch, thanks to the fine weather. He loved to eat there, the food was good and made him think that he looked healthy. The African-American detective finished his vegetarian bowl, and his phone rang. It was James.

"Hi James, how are you doing, baby?" Jackson said, cheerfully.

"I'm fine. I need to talk to you. Where you at?" James spoke hurriedly as if it was an emergency.

"Why, what happened?" Jackson asked. He didn't get a straight answer because James wanted to speak with him in person. At precisely half-past two in the afternoon, they met at the parking lot of Home Depot, located on North Avenue.

"James! You've got a new ride! What happened to the Hyundai?" Jackson spoke, exposing a charming smile.

"It's a rental. I called a junk company to take my vehicle," James explained.

"Huh? It broke down?"

"Not really," James said and talked about the conversation that he had with Jake. He lied about seeing Jake in person. Instead, he said that they spoke over the phone. Jackson listened carefully because the information had an essential key to resolving the case.

Unfortunately, there was a problem. James didn't have any evidence to prove that Jake was telling the truth.

"Okay, this guy Jake, where is he now? Do you have any contact information," Jackson made a good point.

"I have no idea! He said he would contact me," James said, and Jackson nodded.

"There is one more thing that you need to know," James went on. He talked about the unpleasant encounter that he had with Anton, the Russian Mob boss. Dobrev knew that revealing the information about Anton could be dicey. He decided to take the risk, even though that could jeopardize the life of his family. Listening to James, Jackson was dumbstruck, trying to connect the dots.

"So, Anton is looking for Boris' murderer, but for what reason?" Jackson asked, and James shrugged.

"Let me get this straight! Jake said that Boris could live longer and have the ability to look the same age as he was 40 years ago! That's insane!" Jackson snapped, and James agreed.

"And Mr. D killed Boris because he was about to reveal the covert information about the entire project!" Jackson continued.

"I would guess so!" James said.

"Okay, I'll have to look for a guy with the quirky pseudonym," Jackson spoke with a face that looked like he had unpleasant diarrhea. The information given by James was making him sick. He had never worked on such a knotted case.

"Have you changed the locks of your building?" Jackson asked. James had not only changed the locks, but he had installed the most expensive locks that could be found in the industry. Also, the writer announced to the Mexican tenants that he was selling the building, and they had to move out by the end of the next month. James didn't actually intend to sell his building; it was a polite way to kick out the tenants—this was a common cycle practiced by many landlords. James didn't want to get rid of the Mexicans. They were cordial and respectful. That family had been living in his building for three years, and he hadn't had any problems with them. But the writer didn't have a choice. He had to make sure that his building was empty until the nightmare was over.

"Did you install security cameras in the building?" Jackson asked.

"Not yet!"

"What! You Bulgarians are cheap," Jackson joked. He needed to break the ice because the situation wasn't funny at all.

"Nah! We are smart cheapheads!" James replied.

"What's a cheaphead?" Jackson asked. His expression was something like, *"What the heck are you talking about?"*

"It's a person who only spends money when he has to. I've just made it up." James stated, mirroring his polite smile. Jackson cracked a smile. Instantly, a ringing phone interrupted their conversation.

"Is that yours?" James asked, confused.

"Nah, mine doesn't ring like that," Jackson asserted. Then James looked at his phone and saw Frank's name on the screen. The writer picked up the call.

"Hi Frank, what's…"

"James! You need to come over to Schaumburg. It's your mom!"

***

The news about Michelle hit James like a bolt of lightning. It was as if Chicago PD had just uncovered Jimmy Hoffa's long-lost body. Without a moment to waste, James hopped into his car and followed Jackson's Camaro down I-90 westbound. They arrived at Frank's house in Schaumburg much faster than expected. When they pulled in, the house was swarming with police officers. The first floor of the house was filled with a plethora of cops, giving it the appearance of a bustling police department.

Michelle was, crying, and clearly traumatized by what she had experienced the last several days. Frank consoled her by saying that everything was all right, but she couldn't hear his words. She was buried in emotional shock. Frank covered her naked body, and took her to the second floor. Michelle waddled to the master bathroom—she needed a shower. Then Michelle locked herself in the bedroom.

"She doesn't want to speak with anyone," Frank said from behind the bedroom door, as if he was her personal guard.

"Okay. Listen, call me when she feels ready to talk. I'll send a police patrol to watch the house for 24 hours," Jackson declared.

"Jackson, please, don't tell the media," James implored.

"I'll see what I can do! Can't promise much," Jackson said and went to the first floor, where a bunch of deputies were chatting. He urged the police officers to leave the house and then backed his car out of the driveway. His mind was buried in deep wonder because he sincerely empathized with James' pain. He couldn't imagine what he would have done if he had seen his mother in a similar situation. Later on, Frank went to a prominent restaurant, bought a delicious meal, and served the food to his wife. He was attentive and would do anything to please Michelle. It took a couple of hours before Michelle could say anything.

"It was horrible! I can't even tell you how I'm feeling," Michelle said, sobbing.

"It's fine, honey! You can talk when you're feeling better," Frank suggested.

"It's NOT FINE!" Michelle yelled. Her anger burst out loud, and Frank zipped. She was a strong woman, but her mind became weak. Michelle had been facing many issues in her life, yet nothing could compare to what she had experienced in the past few days. She was terrified and couldn't sleep that night, fidgeting in her bed until the early hours of the next day.

Two days later, Michelle called James and Frank. They came to her bedside and checked on her.

"Here's what happened," Michelle started. "I stopped at McDonald's to get a large fries. As I was walking back to my car, I saw a few trucks that were parked next to my vehicle. I thought it wasn't a big deal. I unlocked my vehicle and opened the driver's door. As soon as I opened the door, someone pushed me into the car. I wanted to scream, but I couldn't. They put some kind of a plastic bag on my head, and I literally freaked out. I felt the edge of a knife pressing on my throat and I heard a voice saying, 'Don't move a muscle, and don't make any noises.' I did what the voice told me. Someone must have grabbed my car keys because I heard all of the doors opening at the same time. Another man pushed me to the passenger seat and held my hands. There must have been three or four guys, at least. It was so scary!" Michelle sobbed. Frank hugged her; she leaned her head against his chest. Michelle wept for a few seconds more, and then she continued. "They drove me to some kind of a factory or warehouse. The building was empty, though. There were no workers. They tied my hands with some cheap zip ties as if I was a prisoner. They walked me to an empty room. That room was bright. It had many lights like we were about to shoot pictures for a magazine or something like that. And then the worst happened," Michelle said and sobbed continually.

"Mom, you're saying that this room looked like a photography studio?" James asked quietly.

"Yeah, something like that. Then… those bastards took their pants off and raped me. One after another. It was horrible!" Michelle almost screamed and started crying.

"Mom, those guys, did you see their faces?" James chimed in.

"No. They were wearing ski masks, covering their faces. They had cameras and recorded everything. They were having fun, and I was devastated." Michelle wept even more. James and Frank were in disbelief.

"Motherfuckers!" James blurted out. His mind blacked out. The desire for retaliation made him walk around angrily in the bedroom.

"Honey, how many did you say they were?" Frank asked. His question was kind of pointless, but Michelle answered.

"They were four in that room."

"After that, what happened?" Frank asked.

"They kept me locked in that room and gave me food, which I refused. They also took my belongings. I cannot tell how long I had been there. Later, they took me out of the room and drove me to Schaumburg. The bastards dropped me a few blocks away from our house. I had to walk naked in my own neighborhood. I'm so embarrassed," Michelle cried out and continually shed tears.

"Mom, where's your car?" James asked.

"Can't tell! They took me in a black van that had no license plates. It was a nightmare, James!" Michelle cried out, and the writer hugged her.

"Mom, can you tell the same story to the police inspector?"

"Yes, I believe so," Michelle said sobbingly.

***

It was Friday, three days after Michelle returned home. Jackson's Camaro was parked in the driveway of the house in Schaumburg. Michelle didn't want to go to the police station. She preferred to speak with Jackson at her house. As he walked to the house, Jackson looked as presentable as usual, and his Gucci coat looked outstanding. Politely, he asked Michelle if he could record their conversation, to which she agreed. Michelle then proceeded, telling him the entire story in a verbatim statement, and the detective listened carefully, nodding along as she spoke. He then asked.

"Michelle, do you have any idea where this warehouse was located?"

"I can't tell. I was so scared. The guy from behind was pressing a knife to my throat, and I could barely breathe. It was awful," Michelle explained and started crying again.

"I can only imagine. Okay, I'll ring if something comes up," the detective stated, and James walked him to the driveway.

"Have you heard anything about Mr. D?" James asked.

"Working on it. Listen, whatever he is, we will trace him to his whereabouts. Mr. D is someone powerful and influential. I wouldn't be surprised if he is an alderman or some official that works in the government."

"In this case, how are you planning to identify a mogul like him?" James questioned.

"There is not a straight answer to your question. It may take years. The only way to puzzle out this case is if someone snitches about Mr. D. As a matter of fact, I believe that many people work for him, and the key is to find somebody who would tell us more. You know like…"

"Jake!" James intervened.

"Yeah! That's right. But we don't have any contact information for him. We also don't know what his real name is. So Jake Kohan might be a false name or nickname like Mr. D. What can I say… we're working on…Hold on!" Jackson's phone interrupted his conversation with James.

"Excuse me for a second!" the detective said. The African-American man picked up the phone, and in the next second his face froze.

"Wait! What! Are you for real?" Jackson asked.

***

Jackson was in shock. The news spoken over the phone had terrified him. Teresa, Paul's wife, called to inform him that Paul had passed away the night before. He never woke up from the coma. Paul had dedicated his life to investigating crimes and loved his job. Despite occasionally complaining about his position as a homicide detective, he was generally a happy camper. He also was a devoted husband and a loving father of two boys. Paul made many friendships over the years and enjoyed going to Cubs games with his buddies. Baseball was his religion. His father had been taking him to baseball games since he was a child. Teresa was devastated because she had prayed for her husband's recovery, and now he was gone. She remained strong during daylight to prove how stoic she was for the sake of her kids. But when nightfall came, she cried a lot. She couldn't imagine what her life could be without Paul. Teresa was in her late thirties, her boobs flopped a bit and looked like they were about to fall, but she was still voluptuous and aware that she could have another man at any minute. However, she knew that no one could replace her husband as the father of her kids. Jackson expressed his condolences and asked when the funeral would take place.

****

The funeral was held two days after Paul went to be with the Lord. Many of his friends, including a bunch of police deputies, wanted to pay tribute and came to the funeral. Before the ceremony, Paul's parents gathered everyone at their house in Glencoe. There was so much food that it made the house look like a grocery store. Over 300 vehicles drove to the cemetery, and the ceremony started at noon. A prominent brass band was playing at the cemetery. Most people attending the funeral looked down to the ground as if they were ashamed of doing something wrong. Teresa, dressed all in black, covered her sons as if to protect them from rain. Her sons were children, but they were old enough to understand that their father wouldn't be around anymore. Eight people carried the casket and Jackson was one of them. After the brass band stopped playing, a few police officers including the chief of Chicago PD, gave a speech, addressing their condolences for Paul's family.

At the end of the funeral ceremony, Harry approached Jackson and whispered, "Lawrence Fisher and I want to talk with you!"

"About what?" Jackson asked.

"Can't talk here. I'll meet you tomorrow at Lawrence's office at 4:00 p.m.," Harry explained, and Jackson nodded. An hour later, the cemetery was over. People left Paul to rest in peace.

Sometimes, relatives and members of the family leave this world suddenly, making it important for people to express their love to them.

10

Jackson knocked on the door with the sign saying 'Chief of the Police.' His phone clock read 4:30 p.m.

"Come in," Lawrence hollered from behind the door. Jackson entered through the threshold and surveyed the office. Lawrence's office was airy, bigger than a one-bedroom apartment. It had a couple of bookshelves, implying that Lawrence was an avid reader. In the corner on the north side was a classy vinyl record player with speakers placed on top of a vintage stand. A huge rug sprawled on the floor that came from the Middle East, on which the price tag exceeded $5,000. On the ceiling was a crystal rain chandelier that looked like it could fall at any second. On the wall of the south side were mounted a few abstract paintings that gave an interesting contrast to the office. Lawrence's desk was bigger than a single bed. Behind his desk was a black leather massage chair that was worth over $6,000. That chair had more features than Jackson's vehicle. It had ten massage modes, and six massaging styles. Behind the massage chair were windows along the wall that spanned the width of the entire room. The view was splendid; it showed the loop of downtown Chicago.

Jackson saw that Harry and Lawrence had already been speculating something. He stepped in and greeted the lieutenant of the Northside PD and the chief of Chicago PD.

"Jackson, you're late!" Lawrence cracked a smile.

"You know how the traffic in Chi…is," Jackson shrugged. Harry smiled at Jackson and laid out a map that had red pins, indicating the investigation crime scenes of the murders committed a few months ago.

"Gentlemen! Shall we begin?" Harry asked, looking at Lawrence as if he was asking for permission to proceed. Lawrence gave a sign, and Harry nodded. There was a huge TV screen attached to the wall on the south side. Harry used a Bluetooth keyboard and a mouse. On the screen were displayed the evidence and the victims. Lawrence and Jackson gawked at the TV screen. Harry spoke as fast as he could. He knew that Lawrence had to leave in an hour or so.

"Let's start over: On the 20th of November, Boris Gurmanov was murdered, and the writer, James Dobrev, survived at the liquor store located at the corner of Belmont and Halsted. On December first, Charles, James' friend, was brutally murdered by the delivery guy. What was his name?" Harry asked and automatically answered himself. "Kevin Mills! Yeah, that was the name of the delivery driver who had slashed Charles' throat. Then, on February 23rd, Kevin Mills was found dead in his apartment. At this point, we don't have any trace of Kevin's murder. Next, on March 31st, Thomas Macintosh, aka, Thomas The Daggers, aka Thomas The Fucker was burned to death as a result of an explosion in his car. The bomb made it hard for the coroner to identify the body. At this point, we don't have anything that could lead us to the murderer either. Am I missing something?" Harry asked in a state of confusion.

"Paul!" Jackson's voice echoed through the entire office.

"Oh, Gosh. Yeah, Paul passed away on April 26th, which was yesterday. So, let me make it clear. Up until this point, are we clear that all of those murders were committed by one person?"

"Allegedly!" Lawrence Fisher answered.

"Yes, this statement could be described as circumstantial. And what do we have? Mr. D, who is allegedly responsible for those murders, and Jake Kohen, who can allegedly give us information about Mr. D. So, we have the nickname of a suspect and the false name of the guy who claims he knows that murderer. And no witnesses, except Michelle who's memory is hazy," Harry finished his thoughts.

"What a great story! Maybe James could write a book about it," Jackson said skeptically. At first, Harry guffawed at Jackson's remark. He then realized that it wasn't funny at all.

"You don't play games with the player! Does that make any sense?" Lawrence spilled his profound knowledge.

"Not really! What do you mean by that?" Harry asked and the chief of the Chicago PD rolled his eyes as if to say, *Do I have to explain everything?"*

"It means that you don't mess around with the player who has created the game. It's a way of saying: hey, we can't afford any mistakes," Lawrence finished his speech.

"Got it! Okay, perhaps Jake has already left the country, but we don't know what he looks like," Harry declared.

"James said that he had spoken with him over the phone," Jackson said.

"Can we get a copy of that phone call?" Harry asked.

"I don't think so. James said that Jake had called with NO CALLER ID."

"Okay, why would Jake talk to James and not the police?" Harry asked.

"That's a good question!" Jackson snapped.

"He's probably scared," Lawrence asserted.

"Okay, but what is the difference? James would talk to us no matter what, and Jake knew that," Harry wondered.

"He needed more time!" Jackson said.

"Time for what?" Harry questioned.

"To leave the country," Lawrence declared. He felt relaxed, the massage chair was on Shiatsu mode, and Lawrence loved it.

"Why are you so sure that he had left the country?" Harry questioned.

Jackson replied, "Of course he did. Mr. D would kill him. Jake is a tattler, and he wants Mr. D to be locked behind the bars." There was a pause. The three police officials were silent. Then Lawrence broke the silence.

"This guy, Mr. D or whatever his name is, someone should know that name. What about the penitentiary? Someone should have heard that nickname before."

"I'll swing by," Jackson said.

"You'll need help!" Lawrence added.

"Huh? What do you mean by that?" Jackson was confused. Lawrence looked at Harry and gave him a tacit sign. Harry made a quick phone call. Two minutes later, a young man unfamiliar to Jackson entered the office. The name of the young man was Jacob Bartek. He was 25 years old, slender with an expensive haircut, and handsome like Chris Evans. His parents had emigrated from Poland back in the 1970s. His father worked his ass off to send him to a good school. Bartek had just gotten his Master's in investigations, graduating from a prominent university in Boston and now was starting his career as a homicide detective. He could have had many girlfriends, but alas he had had a shotgun marriage. His wife gave birth to an adorable daughter. Jacob needed to work hard for his family. He stepped inside the office and introduced himself to Jackson. They exchanged a few kind words. Jackson mirrored an amiable expression toward Jacob, but he was flustered. He didn't expect to meet someone at that time. Lawrence, Harry, and Jackson chatted with Jacob for a bit, then the chief of the police announced.

"Okay, kid. Wait for us outside. I'll be back with you in a minute."

Jacob looked a little confused that he had to leave so early. He sauntered to the door, but then turned back to the gentlemen in the office and proclaimed "I appreciate your time, sir! I'll do anything possible to catch this diabolical man." Bartek clenched his fists as if he was a boxer posting his weight in a press conference, and continued, "Jackson, it was nice to meet you. See you later."

"My pleasure," Jackson replied before watching Jacob close the door. He then exclaimed, "With all due respect, that is unacceptable!"

"What do you mean?" Harry couldn't comprehend Jackson's words.

"Why would it be unacceptable?" Lawrence asked.

"Looked at him! He is so sexy! I don't like it," Jackson stated, and Lawrence nodded.

"Guys! What are you talking about?" Harry repeated his question. Jackson and Lawrence looked at each other as if they were saying, *"You tell him!"* Then Lawrence called Harry to step closer and whispered. "Jackson doesn't like his partner because he has a crush on him and that could be a problem with work." At first, Harry laughed. He then realized that his laugh was inappropriate.

"Jackson, we can transfer Jacob to a different department. That wouldn't be an issue," Harry suggested.

"Nah, it's cool. I'm fine."

"You sure!" Harry asked.

"I'm positive!" Jackson declared confidently. Despite his ability to handle anything, he couldn't shake the feeling of loneliness.

"Is there anything else? Am I missing something?" Lawrence asked. He tried to sound less agitated.

"Not really. I mean, the case is in abeyance until we find out who

Mr. D is," Harry declared, realizing that he hadn't eaten since noon as his belly made strange noises.

"And Jake too!" Jackson added.

"Okay, here is my last question. What connects all of those murdered people?" Lawrence asked.

"Boris!" Jackson answered automatically, as if Siri was talking.

"Yes! That's right! Okay, guys, I'm running late for dinner. I'll set up another meeting on next Tuesday, okay?" Lawrence sounded as if he was asking, but actually, he was laying out his statement. Five minutes later, Harry and Jackson left Fisher's office.

***

It was a Saturday morning in Chicago, the sky looked ominous with large, dark clouds that made it seem as though the sun had been destroyed. The temperature hovered in the mid-fifties, and the forecast predicted possible storms later in the day, but Jackson had no issues with the weather as he was waiting in his Camaro. His vehicle was parked at the lot of Dunkin Donut located on South California. He glanced at his smartphone and saw that the clock read 9:30 a.m. A few minutes later, an Uber driver pulled up in his Honda Accord a few feet away. Jacob quickly exited the rideshare vehicle and rushed over to Jackson's Camaro.

"I'm late! Sorry about that. The traffic was horrible," Jacob stated.

"That's fine. Let's get a cup of coffee. Today, I'm buying it," Jackson said and Jacob smiled. They went into the coffee shop. Jackson ordered tea and coffee for his new partner. After that, they took seats at an abandoned table.

"So, tell me, where did you grow up?" Jackson asked.

"I grew up on Long Island and graduated from one of the most eminent schools there, Wellington," Jacob blabbered on about his childhood. Jackson just asked questions and listened to Jacob's answers.

"What are we doing today?" Jacob questioned.

"We need to see someone."

"I don't understand! Where are we going?" Jacob politely asked.

"To Cook County Jail," Jackson said, and Jacob's eyes twinkled with excitement.

"Cool! Let's go."

"Hold on for a second. What do you know about the Cold Murder case? Have you read the reports yet?"

"Oh, yea. That was easy. I read them in seven days," Jacob claimed.

"Hold on. You're telling me that you've read three reports of about 600 pages each in a week?

"Yes, sir. I've read since I was a kid. My father encouraged me to read and study since I remembered my name."

"That's what's up! I'm impressed, though," Jackson said.

"Thank you. I'm sorry for asking, but who are we going to see? Does it have anything to do with Boris' murder?"

"Good question. Uh… I'm not sure yet. That's what we are about to find out. Let's bounce, baby. We need to do some work." Jackson and Jacob ambled to the Camaro. There was a moment of silence, then Jacob asked a question that left Jackson dumbfounded.

"Jackson, do you have kids?"

"Nah. No kids, no wife. My partner and I had many issues and we decided to end our relationship."

"That means you'll meet a better person." Jacob tried to sound sympathetic. He was glad that he was learning more about his colleague. Jackson thanked him and started the engine. They drove about a mile to a parking space which was designated for officials only. They walked through a few gates guarded by uniformed jailers. A few minutes later, both detectives were escorted to an empty room that had no windows but was wired and captured by a few cameras.

The homicide detectives waited impatiently; Jacob looked calm, but his heart was racing as he paced nervously around the room. As for Jackson, he held a folder containing a few pages. A few minutes later, the door opened, and a jailer brought in a bald man with a pencil style mustache. The prisoner looked like he had a Latin lineage. He resembled a furious pit bull with his dagger-like eyes showing his anger.

"Who the fuck are you, and what do you want from me?" the prisoner grumbled. He was in his mid-forties, six feet tall, slender with big black eyes who scared the shit out of Jacob.

"Watch your language!" the jailer grunted while holding the handcuffed prisoner.

"I didn't ask to be here. Who are these people?" the Latin prisoner asked. He looked like he wanted to beat the shit out of the detectives.

"Behave!" The jailer, who was also a bodybuilder, raised his voice.

Jacob looked at Jackson as if he was saying, "*What the fuck is going on here?*"

"All right. Please, leave us," Jackson said to the jailer and pointed to the Latin prisoner.

"Okay! I'll be at the door," the burly jailer declared and left the room. Jackson looked at the inmate and start reading the report he held in his hand,

"Carlos Santana, born and raised in Indiana. Your mother deceased from cancer in 2010. Father undetermined. No brothers or sisters. You were sentenced for carjacking in 2013. You filed for clemency, and the judge let you out of prison in 2017. Then you were charged with rape felony: a seventeen-year-old girl. Your case started in 2021, and you were convicted of child molestation. Your report doesn't look good, my friend. You'll be in Cook County Jail for more than ten years," Jackson finished.

"So what! Tell me something that I don't know," Carlos grumbled. He was still handcuffed at Jackson's request.

"I can change that," Jackson said quietly.

"Bullshit! Y'all the same bloodsuckers. Why am I here? What the fuck you want from me?" Carlos Santana asked aggressively. He was confused and angry, as he had hated Cook County Jail since day one. Carlos Santana had encountered some obstacles in his first days in Cook County. At first, he didn't know that he had to eat only with people of his race. He couldn't eat at the same table with African-Americans and White Wonder Breads. Otherwise, the Latin gangs would turn against him and wallop his ass. Carlos had a rough time in prison—every now and then, other inmates were breaking his balls. Santana had been beaten up a couple of times. Once, his face looked so bad that a correctional physician had to check him out. Jackson knew that the prisoner reports were hidden and covert, and only a few officials could have all the information about what was happening to each perpetrator kept in jail.

"I can shrink your time here up to three years," Jackson said.

"You're shitting me. How am I supposed to trust you?" Santana grunted aggressively. Jackson stepped closer and whispered to him. "Because I'm your only chance to get you out of here." Hearing those words, Carlos Santana's expression changed. His eyes rolled in a state of confusion. Jacob was observing the interrogation. He was as quiet as if he wasn't in the room.

"What you wanna know?" Carlos Santana asked. This time his voice sounded calm.

"Who is Mr. D?"

"Dunno. Never heard of that name," Santana said, his eyes looked in a different direction. Jackson surveyed the prisoner.

"You're lying to me, Carlos. Tell me who Mr. D is. Save some lives, including yours." Hearing this, Carlos Santana burst into hellish laughter.

"Y' all ain't shit. You think that you can come here with your expensive clothes and you know everything. You know shit. If I tell you who this guy is… it ain't gonna change anything."

"So, you do know him?" Jackson asked.

"I didn't say that," Carlos Santana retorted.

"You've just told me that if you tell me who he is, that won't change anything. That implies that you do know him."

"Listen, I don't know shit about this man. You got the wrong guy," Santana raised his voice.

"Let me tell you something. Carlos, your boy snitched on you already. Why do you think I'm here? I don't have time to waste in prison. You think I like to come here and talk with criminals?"

"Who snitched on me?" Carlos burst out loud.

"You know prisoners sell information just like people sell drugs on the street. That's why I'm here. Criminals like you would never understand how information leaks from jail."

"I'm not a criminal!" Santana grunted.

"Yea, and I am not Kris Kringle either!" Jackson piped up.

"Huh?" Santana exclaimed. He couldn't understand Jackson's levity. Jackson sighed, getting a bit frustrated.

"Listen, your best choice is to give me some information, and I'll take care of you. Unless you want to rot in this jail for ten plus years," Jackson made a good point. Carlos Santana was dead quiet, but his mind was speaking.

"Okay. In 2016 a guy called me for a job. I had to pick up some load from a pharmaceutical factory in Illinois. The guy who calls himself Mr. D owned that factory." Carlos explained.

"Did you talk or see Mr. D?" Jackson asked.

"Never spoke to him. I have no idea what he looks like."

"What kind of cargo did you have to pick up, and where did you drop it?" Jackson continued.

"I don't frigging know, man. They gave me some van that looked like shit and $7,000 to drop a package somewhere in Wisconsin. My guy asked me if I wanted the job, and I took it."

"Where in Wisconsin?"

"I don't fucking remember. I do remember the address of the pharmaceutical company. That's all I know."

"Can you write it down?" Jackson asked excitedly.

"Yea!" Carlos said. Jackson called the jailer to remove the handcuffs, and Carlos Santana wrote an address that was in Elgin.

"Great, I'll send a lawyer. He will give you paperwork and explain how it works," Jackson said and gave a sign to the jailer to take Carlos out. Jacob was impressed by how smoothly Jackson had handled the interrogation. The detectives immediately headed out from Cook County. They had work to do.

***

Later on the same day, Jackson and Jacob went to the police department in downtown Chicago. They checked the address that Carlos had given them. Google couldn't identify the place. It turned out that the address was an old industrial building that had been abandoned for five years. Jackson contacted the owner of that building. His name was Don Morrison. Don had inherited the building from his father who migrated to the U.S. from Germany back in the 1950s. Don Morrison had a restaurant business. He revealed that the building was for sale, and that he wanted to get rid of it as soon as possible. Jackson checked Don's social security. His ass was clean. He had been arrested for a DUI back in 2016. Other than that, Morrison hadn't violated the law. He had three kids and a wife and they had lived in Carol Stream since 2001.

"That's not our guy! Santana lied to us," Jackson said to Jacob.

"What are we going to do?" Jacob asked. Jackson combed his

short curly hair and looked around as if he was searching for something. In the meantime, Jacob was reading his movements.

"What time is it?"

"4:30 p.m.," Jacob answered.

"Tomorrow, we will drive back to Cook County Jail and have a word with our friend."

"Uh…you mean Santana?" Jacob questioned. Jackson didn't answer, just nodded.

***

In the evening of the same day, five guys barged into Santana's cell and immediately jumped on him. Santana couldn't escape. He was stabbed seven times while he was still lying on a dirty mattress. It happened so fast that most of the inmates misunderstood the scenario. At first, the prisoners thought that a fight between inmates had occurred. No one found out who killed Santana, nor the murderer's weapon. The coroner examined Santana's body and found that he was stabbed three times in his neck and four times in his chest, which gave an assumption that he struggled before he died. That was how snitches were dealt with.

11

It was Monday, the second week of May. James Dobrev had exciting news. Carl, his agent, told him that his book was in the last stage of the page design. The release was scheduled for the 25th of July. James was thrilled to see how his project was moving forward. He thought about narrating his first audiobook version and shared his idea with Carl. His agent was ambivalent about the suggestion. In the contract signed by James and his publisher, it was written that the publisher would take care of the audiobooks.

***

On Wednesday, James decided to spoil himself and bought a ticket for a Bulls game. The Chicago Bulls hadn't been having their best season, but there was some hope for the playoffs and James was enthusiastic about the game. He hadn't been to a Bulls game for years. He had to meet his buddy, Bob Shuimmer, from college at the United Center. Bob was Jewish and the same age as James. They had both studied English literature. Bob worked for a renowned local real estate magazine. He wrote short articles for the magazine, and he was making decent money. He also had assets in the real estate biz—it was his side hustle. Bob was doing fine financially and had never been married. His ex-girlfriend had cheated on him, so he gave her the cold shoulder. Bob was in his early thirties and still lived with his parents. He was still jerking off to the same porn videos that he had downloaded illegally from internet.

The game kicked off on Friday. James had to meet Bob at Gate 2, located on the north side. James drove his rental Kia to the Center. The traffic was bad, as usual, but that didn't bother him because he had time. At 7:30 p.m., James drove slowly into the parking lot of the United Center. He saw a few deputies chilling out by the lot. They were waving and making signs at him to stop his vehicle. Then the deputies approached James' car.

"Good evening, sir! Are you coming in to park your car?" One of the deputies asked. He was a tall and hefty man who looked as big as a WWE superstar. He also was a bald man who had a big combed beard.

"Yes, sir," James stated.

"Okay. I need you to step out of the vehicle, please. We have to search your vehicle for weapons. It's a standard procedure that each vehicle has to pass before using the parking lot."

"I've never heard about that procedure. Am I doing something wrong?" James asked.

"No, sir. It's required by the management of the United Center. We just follow the rules," the tall man explained. James looked shocked.

"Then why is the car up there entering the lot without being checked?" James pointed to a black BMW that was coming through the entrance of the parking lot.

"That vehicle has already been checked by the patrol on the east side. Sir, I'll repeat. Please, step out of the vehicle." The voice of the tall police officer was imperative. James did what the police officer asked and stepped out of the vehicle, completely confused. Another officer walked around the car and opened the passenger door. He pulled out a flashlight to survey the vehicle, and took an 8-ball baggie from his pocket, and placed it under the passenger seat.

"Hey, I found something here!" the same police officer searching the vehicle announced. "What is it?" the tall man asked.

"I don't know. It looks like cocaine to me," the policeman who had left the 8-ball said. The tall man stepped closer and looked at the 8-ball baggie.

"Mr. Dobrev, is this bag yours?" the tall officer asked after checking Dobrev's ID.

"What are you talking about? I don't take drugs. This is ridiculous." James panicked, trying to figure out what was happening.

"So if you don't take drugs, then what is this bag doing in your car? Mr. Dobrev, are you selling drugs?" the tall man asked, while studying James.

"Naw! Absolutely not! I've written a couple of books, and I'm fine with the money I make. Why would I sell drugs?" James asked rhetorically.

"That's why I'm asking. Mr. Dobrev, you need to come with us to the police department. I need to ask you a couple of questions." Being arrested was the last thing that James was expecting. He knew that there was no reason to argue with the deputies. He would stay silent until he had the chance to use his phone call.

"What about the car?" James asked.

"Don't worry about it. We'll take care of that," the tall police officer said, while he was handcuffing the writer. The police officer opened the door of the police vehicle, and James sat in the rear. But there wasn't any cushion on the back seat, making it incredibly uncomfortable and causing him pain in his buttocks. Two police officers jumped into the car, and the vehicle headed up north. A couple of minutes later, James became confused. He was looking around to see which streets the cops were taking.

"Where are you taking me?" James asked. There was no answer and that annoyed him.

"Excuse me! To which department are we going?" James repeated his question, his voice filled with frustration.

"Shut your pie hole!" One of the officers hollered. It wasn't too long before James realized that he was the victim of a setup.

***

Jackson sped his Camaro on 290 Eisenhower Expressway. He drove so fast that he almost caused a car accident. The United Center turned into a chaotic scene as if a terrorist attack had transpired. There were more than forty police vehicles patrolling the area as officers tried to control the unruly crowd. The game had already started, and people were still trying to catch the first half. Many of them were confused Chicagoans, wondering why there were so many police vehicles around the premises. Jackson parked his vehicle close to the parking lot of the United Center. Jacob and Harry had gotten there already. They talked with Bob Shuimmer. Bob realized that James' phone had no signal when he tried to contact him, which made him panic. He called Michelle, and she told him to call the cops.

"Do you know where his car is?' Jackson asked Bob.

"No! James sent me a text. Here, look at the text." The text implied that James had already arrived at the United Center and he was looking for parking. Jackson urged the police officers to look around for a silver Kia K5 LXS model 2021.

"Here! There it is!" a deputy exclaimed. Jackson approached the vehicle and checked the license plate and the VIN number. The information matched, and that fazed Jackson. The police had found James' vehicle, but there was no sign of him. Jackson scavenged every inch of the rental vehicle, but he couldn't find anything that could be useful. James' belongings were missing. After the game was finished, the police impounded James' vehicle. Jackson, Jacob, and Harry brainstormed the disappearance of the writer.

"What do you think, Harry?" Jackson asked.

"Evidently, James has been kidnaped. That's all I can come up with," Harry asserted, and Jackson nodded in agreement.

"Do we all agree that Mr. D is involved?" Jackson asked, and the other two nodded.

"So what are we going to do about it?" Jacob managed to say something.

"Hold your horses, young man," Harry exclaimed. His expression made Jacob frown. It was inarguable to everyone that Jacob had the zeal to unravel the puzzle of the Cold Murder which could make him a star and put him in the media spotlight. The Polish-American detective wanted to make his parents proud and also wanted his kid to remember her daddy as the most renowned detective in the U.S.

"We don't have any fingerprints other than James'. It doesn't make any sense, though," Jackson pointed out.

"I guess we need to talk with Lawrence Fisher and pick his brain," Harry announced.

The homicide detectives and the lieutenant left the parking lot of the United Center at midnight.

***

The next couple of days, Jackson was frustrated about the shocking news related to the missing writer. He searched for the essential piece that could solve the puzzle. His mind was congested with possibilities of what might have happened to James. Jackson couldn't remember the last time he was not thinking about The Cold Murder.

Michelle kept crying over her missing son. Frank persistently soothed her by saying that everything was about to be fine, but Michelle didn't pay attention to his phony sympathy. Her eyes were filled with tears as she was stuck in emotional breakdown. Two weeks ago, she was kidnapped and brutally raped and now her son had mysteriously disappeared.

Jacob spent some quality time with his family. They went to a movie theater to watch *Fireheart*. Jacob looked at the big screen at the theater, but he wasn't watching. He thought about how he could find James. Although he was too impatient, Jacob had faith that he would find the writer and the identity of Mr. D.

Lieutenant Harry Burns was making a bunch of phone calls and looked for information. He also licked an ice cream stick and thought about how fat he was. Harry wanted to be on a diet and lose some weight. There was a problem, though—he loved chocolate too much.

Lawrence Fisher was at his house in Deerfield, writing the speech he had to give about James' disappearance. On the following day, he would give an interview about the missing writer. Writing was one of the Lawrence's passions. Often, he posted what was on his agenda on social media. Fisher looked out the window office. The tree in his front yard was shaking as if it was a shivering human. Lawrence didn't know that he was being watched.

12

James couldn't precisely tell where he had been taken. The police patrol drove westbound toward Barrington. Actually, those police officers were Joe, Rocco, and a few more that worked for Mr. D. The sky darkened and James couldn't tell what time it was. His belongings were captured by the fake police officers. They screamed at James every time he opened his mouth. The fake police patrol passed through a security booth. A man inside waved at them and opened the gate. The vehicle parked at the door of what seemed to be a gargantuan factory, encircled with a high fence that had signs that read: PRIVATE PROPERTY. NO TRESPASSING! It was located in a rural area, with several other industrial buildings in the vicinity, but not as close as the nearby turnpike, I-90. James was taken out of the police vehicle, and Joe smiled at him hellishly. He disliked James and dug a few body shots on the writer's ribs. The beef between the two of them grew exponentially. James took Joe's punches like a man. He was still handcuffed and that frustrated him. James spilled blood and said, "Take off those handcuffs and I'll wallop your ass, motherfucker."

"Oh, yeah! You think you're a tough guy. I'll make you my bitch. You'll bow when you see me. Rocco, remove the frigging handcuffs. This fucker needs a lesson." Joe commanded, ready to fight at that very moment.

"No, no, no. Joe, remember the orders," Rocco protested peacefully. "Fuck the orders. I'll fuck him up," Joe raised his voice and accosted James, and just before he swing a hook, the other guys grabbed hold of him.

"I'll change your pretty face. Fucking writer!" Joe snarled, as the other guys struggled to hold him back.

"Knock it off!" a voice echoed. All of them turned around to see who had spoken. A man with curly hair was standing at the door. The man was short, with a plump body, but his hands looked as big as hammers. A huge scar lined his entire cheek, which had been made by a knife.

"Who the heck are you?" James questioned, wanting to show that he was fearless. He wasn't just putting on an act; he was naturally ballsy. However, the sense of trepidation about what could happen made him nervous. Hearing James' question, the man with the scar burst into laughter.

"Who am I? Hahaha. I'm Freddy Limo. The last person in the world that you want to fuck with."

"You are all the same to me. Frigging scumbags," James bawled.

"You need to correct yourself, young man! We are the greatest scumbags you can ever meet."

"What are you talking about?" the writer asked.

"You'll see," Freddy Limo replied and smiled. They took James through the factory. The writer observed the premises. There were a bunch of employees who wore masks, gloves, and hooded disposable coveralls to protect themselves from radiation or viruses. The employees were working with hundreds of high tech machines and expensive equipment. All of those machines looked squeaky clean, as if they were manufactured the day before. James realized that the machines outnumbered the employees. He saw a bunch of chambers that needed a specific code or finger print to let someone in. James figured that he was in the pharmaceutical company, the one that Jake Kohen had talked about.

"What do you want from me?" James asked. At the next moment, Joe couldn't restrain himself and punched James in the stomach.

"Knock it off! I said. Joe, go to the office on the second floor," Freddy grumbled.

"I'll see you later, wuss," Joe said, looking at the writer. He split from the group and walked in a different direction.

"You didn't answer my question!" James protested. Freddy Limo was walking ahead, looking like a leader of a wolf pack. He turned around and said, "Mr. D has some interesting plans for you."

"Oh, I see. And what's on his mind?"

"You'll see," Freddy Limo kept giving short answers. It was his mind game that worked well on James.

"And when will I meet him?"

"Soon!" Freddy declared. Rocco and the other two guys walked the writer to a small restroom. They shackled James' hands to the grab bar that was next to the toilet. James lost it. He was laughing his ass off. It was so ridiculous that he couldn't hold himself any longer.

"So, you guys will be keeping me here, in this restroom. That's very innovative," James said sarcastically.

"HEY! Zip it," Rocco raised his voice. James wanted to talk more, but he remained speechless.

"At least you don't have to worry if you need to use the toilet," Freddy said and smiled. He was an obnoxious cheeseball. James asked if he could have a book to kill some time, but Freddy refused his appeal. The guys then left the restroom, leaving James trapped next to the toilet.

***

Day 1: James sat on the toilet, thinking about what he could do. He had no idea what time it was and how long he had been shackled by the toilet. His legs became numb and the pain in his hands became unbearable. The handcuffs were tight. James screamed, demanding that someone loosen his handcuffs, but no one responded to his request. However, that didn't discourage him. Actually, he was more strongly motivated and kept screaming.

"Hey, loosen those handcuffs, dammit! My hands hurt. C'mon, man! Are you listening to me? I know you are. Just loosen them up. Please!" Still no answer. James didn't quit. He pushed harder, and he wasn't rushing. He raised his voice, trying be more disturbing. It seemed that his plan wasn't working, but then Rocco opened the door.

"What?" Rocco cried out. James explained how his hands hurt.

Rocco stepped closer and said, "If you do somethin' stupid, I'll break your neck. You hear me?" He was so big that made James think about how he could beat him in a fight. Rocco loosened the handcuffs and said, "Are you happy? Now, shut your pie hole! You miserable fuck!" His words agitated James even more. As Rocco closed the door, James started screaming again. This time, he wanted water. The writer had been screaming for three hours and his voice became hoarse. He was impressed by his vocal overuse. Thirty minutes later, Rocco burst through the door and gave him water. James was relieved, unaware that the water he drank had been mixed with Adderall and Xanax.

Day 2: James awoke from a long nap, looking around with hazy vision and feeling dizzy. The medications were making him drowsy and content. Dobrev had been staring at the door handle for a couple of hours, without any particular reason or thoughts on his mind. He was awake but his brain was shut off, moving his head left and right. The Adderall was kicking in harder.

His head felt as if he was in a broken helicopter that was falling. His eyes were heavy, and James drifted off to sleep once again. However, an uncomfortable feeling woke him up. He had an urgent call for a bowel movement. He sat on the toilet, but his pants were on. The writer couldn't take them off because his hands were tied to the grab bar. It would be quite embarrassing if he shit in his pants while sitting on the toilet.

"Hey! I need to use the restroom. I have to drop a Mondo Duke! Someone has to help me. I can't take my pants off! Help me! Please!" James screamed. He could barely talk. His throat hurt, but that didn't discourage him. A few minutes later, two guys opened the door. One of them was a tall dude. He was a middle-aged man with a scrawny type of body. He held a firearm. He kept around ten feet distance and pointed the gun at James. The other guy had to do the dirty work. He took off James' pants without looking at him.

"When will I meet your boss, Mr. D?" James asked.

"Soon!" the man who was taking his jeans off mumbled.

"Why don't you release my hands and then I can take care of myself?" James pointed out. It was peculiar that someone else was taking his pants off, especially when James could have done it on his own.

"That's the orders! Now, shut up!" the man replied with a frown on his face, purposely avoided looking at James' genitals.

"Done!" the man said and hurriedly stepped out. A few hours later, a guy with a man bun stepped in. His body looked like a pear and his belly was shaking as he was walking. The pear man poured water into James' mouth. Again, the water was mixed with Xanax. James became drowsy. He felt uncomfortable sitting on the toilet for many hours, but the pill relaxed his muscles, and he drifted off into a deep sleep.

Day 3: James opened his eyes slowly, feeling lethargic and disoriented. His mind seemed to be stuck on autopilot, and he struggled to think clearly. His common sense flew like an intimidated pigeon. Dobrev looked around to survey the room and noticed that he had an IV injected onto his right forearm. Next to him, there was an IV drip bag filled with colorless liquid that was hanging on the medical stand.

"What the heck is that?" James asked in shock. *"I've got to find out what medication they are giving me!"* he thought.

"Hey! Why do I have an IV poked into my forearm? Answer me! Dadgummit!" James screamed at the top of his lungs. He disliked medications, especially when he didn't know what they were. Half an hour later, the pear man opened the door.

"What?" he blustered.

"What is this medication? Why are you treating me like I am a patient?" James asked fearfully.

"Our doctors have checked you out and determined that you're sick."

"Who are these doctors? I'd like to speak with them. And what medication you're giving me?" James was getting bent out of shape.

"The doctors will come to talk with you later. They prescribed you an antibiotic. That's all I know," the pear man lied.

"What kind of antibiotic? And why am I still chained to this frigging toilet?" James was raging.

"Uh… the doctors will tell you. I'm not a nurse," the pear man said, and left James alone. This information sounded ridiculous to him. Half an hour later, James felt exhausted and passed out.

Day 4: James woke up after a long nap. His eyes could barely stay open. He had no idea what time or what day it was. There was a small camera installed on the ceiling at the restroom monitoring the writer 24/7. James didn't know that and he also, didn't realize that the drip didn't contain an antibiotic. They were giving him Fentanyl to keep him sedated—those were the orders. The controlled substance (Fentanyl) was making him happy as a clam and he kept smiling as if he was watching stand-up comedy. James envisioned that he was chilling somewhere on a sunny beach. A bottle of scotch was keeping him company. He was so happy, as if he had just gotten laid by a gorgeous woman. He even forgot about his family and what was going on in his life. He failed to remember that he was a captive. James didn't even notice that he was sleeping.

Day 5: James watched as his son was playing soccer. Patrick was significantly taller than most of the other players. His height gave him an advantage. The game was held in Denver, Colorado and the soccer field was encircled by many spectators. They looked like a flock of ravens. It was a tight game, with no goals scored until ten minutes before the end, when the referee blew the whistle and wrapped the game with a draw. Patrick was disappointed, but his father was proud of him. James' son had been the most active player, and the horde acknowledged his skills. James couldn't hide his smile. He was happy in his dream. He tried to grab his son and embrace him like a loving father would. Patrick wasn't there and James was still shackled to the toilet. He was talking in his sleep. Two male and one female physician were observing his reactions closely. They were scrawling something on their clipboards. The female physician, Sarah Kimble, was a sweet bespectacled brunette with an athletic build due to her veganism. She was also one of the most scholarly and educated physicians working for Mr. D, and was in charge of James' medical treatments. Sarah kept explaining what the following procedures should be. James was shaking, as he had cold chills. His eyes were open, but his mind was sleeping.

Day 6: James opened his eyes, but he couldn't move his body. His legs and hands were sore. *"Where the heck am I?"* his inner voice questioned. James lay on a large operating table that looked expensive and was only found in a few medical facilities across the world. He moved his head left and right, surveying his surroundings to see where he had been taken. He found himself in a surgical room equipped with cutting-edge technology that he had never seen before.

The writer wanted to scream, but he was weak. He could only grunt gibberish as if he was an extraterrestrial creature that came from another galaxy. His muscles were impotent and his vision was hazy. He had a severe headache that made him somnolent.

Day 7: James could barely open his eyes. He saw a bunch of people walking in different directions in the surgical room. He had no idea what was happening. His body was fragile. He also had a headache that made him feel sluggish. James was so sedated that he could barely remember his name. His hands were shaking as if he had Parkinson's. James could overhear the voices of the people that were dressed like doctors, but he couldn't comprehend what they were saying. He was exhausted and felt simultaneously warm and cold. He didn't know that they kept changing the temperature in the room on purpose to give him cold sweats.

Day 8: James woke up and looked around like an intimidated squirrel. He realized that he was in a different room with no windows. The room was a small and resembled a cell in a penitentiary. Dobrev slept on a thin mattress. There were no cushions, no blanket, and no toilet. James looked down and noticed that he had been undressed and given a blue jumpsuit to wear. Then the writer looked around, mouth agape, feeling slightly better and more energized than in the previous days. However, his hands were still handcuffed. A knock on the door disturbed him, and James cried out, "Yeah!" He was freaking out at being confined like a prisoner. The door opened, and Freddy Limo burst in followed by two men. Freddy Limo always walked with security. He was a chicken-shit, and James knew it.

"Hey, James! How you doing? Are you making yourself comfortable?" Freddy asked.

"Yeah, I feel like I am ten year old at Disneyland," James responded, and Freddy cracked up.

"You see, it's never too late for some levity. I can tell that you like your vacation," Freddy was being sarcastic.

"Absolutely! Only the call girls are missing. What the heck you want?"

"I don't want anything… Mr. D will be flying tomorrow in his private jet. He wants to talk with you."

"I bet! Tell him that he needs another taintkisser, cuz you suck!" James sounded aggressive, but he was smiling.

"Taintkisser! What the fuck is that?" Freddy Limo was pushed onto the ropes of this verbal battle, looking somewhat embarrassed.

"Google it, sucka!" James snapped. He had fun chatting with Freddy Limo. Freddy was illiterate. He had dropped out of elementary school a long time ago. That was why he got frustrated and hated when people called him names that he wasn't familiar with. Freddy Limo leaned forward and said, "You won't live much longer, toughhead! You know that, right." His words didn't mean anything to James and he didn't respond. He then spat in Freddy's face, and one of the security started laughing.

"You think that's funny?" Freddy yelled to the guy who was laughing.

"I'll talk with you later," Freddy said, and left the room. The security remained in the cubbyhole and started beating James. They weren't hard hitters, but James could feel the pain. A minute later, Joe burst in.

"Move, idiots!" Joe hollered to the guys who were beating James. Joe took a lateral step and dug a body shot at James' ribs. The writer blocked a few punches that Joe landed, but his legs were shackled, making it difficult to defend himself.

"No, Joe!" one of the guys screamed. A few more guys came into the room to stop Joe from beating James. It was like they were holding a wild animal.

"Joe. Knock it off!" Freddy limo yelled. He was pissed because Joe wasn't following his orders. The other guys could barely hold the raging animal, Joe. Rocco burst in and grabbed Joe. He was a sturdy man, big enough to thwart Joe's uncontrollable rage.

"I'll make you my bitch. You hear me?" Joe screamed at James as he was held by the burly Rocco. The writer didn't flinch, he was ready to fight at any second.

A few hours later, a woman wearing a white lab coat entered the room where James was being kept. Her name was Jazmine. She had an Indian lineage. She was a successful physician and was considered one of the best working in that facility. Jazmine's body was athletic because she loved to take care of herself. She was a single mom; her ex-husband was a junkie sentenced to life in prison. While Jazmine checked James' condition, she was asking him personal questions.

"You'll be fine! I promise," she declared. James lifted his eyebrows in surprise. Jazmine was a hot chick, but James wasn't interested. His mind was overwhelmed.

"What will they do to me?" James asked quietly.

"I really don't know! They give us orders without much explanation," Jazmine replied. She kept staring at James as if she wanted to tell him something personal.

"You're all the same!" James said apathetically.

"No! You're wrong about that. Listen, I volunteered to come and check on you," Jazmine said and tapped James' shoulder.

"Why?" the writer asked.

"Because I care for people like you," Jazmine replied with a low voice and asked. "Do you need me to bring you somethin'?"

"Yea. A bottle of Scotch!" James said. The writer sounded as if he was joking, but he was dead serious. Jazmine froze. She was dumbstruck as if she was told to buzz off from the room. She then leaned forward and whispered,

"I'll try my best, stud! I'll see you soon." Jazmine slid out of the room wearing a smirk on her face. Usually, physicians working in that facility were escorted by guards, but Jazmine came on her own. However, James didn't care about that. His only thought was about getting alcohol. The desire for alcohol was making him lose his mind. James was certain that he was about to die there. He didn't know what to think and what to expect. He had no idea what was about to happen.

Day 9: James woke up after having a nightmare. He was sweating; his body reeked. He was losing his faith. He asked God for mercy and prayed for his family and mostly for Patrick. He missed him a lot. The room was quiet. James could hear the buzzing sound of the light fixture above his head. He used the time he had to count his blessings. He thought about how poorly he had treated his mother and Frank. James thought about how he could be a better person and how he could contribute to society. *Bullshit! I'll never gonna get out of here. Not alive!* his inner voice declared. His sanity was shaking off. He tried not to go apeshit as he could barely restrain himself. A couple of hours later, Jazmine burst through the door, alone, with her hair tousled. Jazmine smiled at James. She had wanted to see him. The physician handed James three small vodka bottles and his eyes lit up.

"Thank you so much! Honestly, I thought you would never come back," James confessed.

"Are you kidding? I told you that I'd take care of you. I have to get back to work. I'll see you later," Jazmine announced and James nodded. He couldn't remember her name. He was concentrating on the gift she'd brought. James' hands were cuffed, but that didn't stop him drinking from the bottle. He drained almost all of the bottles. The alcohol made him dizzy, and he quickly fell asleep.

Day 10: The writer opened his eyes, feeling the effects of a hangover that gave him an annoying headache. James looked around and felt as though he was being crucified on a wall, like Jesus. He found himself in a different room with the lights off, as if he was in an ancient cave. It appeared to be a storage room, with a few aisles spread across, creating an airy space.

"Water! Water!" James screamed out loud, his throat dry and parched. He kept yelling for water, but no one answered. The writer looked down at his feet and clenched his eyelids, feeling the sweat on his body as his temperature rose above 101 Fahrenheit. His breathing became heavy, and he found himself dozing off every five minutes or so. His muscles were in great pain, and James floundered, begging God to let him die without more affliction.

"Water! I need water! Please!" he screamed. James didn't have energy, but he didn't stop yelling. His faith was still keeping him alive. However, he questioned his mental stamina. A few hours later, the sound of a door opening disturbed him.

"Hey! Water! I need water. I'm not asking for much! Just give me water. Please!" James screamed. The footsteps were pounding harder. A person was approaching. It was Jazmine.

"Hey! Thank God you are here. Do you have water? May I have some, please?" James saw that Jazmine was holding a bottle of water.

"Here. I'm worried about you, stud. How are you feeling?" the physician asked. James cracked a smile. *"How am I feeling? Great! Like I'm on a cruise to the Caribbean!"* he thought.

"Great!" James snapped in a sardonic way.

"Take this! It will make you feel better. Trust me," Jazmine uttered.

"What is it?"

"Just take it. I promise it will help you." Jazmine continued her persuasive speech. James stared at her. *"What the heck does she want?"* his inner voice whispered.

"Okay, whatever!" James cried out. He didn't care what he was taking. Not anymore. The writer was certain that he wouldn't make it. "*I'll die like a rat!*" his inner voice snapped. Jazmine had given him Xanax, and the writer nodded off as quickly as a snap of a finger.

Day 11: James woke up with an intolerable headache, feeling his body frail and weak. He still felt crucified on the wall as if he was responsible for shooting 20 kids in a school for no reason. The storage room was as dark as if lights had never existed.

"Food and Water! Please, I need food and water!" James yelled. The writer was ravenous for food; he was at the edge of turning ballistic, fighting against the hunger and the pain. He prayed to God that if he died there, it wouldn't be painful. A few hours later, footsteps disturbed James' nap. Someone was walking, but not in a rush. James squinted and surveyed who was approaching. The person stopped at a safe distance. James could only see the stranger's shoes. "*That's pricey shoes!*" he thought.

"Hello, James! It's nice to meet ya," a male voice said fearlessly.

"Give me food and water. Please!" James cried out. The stranger waved, and another guy came holding water and a sandwich. James took a few bites and gulped a bit of the water. Mr. D waved to the guy, and he left the room. Then James asked, "Who are you?"

"I think you already know the answer," the stranger said. There was a pause.

"Mr. D!" James exclaimed.

"Bingo!" the stranger snapped sarcastically.

"Oh! So, you're the ignorant freak who has killed so many people and has been torturing my family and me." James stated. Mr. D didn't answer. Instead, he burst into hellish laughter and clapped his hands sardonically.

"Who the heck are you, and why have you been killing innocent people?" James questioned. "I'm the most successful entrepreneur and philanthropist on earth," Mr. D proclaimed.

"Really! What do you do?" James asked, deeply interested in

having a conversation with the man who was responsible for so many transgressions.

"My pharmaceutical company makes billions of dollars annually. I also created Zener, you know, the virus that has plagued the entire world for about a year."

"How did you do that?" James was in shock. Mr. D went on. "Well, I'm a very powerful and wealthy man. I had an idea to make some extra money and the US government had approved my plan. We've told the tabloids what to say to the world, and they scared people on purpose. We wanted to make sure that Zener would be classified as a destructive and dangerous virus. Also Zener had to be known as the most destructive virus in the history of mankind. A few buddies of mine didn't like the idea. They control the gasoline flow, pretty much over the entire world. But I assured them that they would double their money. That's the reason why today the gas price is at a record high. We had to tell the people that vaccinations would cure and protect them against Zener. I created those vaccines and sold them to governments in different countries."

"Where is the catch? Why would the government pay you for those vaccines and give them free to the people? I don't get it!" James protested. Mr. D paused. He then continued his speech.

"After the government forced the people to get vaccinated, we established inflation and raised the prices of everything starting with gasoline. In that case, the taxes became higher and that's how the government takes its portion. Furthermore, the government collects $500 for each positive Zener's test made in the entire country. Health Insurance Corporations pay the government and charge the people. Bottom line; we trickled down and got richer by taking people's money and no one could find out about our conspiracy. It's a legal way of stealing people's savings."

"But you've killed millions of innocent people! You're a despicable egomaniac!" James snapped. Mr. D remained quiet, then he cackled.

"Zener doesn't necessarily kill people. We spread this falsehood through the media. If someone dies, it wouldn't have anything to do with me. I mean whatever. People die and get born every day. That's life."

"You are a very sick person! A diabolical man that will burn in hell," James spoke slowly, but in an aggressive tone. Mr. D laughed his ass off—it seemed like he was enjoying this conversation. James was getting bent out of shape, but just a tad. Mr. D walked around in the dark. James still couldn't see him.

"You know, James. I've read a few of your books. Got to tell, ya. As a writer, you suck," Mr. D declared. This time, James was the one who laughed.

"Your opinion doesn't mean anything to me," the writer went on.

Mr. D didn't respond, and James continued, "What about Boris? Why was he so important to you?"

"Boris! Yeah, this motherfucker had caused a lot of trouble. I'll tell you since you are about to be killed. Back in the 1960s, Russia was working on a secret project that drew my attention. They called it 'The Rejuvenation Order' or something like that. Anyway, this project was about making people stay the same age for a very long time and Boris was the first human who was tested in this project. Russians did a good job, and Boris became my target. I kidnapped and brought him to the US. I wanted to mimic what the Russians had done with him. Boris was under my authority for more than twenty years. He then escaped from one of my properties, and I had to wipe him out. I traced him to the liquor store, and *Boom!* End of the story."

"And what has this got to do with me?" James asked. Mr. D laughed again.

"Well, I didn't invite you to the dinner! You were behind Boris at the time of the shooting. You shouldn't have been there.

"So…!" James interrupted him.

"So, I had to remove everything that was connected with Boris' murder."

"What about Charles? He didn't have anything to do with Boris!"

"No! You're wrong! Charles wasn't your friend; he was working for me. But he was about to snitch on me. He didn't leave me any choices. I had to whack his killer too. It's a business." Mr. D was smiling, but James couldn't see him.

"So why didn't you just kill me, after you found out that I was behind Boris at the liquor store?"

"I can't just kill random people. I had to check you out before I could do anything."

"You're a good liar," James antagonized the pharmaceutical boss. Mr. D laughed even harder. He then continued, "I know everything about you. You don't understand. I have the power and access to any sort of information. I have your social security number. I know how many cars you've driven over the past ten years. I also know how your ex died and what happened to your son, Patrick. I know why your father was killed.

"What? You knew my father!" James snapped in confusion.

"I didn't personally know him. I said I know why he was killed. Ivan Dobrev often played cards with people who I know. One night, Ivan Dobrev was playing poker, and he was winning throughout the entire game. He pissed off the other players. After the game, Ivan Dobrev took his winnings and left the casino. Well, he didn't go far. You get the picture," Mr. D finished his monologue. James was speechless. Mr. D continued, "Also, your mother, Michelle, is not your biological mother. Ivan Dobrev met her when you were around four years old."

"What the heck are you talking about? No! You're lying to me!" James cried out.

"Am I? Ask Michelle to show you a picture of her holding you as a baby on the day of your birth."

"No, no, no! Okay, let's presume that you are telling the truth. Where is my biological mother?" James asked.

"She passed away. Terminal cancer. Too bad. But look at the bright side; Michelle is a pretty lady. Old but pretty. She was being kept here, in this building. Oh, wait, you don't know that," Mr. D said. He kept teasing the writer. James clenched his eyelids, his face frowning in disbelief. He couldn't believe what he had just heard as it made no sense to him. But Mr. D made a good point. James had never seen a picture of himself with Michelle on the day of his birth.

"This is all bullshit. You're a good manipulator. What makes you think that I will buy any of this crap? Do you think I'm an idiot?" James kept asking questions as if he was in elementary school asking his teacher about a subject he was interested in. Mr. D laughed again. His laughter became annoying.

"I'm not trying to convince you. You don't understand! The truth is that you're living in a world of lies."

"What?" James snapped.

"It's actually simple. You're living in a world where the tabloids and social media are controlled by powerful people like me. Any source of news posted on social media has been checked by CEOs and executives who work on the payroll. They are people who make more than average but still, they are employees on a paycheck. The same thing applies for newscasters. They are telling the world what people like me and the government have ordered. I have the power, influence, and resources to rule the world. Or let's say most of the world."

"Most of the world? What do you mean by that?" the writer asked.

"Well, Russia is competitor. They are too powerful to be controlled. Most Scandinavian countries are on their own. For instance, no one messes around with Switzerland. Why bother? Every billionaire, including me, keeps his money in Swiss banks. Even Hitler didn't cross that country. He also kept his money there."

"What do you know about Hitler? You weren't born yet!" James started to tease Mr. D.

"I was six years old during the World War II," Mr. D retorted as he sounded offended.

"What! Are you telling me that you are eighty-three years old?" James grilled.

"Bingo!" Mr. D. snapped. James didn't believe Mr. D's words.

"Step closer. I want to see your face," James said. It's been many years since someone had given orders to Mr. D and he didn't like it. His father was a gangster back in the 1930s. He came from Ireland in the last years of the 19th century. Mr. D had never worked for anybody, except his old man. At the age of twenty, Mr. D managed one of his father's restaurants in Brooklyn, New York. While he worked in restaurants, Mr. D graduated from school as a pharmacist. He always had that ambition in the pharmaceutical business. His father gave him a huge loan to start a pharmaceutical business. Years later, Mr. D became one of the richest men in this industry, but he never paid his father back. In 1986, his father was found shot in the alley behind one of his restaurants. Mr. D got into close relationships with the organized crime of New York. He agreed to kill his father for business reasons.

"Let me see your face," James repeated.

"What for?" Mr. D replied. His voice became sketchy, and that was what James looked for.

"Since you're going to kill me, can I at least see your face?" James asked. Mr. D laughed. He thought James was a funny guy. A few seconds later, Mr. D stepped forward. James was puzzled. He saw a man approaching with curly hair and a slender type of body. Mr. D was bespectacled and wore a blue suit made from silk. He looked like a gangster. The pharmaceutical boss looked to be in his early forties. *"How is that possible?"* the voice in James' head asked. The writer realized that Mr. D had been treated with the Rejuvenation Order, just like Boris.

"So, how long have you been on this treatment?" James asked, staring at Mr. D with great enthusiasm.

"It's been a while. James, you don't understand. I have to live longer. A few buddies and I rule this world. We tell you how much per gallon of gas you'll pay, or how long you will wear a mask. And also how long this virus will hover around. The truth is, viruses like Zener have been around us for a long time. We've just blown the whistle and made it public to make a profit off of simple people like you. But people like you cannot grasp the concept. This is what we wanted. We don't want people to understand what really is going on. We want you to believe what you've been told; whether from the TV or social media. And to be honest with you, I feel great at the age of eighty-three." Mr. D lied. Actually, he was in great pain. The Rejuvenation Order made him look younger, but his bones were bothering him. Also, his internal organs weren't the same as a young person's. Mr. D had had a heart attack last year. His time on earth was limited, just like everyone else's. James thought for a moment. He needed to tease Mr. D and get him pissed.

"Yeah, your buddy told me about this Rejuvenation Order," James declared. Mr. D rose his eyebrows, caught off guard. There was a pause.

"Listen, young man. I don't care what you know about me. Dead people cannot snitch!"

"You mad?" James continued to play his mind games. Mr. D burst into laughter.

"Why would I be? You're a corpse. Listen, young man, I don't have time for casual chats. Besides, you need to get ready for the fight."

"What fight? What are you talking about?" James was perplexed. His mind games didn't work. Mr. D laughed harder. He was having fun. "What's the matter, smart boy? Are you surprised? You will be fighting Joe. I'll organize a boxing event, here in this building. I'll invite a few buddies of mine. We'll have fun watching how Joe changes your face. Don't worry, it will be fun. I'll make this event look like you're fighting in Las Vegas." Mr. D finished his speech with excitement.

"I'm not going to fight!" James exclaimed.

"I don't think you'll have much choice when you jump in the ring. Whatever. I don't care. Joe will beat the shit of you. I'll promise that. He is a good boxer. He is a hot-head, and has some problems with anger. I think is because he wants to kill someone in the ring. And that will be you," Mr. D finished his speech with laughter.

"Fuck you!" James hollered and Mr. D laughed even harder. He turned around and walked to the door.

"See you later, James!" Mr. D said over his shoulder.

"Go to hell!" James exclaimed.

13

Michelle walked into her house, weighed down with trepidation. She was worried about James who had been missing for two weeks. She had no idea if he was still alive, and that made her feel queasy. Mr. D was right, Michelle hadn't given birth to James, but she had been taking care of him since he was four. She loved him as if he was her own child. Michelle had a few miscarriages when she was in her mid-twenties. The doctors told her that she would be barren. Michelle didn't like that news, but she had to live with it. James was her only child, and he was gone. Michelle didn't know if she would see him again. Frustration drove her into a restless spot. Frank was trying to console her, and that made her angrier. One day, Frank came back home carrying groceries, as Michelle had requested. Frank had bought the wrong items, and Michelle screamed at him. He made excuses, and apologized but that didn't make her happy. Frank failed to acknowledge the fear and the pain of his wife. He was confused, so he left the house and drove to the nearest bar. Frank loved Michelle and wanted to do something nice for her, so he decided to give her some space for the night.

***

It was Monday morning, June 10th, and he sky in Chicago was overcast. It looked like a severe downpour was about to hit the Windy City. Despite the dark forecast, it was hot and humid, but that was fine with Jackson. He looked at his watch. The time was quarter to ten. He sat in a Starbucks staring into a cup of coffee which he had ordered a few minutes earlier. He looked at the cup as if he was about to move it using his telekinesis power. Jackson thought about how he could find James. His intuitive mind was telling him that the writer was still alive but he couldn't ignore the possibility of James' body being found at any moment. Jackson thought that if he found Mr. D, he would discover James' whereabouts. The detective told himself that the main priority was to find Mr. D. He thought about contacting Jake, the techie guy who used to work for Mr. D. The problem was that Jackson had no idea where Jake could be. He wasn't in the country, but then where he could be hiding? Jackson kept pondering over Jake's whereabouts. But after a few minutes, Jacob burst through the door of the Starbucks. He was rushing as if he needed to use the restroom. He was wearing a black raincoat and black trousers that made him looked like a yuppie.

"I know I'm late, sorry. Traffic was horrible," Jacob said, out of breath and Jackson nodded.

"You want something for breakfast? Or a refill?" Jacob asked, his voice sounded as if he was still apologizing.

"Yeah, get me a bacon and egg sandwich," Jackson said, and Jacob immediately went to the cashier. A couple of minutes later, both homicide detectives sank into deep discussion.

"So, how can we find Mr. D?" Jacob asked as if he was a student in elementary school.

"We've got to cyberstalk this guy, Jake. We need to find out everything about him; what he likes, where his favorite place is, and so on. There has to be something in his past that could help us trace him," Jackson said, and Jacob agreed. The homicide detective didn't have much choice, as Jake Kohen seemed to be the only chance they had. Jackson hoped that his intuition would not lie to him.

No one could tell what was about to happen.

***

James was transported to another room. He was cuffed and escorted by two Mexican guys. The writer was asking tons of questions, but the Mexican guys didn't pay attention. The room where he was taken was a small 5 by 10 storage space. In that room, there was a single light bulb above him and an old bench where he sat. James was left alone, still handcuffed. He was dressed all in white as if he was an angel that had come to earth on a mission. Not too long ago, James was hitting the back of his head against the wall made from stainless steel panels and started screaming about water

"Water! I need water, please!" James kept yelling. It looked like he was freaking out, but actually, that was part of his plan. What was his plan about? James had no idea. He wanted to create chaos and get the Mexicans' attention. A voice deep inside was telling him that he was done, but his faith in God didn't leave him. He kept praying and trying to pull himself together. Although, his sanity was seriously tested.

"Water, please!" James reiterated. Despite his screaming, no one answered. James used all the time he had to think about his mother, who was actually his stepmom and that made him feel weird. "*How come in all of those years she had never found the guts to tell me the truth? I guess she hoped that I would never find out,"* James was talking to himself as he contemplated how he would react if he ever saw her again. That didn't matter to him; he loved Michelle. She was the only mom he had. The writer wondered why his father, Ivan Dobrev and Michelle had kept that secret from him. Thinking about his stepmom, James realized that the time in that room was passing slowly. He tried to sleep, but he couldn't put his mind at ease.

"Water! Can anyone hear me? Please, I need water," James cried out again. Yet, no one responded. James was getting pissed. He started thinking deeply, *"They're doing it on purpose! They want me to lose my shit."* James couldn't remember the last time he had used the word *'shit.'* He hated that word. Suddenly, the light bulb above him started to blink. He looked at it and frowned. He had precognition that something bad was about to happen. James knew that at some point, someone would come to see him—it was just a matter of time. Three hours later, the door handle wiggled, and someone came through. It was Freddy Limo. He was followed in by two sturdy guys. Freddy Limo never walked alone; he was a wuss.

"How are you doing, James?" Freddy asked with sardonic smile that irked James.

"I'm great! Waiting to chat with you," James answered, his sassy words were coming quickly.

"Yeah, that's what I thought. Well, I have some good news, James." Freddy pronounced James' name with a longer 'S' on purpose. It was obvious that he teased the writer.

"Oh, yeah! I cannot wait to hear about it!" James exclaimed.

"As you already know, you'll be the main event for our boxing spectacle. You will be visiting a small boxing gym for the following month. There will be two trainings daily, one in the mornings and one in the evenings. Each training will be no longer than two hours. Of course, we cannot let you work out on your own. There will be armed guards observing you when you train. That's the orders. Any questions?" Freddy asked, still exposing his sardonic smile.

"Yeah. When am I supposed to start?"

"Uh… I believe tomorrow morning. Also, you will be on a special diet to maintain your cruise weight. That's the orders. Here's some water!" Freddy threw a bottle of water at James as if he was an annoyed fan disappointed by the performance of his favorite singer.

"Thanks. Let me ask you something. Were you a Baby Clunt?" James said.

"What did you call me?" Freddy asked. His voice changed. He wasn't smiling anymore.

"A Baby Clunt!" James repeated.

"What do you mean?" Freddy asked, puzzled. Then James cracked a smile. He knew that his plan to tease Freddy was working.

"A baby clunt is a baby that gave an orgasm to his mom at the moment of his birth. I can rephrase that: did you give your mom pleasure when you came out from her genitals?" James asked. He couldn't hold it anymore and burst into laughter. Freddy was dead serious. James' joke didn't sound kind to him.

"I will be the one laughing when Joe smashes your face! How about that?" Freddy snapped, confidently.

"Sure! I don't expect you to cry for me, Susannah," James laugher's became louder. Freddy nodded and bolted out. James' mind games worked, yet it seemed that he was the loser.

***

James started to train just like Freddy had said. At first, he wasn't in training, yet after his second day, he was all over the punching bags. A month wasn't enough to get ready for a fight. It didn't make any sense to James. When he addressed this statement, Freddy Limo refused to listen. The writer was worried about his arm. It had been more than eight months since he got shot. He didn't feel any pain, but that didn't mean that his arm could not get worse.

It had been nine months since James was in a boxing gym, yet his boxing ability hadn't diminished. Dobrev focused on what he would do when he jumped on the canvas. He was taller than Joe which meant that he had a longer reach. That's why he worked on his jab. That would be his weapon. He had an orthodox boxing stance which implies that he would have to use the power of his right hand. He also trained his footwork, moving around the ring showing his shadowboxing skills. Knowing that Joe would chase him in the ring, James focused on refining his footwork. Also, the writer trained his power punches, especially the uppercuts. He worked on fast combinations and counter punches as well. The more he trained, the more excited he became. After two weeks, James began to enjoy his training, and boxing made his time there a bit better. He even requested sparring partners to practice what he had been training for. Freddy disapproved of the idea. Mr. D couldn't bring in any outsiders because then he had to kill them. No one was supposed to know about this event.

***

Joe was taking the fight seriously and trained at a boxing gym that was managed by a notorious mob boss named Mario Colonnochi. Mario was a prosperous entrepreneur who owned a few gas stations, a car dealership, and a funeral home called 'Sweet Dreams.' Mario also had a stake in the gambling business and loved betting on boxing. Mr. D and Mario had been working together for years. The pharmaceutical boss called Mario and asked for a favor. Mario was happy to have Joe at his gym. Not because he liked him, but because he saw an opportunity to make a lot of money as he orchestrated bookies on this fight. Mario had been involved in organized crime for more than thirty years. He was a *made* man in a well-known family.

Mario was in his early seventies. He looked like Jabba the Hutt, the fictional character from *Star Wars*. The mob boss had had a heart attack a few years ago. As a result of his medical condition, he could hardly walk. That didn't bother him because he didn't have to go anywhere as he controlled his business remotely. Mario started working for the Mafia as a driver, and ten years later, he became a *made* man. Many people were kissing his ass because they wanted to work for him.

A few days before the fight, Mario called a former WBC heavyweight world champion to train Joe. The WBC champion gave Joe some helpful strategies, but Joe didn't listen to his trainer, although he paid tribute to him. Joe hit the mitts so hard that the guy holding them needed to go to the ER. The Irish not only wanted to knock James out, but he also wanted to kill him in the ring, literally. Unlike James, Joe sparred three times per week. He knocked down a few professional boxers with insignificant boxing records. His trainer was impressed as he watched how the Irish walloped other boxers in the ring. Joe could sit on his punches and pivot his body to establish maximum power. Mr. D had promised him a big check if he turned in an impeccable performance. That additionally stimulated Joe. He was as excited as a boy who was playing his favorite computer game.

The illegal boxing event was approaching. James seemed to be condemned to a brutal fight. On the other hand, Joe couldn't wait and was counting down the days.

14

On Thursday, June 16th, was just another night leading to the big fight. The event was taking place in one of Mr. D's warehouses, and he had gone to great lengths to make it an unforgettable experience. He had even brought twenty chefs, all of whom worked in famous restaurants, to be present at the event. Mr. D had also built a kitchen right there in the warehouse, which offered a wide range of cuisines, including Mediterranean, Italian, Chinese, Indian, and Turkish food. The ring size measured up to 20 by 20 and was placed at the center of a huge compartment. There were a bunch of tables and chairs scattered around the ring. The VIP lounge was in a commercial cabin stretched over a 1000 square feet. Inside, it looked like a presidential hotel room. The lounge had an expensive carpet, a few large TVs, and a minibar at the corner of the room. The furniture there was worth thousands of dollars. The ceiling was grooved in interesting shapes that had embedded lights, it looked like the ceiling of a spacecraft. The VIP lounge was on the second floor and had a fine view of the ring. The boxing event was going to have three bouts.

The first fight would be between ex-cons that used to be MMA fighters. The illegal event was supposed to start on Saturday, the 18th, at 9 o'clock. More than fifty employees who wore shirts with a logo saying 'Stuff' worked and organized the event. There were about ten electricians working on scissor lifts to install lights and projectors. Mr. D required this boxing event to look flashy, and he had both the money and power to make things happen quickly.

***

At noon on Saturday, Jackson was drinking a coffee from Starbucks. He was in the passenger seat of a 2022 black Chevy Tahoe. He found the car to be comfortable, and he began to think about getting rid of his Camaro. Jacob had just bought this Tahoe from a dealership. The purchase of the car made him happy as someone who got laid for the first time.

"Where are we going?" Jacob asked.

"Drive to Elgin. I've got the feeling that our friend is somewhere there," Jackson said. Jacob stared at him with a confused face. The Polish investigator absorbed every moves or words Jackson said.

"Okay, what's on your mind?" Jacob asked, and Jackson smiled.

"Just drive, homie. You'll see. I think there will be a big party tonight"

"Huh? What are you talking about?" Jacob asked, looking dumbfounded and having no idea what was happening.

"Just drive," Jackson uttered. The Tahoe cruised on I-90 westbound. It was around 1 o'clock in the afternoon. The highway was already jammed, with a disastrous car accident in the left lane. The police had to block two lanes to make space for paramedics and ambulances, causing the cars to move slowly. Jacob was looking around as if he were lost tourist, remaining silent even though he had many questions he was afraid to ask.

***

At 6:00 p.m. on the same day, more than twenty stretch limos drove into a parking lot of the warehouse where the fight event was being held. The limos parked parallel to each other, lined up like soldiers. A bunch of VIP guests hopped out of those limos simultaneously. They were escorted into the building by security. The warehouse was filled with around two hundred spectators. A DJ was playing music, and once in a while, he dropped the beat to announce specific information. No one was allowed to use smartphones, the event was completely illegal, and Mr. D required privacy. The first fight started at 7 o'clock. An African-American heavyweight was fighting against an Armenian immigrant. The referee was a Mexican who worked on Mr. D's payroll and had to follow his instructions. The gong blasted, and both fighters jumped on. The African-American fighter did a phenomenal combination. He stepped in, closed the distance and threw a few body shots, then he swung a brutal uppercut followed by a left hook, and the Armenian man was floored on the canvas. The crowd yelled, intrigued by the brilliant performance. The referee stopped the fight right off the bat because the Armenian man didn't move. The crowd applauded and screamed madly. Mr. D was enjoying the spectacle while being massaged by a few Chinese girls. Next to him, Mario Colonnochi was engaged in a conversation with a man in his forties, who appeared to be dressed like a lawyer. The VIP guests were having a lot of fun. They were drinking expensive wine and ordering lobsters and steaks.

Joe Smith was in a locker room that was made specifically for him. He had his black trunks and black Ringside shoes. He was quiet, but his mind was hollering, *"I'm gonna kill this motherfucker!"* The Irish was warming up and throwing a few fast punches in the mitts. Joe was overexcited, he couldn't wait to jump into the ring.

James was in a different room that used to be a locker room for employees. A short Puerto Rican guy was wrapping his hands. They didn't communicate with each other because the Puerto Rican guy didn't speak English, and James couldn't talk in Spanish. Four armed guards were keeping an eye on James. That was the orders.

The second fight in the event started. A white prisoner, welterweight had to fight against the Mexican state champion. The white guy had a huge nose and small eyes. His name was Jack, but everybody called him *The Animal*. The director of the penitentiary agreed to allow Jack to fight in that event, but after the fight, Jack would be escorted back to the prison. The fight was spectacular. The boxers were beating each other, and the fight went the full eight rounds. Jack, The Animal, won by unanimous decision. He then was ushered to the entrance with a check for $1,500 and a free night at the Hyatt.

***

It was around 9:00 p.m., Jackson was observing an old building that had too many stretch limos left in the parking lot. A group of men, all dressed in black, were seen walking around the parking lot. They appeared to be the security personnel. Jackson and Jacob were sitting in their Tahoe, which was about 400 feet away from the property, carefully observing the men dressed in black.

"What do you think?" Jacob asked, continually staring at Jackson as if he was about to confess the deepest secret in his life. Jackson looked around. He then took off the binoculars that he had been using and said, "Look at the stretch limos!"

"Yeah, I see them. What about them?"

"There are no police escorts. That implies that this is a private event. Something illicit must be going on there," Jackson said, and Jacob nodded.

"Let's get closer then. We may see something that can give us a reason to enter the premises," Jacob suggested, but Jackson shook his head no.

"Hold on! We can't get too close," Jackson replied.

"How come! Why? I don't understand," Jacob protested. His face was frowning, if not yet fuming.

"If we are too close, they will spot us, and then we are screwed! We need to have a reason. We can't just come up and start asking questions," the African-American detective stated. Jacob's face looked disappointed but he had to agree with Jackson's reasoning. Both homicide detectives were quietly observing with great attention, being as quiet as if they were studying in a library.

***

The main event was about to start. A crowd of two hundred people was anticipating the fighters. The VIP area was loud with people lost in animated conversations, as well as with a few aldermen, talking to a former Illinois governor. Mr. D had a lot of friends who worked for the city of Chicago. Lieutenant Harry Burns leaned forward and whispered something to Mr. D. Harry was a rat, snitching every bit of information from the police department to Mr. D, which was why Mr. D was always a few steps ahead of the police. In exchange, Mr. D had given Harry a lot of money, and he also had access to many call girls for free.

The fight was supposed to start in a few minutes. The announcer was a Jewish man in his forties who usually worked at a radio station, but that night was his side hustle. His voice exuded masculinity and a holy spirit. James was the first boxer to walk to the ring, escorted by four armed soldiers. The crowd was booing him, as he was the underdog. Dobrev knew that he would not be welcomed. His white trunks matched his gloves. The Puerto Rican guy would be at his corner. He took off James' shirt. The writer tried to avoid any contact with the crowd. He walked to the corner and made the Sign of Cross. He needed God at this crucial moment.

Joe walked to the ring as if he was the champion of the world. The DJ played Eminem's theme song, 'Lose Yourself' for the Irish man, Joe. The crowd became raucous, screaming Joe's name. The fight was scheduled for eight rounds. James was deadpan. His face didn't flinch. After checking both fighters, the referee made his way to the center of the ring and signaled the start of the bout by waving his hand. Joe jumped onslaught. He was short, but it seemed that he didn't have problems with closing the distance. He moved just like the boxing legend, Mike Tyson. But unlike Iron Mike, Joe took long steps, and that made him look faster. The Irish concentrated on body shots and some uppercuts, switching up his speed and combinations. James showed a remarkable defense, and Joe became frustrated, throwing some roundhouse punches, which seemed to be unsuccessful. Joe wanted to knock James out in the first few seconds of the first round, but James successfully countered and even headbutted Joe. The Irish boxer went nuts. The gong blasted, and the round was over. The referee had to separate the fighters because Joe wanted to keep fighting even though the round had finished.

During the break, gunshots disturbed the boxing event, and everyone panicked. The crowd scattered in many directions like a herd of sheep as the skirmish continued. Voices of people's moaning blasted from everywhere. James decided to run. That was his chance to escape. Joe went ballistic. The fight was over, but he wouldn't quit. Instead, he chased James madly. The VIP room was like a madhouse. Five guards escorted Mr. D and Mario Colonnochi. They were taken to the roof where there was a helipad.

Jacob heard the first few gunshots. He turned around and asked, "Did you hear that?" The question was redundant, but needed to be addressed. Jackson nodded. He pulled out his smartphone and dialed

Harry. The lieutenant didn't pick up the phone because he was running from the gunshots at the warehouse.

"He's not answering!" Jackson cried out.

"Let's go! People are dying!" Jacob exclaimed, his eyes wide open with nervousness, but not fear.

"Hold your horses. I'm calling the operator. Don't try to be a hero!" Jackson declared, but Jacob didn't listen to him.

"I'll see you inside!" Jacob said and ran toward the building. Jackson got frustrated over Jacob's impulsiveness. He hadn't many choices left, and so he followed the young Polish detective.

All of a sudden, more than thirty members of the Russian organized crime had invaded the warehouse. They had been told to shoot at anything that moved. A big Russian man with a bald head and a large beard was screaming "Bitches! Bitches!" That was the only word he knew in English. His name was Oleg, a great marksman and former KGB agent who was ready to die for his country. Rocco made eye contact with the heavyset Russian.

"Bitches!" Oleg said to Rocco.

"You call me a bitch?" Rocco cried out, and Oleg nodded. Without another word, the two men launched at each other and began wrestling. Oleg used to wrestle in the army and had no problem grappling. Actually, he enjoyed it. Rocco had a bigger body, but his wrestling skills sucked. Oleg pulled a small knife from his sock and stabbed Rocco several times. Rocco lay on the floor, throwing up blood. The pain in his body was unendurable and he died like a real soldier with his eyes wide open.

The people in the VIP area were murdered as were the other guests. The warehouse looked like a battlefield from World War II. The carnage looked bad—there were dead bodies everywhere. The Russians were searching the building and terminating the survivors. Out of the blue, an African-American voice echoed from the entrance, "Hey! You ugly motherfuckers! Where is Boris?" the black man yelled. Around ten black guys were behind him. They were armed with AK-47s. The black man who had screamed had long dreadlocks. His name was Randy and his body was muscular, as if he lived in the gym. Randy was the head of a local gang that used to rob small businesses and pimps. Boris Gurmanov had screwed Randy over with a big shipment of weapons that came from Russia. It turned out that those guns were faulty. Randy felt duped. He thought that Boris had robbed him and wanted his money back.

"Where is Boris? I ain't moving anywhere until I have answers. You understand what I'm saying," Randy screamed at Oleg. The former KGB agent started speaking gibberish.

"You say what?" Randy asked, impatiently. Oleg continued speaking in Russian, and Randy kept pontificating.

"Bitches!" Oleg screamed. His Russian accent sounded like a threat, and Randy went ballistic.

"I' ain't no bitch! You fucking motherfucker," Randy screamed back and pointed his rifle at the Russian KGB. Oleg freaked out and started shooting. The Russians and the African-Americans were shooting at each other as if it were the Wild West. While the Russian mafia and African-American gang were killing each other, Jacob was tiptoeing into the warehouse. He was looking for hostages or civilians who might need help. The Polish detective was prudent, walking quietly as if he was a ghost. He went to a storage room on the first floor and looked around. A minute later, he saw a man holding his head.

"Hey! Are you okay?" Jacob whispered. The man turned around and smiled.

"Harry, what's happening here?" Jacob asked, happy to see the Lieutenant.

"Jacob, where is Jackson? Did you call the police?" Harry asked.

"Yeah, they should be here any minute, though… Are you injured?"

"Just a scratch. Hey, Jacob, look behind you," Harry pointed out, and Jacob turned. Then a firearm's shot blasted in the storage. Harry shot Jacob from behind, then left the compartment and ran toward the exit. A Russian guy shot Harry in the head, causing him to collapse on the floor and pass away within milliseconds.

James ran as fast as he could, hearing Joe's voice over his shoulder.

"Wait! You coward. Come back here and fight like a man," Joe yelled. He wanted to fight James even when the fight was over. James made a mistake by entering a random room with no exits. Joe stopped at the threshold of the door.

"Your ass is mine! You can't escape! Fucking writer!" Joe raised his voice, his eyes shooting daggers. His hatred toward James was almost tangible.

"What is this all about? What do you want? Don't you see that the entire building is invaded, and people are shooting at each other?" James tried to sound reasonable, but Joe ignored his statement. The Irish man went bananas, he stepped closer moving his head side to side. James grabbed Joe, holding him to save some time, but Joe snuck around and threw a hard hook, causing James to wobble. Both fighters continually swung punches.

***

Mr. D and Mario Collonochi scurried to the roof. They were both moving slowly as their age required. There was a private helicopter waiting for them. Mr. D had bought this helicopter a few years ago and this was going to be his first flight in the machine. A minute later, both billionaires climbed into the chopper.

"Go!" Mr. D cried out to the pilot. The man who sat in front turned around and said,

"You don't have a ticket!"

217

"Huh? Who the fuck are you? This is my property! Where is Juan?" Mr. D yelled.

"He is on vacation," the pilot said in a Russian accent.

"What are you talking about?" Mr. D snapped. All of a sudden everyone pointed guns at Mr. D. The pharmaceutical billionaire was dumbstruck. He was shot more than twenty times. Mr. D was dead already, but the guards were still shooting him. It turned out that the guards were Russians. The pilot was Anton, the Russian mob boss who smiled hellishly. Mario Collonochi had set up the murder. He needed to get rid of Mr. D. In no time, the helicopter flew from the helipad and disappeared in a few seconds. Mr. D, the diabolical man, lay on the roof, lifeless. He brought so much pain to the entire world, and now he was dead.

***

The warehouse was filled with countless police officers searching for survivors. Some lay on the floor with their eyes open, screaming from the pain they felt. However, most of them died on the way to the ER. The cops took Joe to the police vehicles while paramedics took James to an ambulance, his bloody face looked bad. Jackson was holding his head as if he had a headache. He found Jacob's body, feeling remorse for the death of his partner. Jacob left his daughter fatherless and his family would be missing him. He died like an honorable hero. Jackson was shocked to find Harry's body at the crime scene. He figured that Harry was the rat, giving up information to Mr. D. The warehouse was filled with dead bodies. The final report was shocking: two hundred and twenty-four people died, and eight were in critical condition. When he heard those numbers, the governor of Illinois almost had a heart attack.

***

James rested in the hospital. He wasn't injured badly, yet he was advised to stay in the hospital for a few days. Frank and Michelle stopped by to see him. Michelle cried, but she was so happy to see her stepson. James stared at his stepmom silently, realizing that Michelle would always take care of him. He decided that it would be pointless to reveal his knowledge that she was not his biological mother. The writer was relieved and felt like he was off the hook. The nightmare was over. That was what everybody thought.

15

James left the hospital by the end of June. He was elated to be with his family, especially Patrick. The moment he saw his son, James broke down in tears, weeping from happiness. He had missed him a lot. James had thought he would never see his family again.

Carl, his book agent, notified James about the release date of his novel *The Cold Summer*. James was excited. After the first week of its release, his book sold more than 500,000 copies. That was the biggest hit that James had ever had. The writer traveled to a few states for work assignments such as book signings and meeting the author. In the second week of July, James went to a meet-the-author event in Evanston, Illinois. He talked about his novel and what inspired him to write it. The event finished in an hour. James tucked his books into his backpack, thinking about his son. Then a female voice interrupted his thoughts.

"I like the cover of your book," the female voice said. James recognized the voice and looked straight at the person, becoming dumbstruck.

"Anna! What are you doing here?" James cried out. He gave her a friendly hug as if they were platonic friends.

"Well, I got a job in Chicago in a law firm, and here I am. I also, was thinking about you and decided to stop by," Anna said. James looked shocked.

"I'm so happy for you. Unfortunately, I need to go now. I'm running late," James lied. He wasn't late for anything. He was playing with her emotions.

"Wait! I need to talk to you," Anna said. "Listen, I'm sorry for getting angry a few months ago, I had a lot of heat at work, and I acted kind of standoffish. I need you to know that I care about you and…" James interrupted her by kissing her lips. They couldn't stop kissing for a minute. The love between them hovered around like an angel. She wanted him as much as he missed her. Anna loved him and wanted to spend her life with him. She had chosen James to be her man, and they started dating, spending countless hours together. James took Anna to incredible places in Chicago, not because he was a pushover, but because he loved her in a way that couldn't be described with just a few words.

***

It was Friday night, the weather in Chicago was gorgeous and James wanted to spend more time with his family. Michelle asked him to buy groceries from Mariano's. The traffic was awful that day, as if every Chicagoan was out doing something. It took James an hour to drive back to Schaumburg, and he parked the car in the driveway before hopping out to grab the groceries from the trunk. Then he heard the sound of a gun being racked from behind.

"Don't move a muscle," ordered a male voice that was familiar to James.

"Give me your smartphone and start walking to the garage. Keep your hands up, but not too high," the stranger's voice ordered. James did what the man said. They walked to the garage slowly and James locked it from inside. The writer was sick and tired of his bizarre life. The man, pointing a gun at him, was wearing a black ski mask, but it was clear to James whose face was behind that mask.

"You can take your mask off, Freddy," James uttered.

"You're a slimeball. You've killed my boss, and now I don't have a job. What am I going to do? I got nothing to lose," Freddy complained. He had gotten lucky at the boxing night a few weeks ago. Freddy was driving to the liquor store to get some cigarettes when the bloody firefight began. When he approached the warehouse, the shooting had already started.

"Mom will soon notice that I'm back. She will be here in a minute," James pointed out. It wasn't a bluff, but Freddy didn't care. He was ready to blow James' head off and then shoot himself. He was depressed, his hands were shaking while he held the firearm.

"I'll kill you! You miserable fuck!" Freddy said in a high pitched voice, but he wasn't confident. Actually, he was scared, as if he was about to pee in his pants.

"James, are you in the garage?" Michelle yelled from the house. At that moment, Freddy turned his eyes, distracted by Michelle's voice. James noticed that and jabbed Freddy's nose, causing him to stumble onto the floor. Then the writer took the gun and pointed it at Freddy. It happened so fast that Freddy didn't realize how he had fallen to the ground. In a couple of minutes later, the police came and arrested Freddy.

Jackson stopped by the house and was happy to see James.

"Let me ask you something," Jackson said. "How did you drop him to the floor so fast?"

"It was magic!" James answered. Jackson nodded and said, "There's something you should know. Are you sure that the man shot on the roof was Mr. D, right?"

"Yeah, absolutely. Why are you asking?" James looked like he didn't understand the question. The writer identified Mr. D's body a few days after the shooting at the warehouse.

"That's not him. The man killed on the roof was Irwin Fletcher, a 41-year-old who was born and raised in Columbus, Ohio. He graduated from college in 1998 and had been arrested for possession of marijuana when he was 21. His DNA is clean. Irwin Fletcher was not Mr. D," Jackson finished his speech, showing a deadpan expression and a deep disappointment. James was left speechless and unsure of what to say.

***

Mr. D was drinking a cocktail at his chalet in Switzerland. His thoughtful face looked like he was in a bad mood, having lost an important building in Chicago. This was clearly affecting him.

The pharmaceutical boss didn't know that Jake had contacted Jackson secretly, revealing to the homicide detective information about where the boxing event would be held. Mr. D was pissed. He wanted Jake's body buried on his property.

Mr. D used a body double, just like any other billionaire. Irwin Fletcher was hired by Mr. D a couple of years ago because he was the perfect match. Mr. D was a very wise man. No one could easily outsmart him. He never went anywhere; people came to him. Nobody knew that. Even Freddy Limo, who had worked for him for the past 30 years, had no idea that Mr. D had a body double.

***

Jackson became one of the most honorable and respected homicide detectives in the Land of Lincoln and the entire country. The mayor of Chicago rewarded him with a special trophy and even promoted him within the police division. Jackson became the person he wanted to be: prosperous and honored. His mother and brother were proud of him.

***

James quit drinking and left his problem with alcohol behind him. But the writer couldn't understand one thing; why those lights blinked when things became crucial.

James and Anna got married on a yacht near Hawaii. Anna had always wanted to get married on a boat, and James liked the idea. The yacht had around 150 guests. Anna's dress looked glamorous, which made James the happiest man on earth. The wedding continued over four days. The ceremony went smoothly, except that Frank got so hammered that he jumped overboard for fun. James and Anna bought a beautiful house in Niles, Illinois. Three months after the wedding, Patrick mysteriously recovered from his disease and started to move his body slowly. James couldn't believe his eyes; it was a miracle. The writer kneeled on the floor, looked up at the sky, and said, "Thank you, Lord!"

A year later, Anna got pregnant and gave birth to Gina. The family lived as if they were in heaven. James and his family didn't know that they were being watched. No one could tell what would happen tomorrow.

**Check the other of Dimitry's bestsellers on
Amazon and everywhere books are sold.**

Bridge of Pain: How My Life Become a Roller Coaster

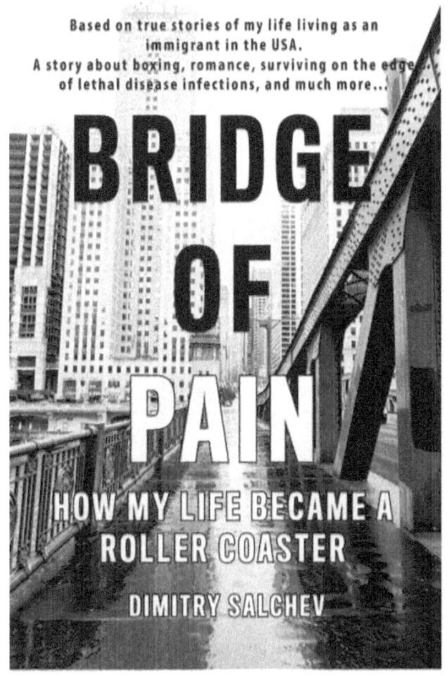

Dimitry's autobiography is based on ten years of his life, and it's primarily focused on the years between 2014 and 2019. Dimitry talks about how he prevailed over countless obstacles in those years. You will witness how his routine life turned into a nightmare. In this book, he portrays how many times he nearly died, and how he returned to life. He also emphasizes how wrong he had been and how important his faith in God was.

On the Fourth of July, a young woman is reported missing. Her family has no idea where she might have gone. The police can find no evidence of where she can be. Robert McCarthur and Lisa Fernandez are the detectives assigned to work on finding the missing woman. Along the way in searching for her, more surprises shock them. Many questions arise which seem impossible to answer. Just when it seems things have become too complicated, something crucial happens that no one can explain. This and much more increases the chaos in Chicago

www.ingramcontent.com/pod-product-compliance
Lightning Source LLC
Chambersburg PA
CBHW031523310726
48971CB00008B/2341